SILVER
TREE
GHOST
HOUSE

Book #3 in the Four Families Series

Merry Brown

Additional books by Merry Brown:
The Four Families Series:
Gold Manor Ghost House
Crimson Hall Ghost House

The Exiled Trilogy:
The Knowers
The Second Fall
The United

YA Books imprint
ISBN: 978-0-9899934-3-2
August 2017

Front and back cover design by Merry Brown.
Front cover photograph, shutterstock.com
Back cover photograph, shutterstock.com

To Beauty.

Don't worry, Beauty *will* redeem
the world.

Prologue

"Grab it! Anna, take it!" Meg yelled, covered in mud, the thunder overhead punctuating her terror.

Meg's arm had a severe slash running the length of it, right down to the tip of her index finger. She was bloody, crying, and frightened. And alone, except for the distant weeping.

"Anna, they're coming. Wake up! Do something! Take it!" she yelled at me again.

I could see and hear Meg, but couldn't move. I was buried underground by piles and mounds of earth, entirely covered except my face. Tree roots had my legs and arms pinned. I could barely breathe.

"What do you want from me?" I rasped.

"Take it! Help me! Please, please, please. I'm so scared!"

"Take what?"

"Anna! Ahhhhhh!" Meg screamed.

In my limited vision I saw her fall to the ground. A shadow passed over the small shaft that was my window to the world.

"Trapped again? Trapped for always, Fifth from the Third. You must hide or my sister will kill more. Power is power is power and it will be stripped. Stripped from your pretty little hands. Death is death is death until it is not. Am I the dead? Are you? Find or all is lost."

"What is lost?" I asked the green specter, the Gold Ghost.

The sky finally opened, letting loose its wealth of rain. If I couldn't find a way out I would drown here. Maybe I wanted to. Easier. No more puzzles to solve. No more danger.

"All who remain, if you lose," the ghost replied. "You must fight and win. Go!"

At the apparition's command, I felt the tree tighten its grip on my arms and legs, new tentacles worked around my torso.

So this was it. I was going to die, crushed to death by nature, blotted out of this world for being unnatural.

I was too tired. I didn't want to fight. I didn't know how to fight or how to be. I closed my eyes as the rain washed my face clean. I took one last breath.

I felt my body being pushed and pulled by the tree, moved through the ground until I was thrown to the surface.

I was in the forest behind Gold Manor. I looked around and Meg was gone, along with the ghost. I patted myself down. No dirt.

A dream, Anna. This must be a dream.

I turned around to find the source of the weeping. Deeper and deeper, the forest drew me in until I saw her, the woman I hated more than the Devil himself.

She was kneeling at the base of the tree I'd tied my scarf to a lifetime ago. I had searched for this spot, but it had seemingly disappeared. Or more likely, didn't want to be found.

I approached on tiptoe. The woman paid me no heed and continued her carving of the helpless tree.

"What are you doing?" I spat.

"Remembering," she said, rocking back and forth, her krim dripping blood as she paused.

"Remembering what?"

"All my evil. All the dead. All I've lost. Only you can stop it," she said, levitating now, exposing what she'd been hiding from me.

"Stop what? Why me?" I asked, disgusted, though I couldn't look away.

"Not you. Both of you," she whimpered. Then she stopped.

Deadly silence descended in the forest. "You want to know the secret?" she whispered, motioning me to draw closer.

Reluctantly I came to her, so close I felt her breath on my face. With a grim grin she winked, "I shall never tell."

Chapter One

The week after my mom's death went as expected. Nothing more than any other family in our position would go through, nothing less. Tears, bargaining, numbness, hatred, plans for the funeral, and lots of silence.

The day after I arrived home, my dad flew back to Tennessee to claim my mom's body. He didn't want to leave me, not that I'd be alone; my entourage would barely let me out of their sight to use the bathroom. I wanted Corey, Echo, Suzanne, and even Adam to just go away, leave me in peace. But they wouldn't.

My dad thought it was nice, and a little weird, that my friends cared so much. I'd been working up to the conversation I'd sworn I'd have with him, after the funeral, that would clear up exactly why this bunch wouldn't let me be. But the funeral had been two weeks ago and I still hadn't said a word.

My excuse was the sudden appearance of Uncle Brandon and Aunt Becky. I only halfway remembered the last time I saw the pair. I was seven, it was Christmas, there was shouting, Aunt Melinda was there. Uncle Brandon and Aunt Becky had been living overseas, military, and it was the first time Aunt Melinda had met them. Not a love connection. I kind of remembered some sort of ultimatum. Aunt Melinda said something like, "It's them or me," but her eyes were really big and it looked like she meant something else. I remembered that part because she'd been holding my hand.

My parents went with Aunt Melinda and I never heard from Uncle Brandon and Aunt Becky again. I'd asked about them, at first, but I could see the question made my stoic dad sad. After a while I stopped.

But my mom and aunt were gone and my dad needed someone.

He was still laboring under the delusion that someone unknown had murdered my mom, his wife. My dad had no idea what'd been going on with me, about the Four Families, the war, my dreams and what I was. Whenever I tried to put it into words, I'd open my mouth, but nothing... I couldn't form a coherent thought.

My uncle and aunt were now living in Kentucky, on a farm, not too far from where we shot *Gold House*. They'd planned to stay longer with us, but they were media shy and seemed allergic to the paparazzi that couldn't wait to get a picture of me and my grieving dad.

The day my mom was murdered in cold blood before my eyes, by Adam's mom, Queen Cora, I was shipped from Martin, TN, to my home in Hollywood, CA, like an expensive piece of Chihuly glass. I'm sure I looked like I might crack, but I didn't feel like it. I didn't feel anything at all. Well, that's not entirely true. I felt hate. Lots and lots of hate, in those moments when I felt.

The first weeks home were dreamless. Numb during the day and dead at night. I didn't know why. I was weak and vulnerable, so I guess someone was drugging me or interfering somehow. I didn't have the energy to find out.

The night my uncle and aunt left town, I dreamt. Nightmare. It wasn't a "reality of things to come" dream, just a nightmare. I remembered only parts, but I woke the house screaming. My dad got to me first, which sent me into hysterics because that was my mom's job. She was the one who soothed me, who helped me work through my nightmares and keep my sanity. But she was gone, leaving me with my shell-shocked dad.

The next night I had a similar nightmare, again waking the house with heart-stopping screams. And again, I could only piece together parts of the night terror. It was maddening! My dad couldn't understand why I was being so hard on myself. "Most people can't remember their dreams, Anna."

"But I'm not most people."

He kissed the top of my head. "You certainly aren't. Can I get you anything?"

"No thanks. I'll try to go back to sleep," I said, lying back down, choked by tears because my mom would've never left me in that state. But I was alone.

On the third night of screams, my dad looked like he'd been hit in the face with a hammer when he showed up at my door. I knew I'd have to find a way to deal that didn't gut him. Why should he have to deal with whatever was tearing me up inside? His insides were already in shreds.

The next morning my dad announced he was going to spend most of the day at the office. Several TA's had taken over his classes for him, and he needed to meet with them and make a plan for the remainder of the semester.

"At this point, I don't know. I don't know if it's better if I stick out the semester or have my colleagues permanently take over my sections."

"Whatever feels best for you, Dad. I'll support whatever you want to do."

"Thanks, dear," he said, pouring one last cup of coffee on the way to the garage, "but I don't think there's any feeling better."

Once I was certain he was gone, I gathered my bodyguards in the living room. "I think it's time you leave. My dad actually shaved this morning. He got dressed and went to work. When he comes home, I want you all gone. He wants a go at normal life and he deserves it."

"You know it doesn't work that way," Suzanne said firmly, but with a sadness in her voice. She was used to death and mourning, but she wasn't jaded.

"Yeah. We're not leaving you. You are in no position to defend yourself. Every night you scream like a banshee. It's getting worse, too," Corey said as I shook my head. "Why are you being like this? Don't deny it. Adam? Little help?"

"She can't look at me."

His wounded voice cut my heart. I realized I hadn't heard him speak, not really, in the past few weeks. He'd been at the house, but in the background.

"I'm sorry you're in pain and your father is hurting, but we can't leave you," Echo said, gently placing his hand on my knee.

I flinched. Suffocated. Buried alive. I needed to get away.

I ran upstairs. Instead of turning into my bedroom, my feet took me to my parents' room. I threw open her closet and stared. How could my best friend be dead?

I spent the rest of the day holed up in my parents' bedroom by myself, planning, figuring out what to say to my dad. Figuring out my next step. Food was delivered to the door, but I didn't go downstairs again, didn't see the people

I'd asked to leave, but who'd stayed. I cried myself to sleep wrapped in my mom's bathrobe.

Chapter Two

"Adam! Adam! Adam!!!" I screamed at the top of my lungs so harshly my vocal cords burned. It was the middle of the night, and within seconds the now-familiar sight of my dad opening the door, out of breath, eyes barely slit, was coupled with the unfamiliar. Adam.

"Honey, are you okay?" came the same question my dad asked every night.

I replied with my rote lie, "Yeah. Sorry, Dad. Bad dream. Go back to sleep."

"Are you sure?"

"Yeah. Goodnight."

Only this time Adam was standing behind him. "You can go back to bed. She's fine," he mumbled to Adam.

"If it's okay with you, Mr. Ellingwood, I'd like to check on her."

My dad's eyes opened further at Adam's request, but he had no energy to question him or reason to suspect any kind of hanky-panky. He nodded and shuffled back to his room.

"Anna? May I come in?"

I propped myself up on my elbows, seeing him illumined by the hallway light my dad had left on. Adam was in a tight, light yellow t-shirt and dark blue jeans. His hair was rumpled, which it was perpetually, but this was a sleepy kind of messy. Though it looked like he'd been asleep moments before, he was wide awake now.

"Please," I answered.

He sat on the edge of my bed, as far away from me as possible.

"Are you okay?" he asked, looking past me to the picture of the two of us on my nightstand.

This morning he'd said I wouldn't look at him, but now I realized *he* wouldn't look at *me*.

"You know the answer," I said softly.

Adam flinched.

I'd been so focused only on what I'd lost and what my dad was suffering, that I hadn't had the space in my brain to consider what was going on with him.

"And you? Are you okay?"

"Irrelevant." His word was crisp and revealing. I allowed myself to feel out, to test the air around him. He was a festering wound.

"Don't do that," he snapped. Stopping himself, he added, "Please."

"And why not?"

"How can you ask me that?"

"I'm so tired, can't think," I said, lying back in bed, curling into a ball.

As the panic of my nightmare subsided, leaving the ever-present hollowness, I somehow found myself asleep.

I was suffocating. It was dark and I was surrounded by something billowy that wouldn't let me go. I beat and tore at it but couldn't find my way to the surface. I was working up a scream when Adam's face appeared.

"Shhh, you're okay. I'm here," he said, leaning over me, freeing me from my sheets.

I grabbed him, throwing him off balance, and he toppled on top of me. He tried to recover himself, but I pulled him close and let loose. I clung to his chest and cried. He held me as I clenched his shirt, his chest muffling my screams and taking my tears.

"You're still here," I sobbed.

"I never left," he whispered.

He held me until I was spent and drifted back to sleep.

Chapter Three

"Anna, you asleep?" my dad asked, tapping on my door and stepping in.

It took me a moment to figure out where I was. First of all, there was a guy in my bed and my dad was staring at us.

"This isn't what it looks like," I yawned.

My dad didn't look mad. In fact, he looked slightly amused. "Do you know what time it is?"

"Did I miss something?" I hadn't been making plans, but I couldn't remember the last time I looked at my calendar.

"It's after noon. I came home for lunch to check on you. Have you been sleeping this entire time?" he asked, amazed.

I sat up, looking at Adam, who was possibly faking sleep. "I guess so."

I arched my back in a deep stretch, feeling rejuvenated. I'd been plagued with either the inability to sleep, dead sleep which was almost worse, or nightmares. It felt amazing to wake up rested.

"I don't want to make it a habit to have Adam sleeping with you, but I'm grateful you got much needed rest. Speaking of which, I think we need to talk. Don't you?"

"Yes," I gulped.

"How about dinner, you and I, tonight? Think your friends will let you go for one night?"

I wanted to say yes, but I saw Adam twitch out of the corner of my eye. Definitely faking sleep, and definitely a 'no' to being out of their sight.

"Well, I think I need to tell you some things too. The continued overbearing presence of my friends will make more sense then."

"Fine. Dinner in, then. Will this discussion be roundtable style?"

"There's no use keeping secrets from them. I know you're a private person, but they know all of this anyway."

"Six. I'll pick up the food on the way home. See you, sweetie. Goodbye, Adam."

Adam rolled over, clearly awake. "Goodbye, sir."

I picked up my phone to confirm the time. Another missed called from Sarah. She was one of my best friends before I left for *Ghost House* last year. A lot can happen in a year.

"Sarah called again. I wish she'd leave me alone."

"Do you really wish it?" Adam asked, knowing my internal conflict.

"Yes and no. I really wish I could still be friends with her. She loved my mom too. I just think it's best this way. The last thing I want to do is get her mixed up in my life." I tried to make my next observation causal. "You stayed."

"Yes."

"Thank you," I said, scrolling nervously through my phone.

"You want to put that down and talk to me?"

"Do you want to talk to me?" I asked, feeling self-conscious, unsure.

There was a gulf between the two of us and an elephant in the room. The elephant was his murderous, powerful, psychotic mother.

He took the cell out of my hand, careful not to touch me. "I'm sorry."

"For what?"

"I wish," he said, rolling onto his back, staring up at the ceiling, "I wish that when I saw your picture in the packet my agent sent, that I had driven the other way, straight out of Martin. I wish you'd never met me."

"I don't wish that," I said in a hushed voice.

"How can you say that?" he asked, eyes cutting to me.

I met his eyes. "Despite everything, my feelings for you haven't changed. When I have feelings, that is. I mostly feel numb. But after last night, I feel better. Thank you."

He broke eye contact. "I should've listened. I thought, somehow, she'd let me go. I honestly didn't believe she'd … and you, you tried to do the right thing. You left me. I tried to let you go. But I'm not as strong as you. I'm sorry."

"Don't. You did nothing wrong."

"I sure as hell did. I wanted you more than anything else. More than reason. And look what happened. There are no happy endings in my world, Anna, only endings."

"Have you changed your mind about me?"

"That's not the point. We tried to be clever before, outsmart the fox, and we failed. I may be handsome and daring," he said wryly, "but not bright enough to figure out how we can work out."

"You know what's crystalized for me since my mom.…" I still couldn't say "died." "I know that I love my dad, Corey, and you. I will not give up any of you."

I didn't mean to cry, but the tears came and went as they pleased these days, not as I bid. They ran down my face and caught in my throat. "It's not fair. I feel like I just figured out how to have you and Corey," I shuddered. "You can't go, Adam. I feel you, I know what you're about to say."

"What's that?"

"That you can't take it. You can't take looking at me and seeing what your mom did. Well, too bad. This is the hard side of love. This is the 'as bad as it gets.' This is the price you have to pay. I lost my mom and your mom did it. We both – "

"Don't you feel sorry for me," he said though gritted teeth.

"You see that?" I asked, reaching out to him in my mind. A charge of electricity ran from my fingers to his. "We are."

"We don't have to be. It can be severed. It has to be. You may not hate me now, though I don't know why, but you will. My mother will not disappear, no matter how much I wish. She will, more than ever, pursue you. And she will do what it takes to get me on her side. You will hate me and I can't be around when that happens."

"You know what my mom taught me? Live one day at a time. She also showed me how to be courageous. She never gave up on me. I'll be damned before I let yours tell me how to live my life."

"Be reasonable, Anna," Adam said. "But I can see you won't listen to reason. Literally."

"You can't see anything. Your eyes are closed."

He looked up at me. "Your hair. It's enormous. It's standing on end. And the zap, sizzle fingers? What are you up to?"

I felt my hair and sure enough it probably looked like I'd stuck my finger in a light socket. I bet that was why my dad looked like he wanted to laugh when he woke me up.

"I refuse to be helpless. I'm not doing it. I've got this power and your uncle told me to dump it, just throw it away. If I hadn't listened to him, I might've been able to do something, anything other than what I did. I can tell you that's not happening again."

It wasn't the first time I'd felt helpless, but it would be the last. The first time I did nothing I was eleven. I'd watched my aunt murdered as I hid. I'd finally come to terms with the fact that her death wasn't my fault. I really couldn't have done anything to stop the Fourth from killing her.

"Anna, that's a losing game. I should know. I've played it my entire life."

"You know I don't blame myself, not really, for what happened to Mom. And I certainly don't blame you. But next time I'm fighting."

"I don't understand you. You should hate me. Loathe me. My life is Family against Family. My family did this to yours. You are supposed to retaliate."

"Good thing I don't play by your stupid blood-rules. Tell me, if my dad killed your sister, would you hate me? Try to kill me?"

"I can't answer that," he breathed as I felt out for the real answer. I could feel the conflict in him as he carefully spun the horrible scenario in his mind. I could feel both his attachment to me and his obligation to his sister. Which would win? He immediately shut me out.

"Stop doing that!" I snapped. I was the one trying to be big, showing him I still loved him and wanted to be together. Why was he being so difficult?

"I'm not like you, Anna. I can't turn on a dime. I've been waiting and preparing for you to kick me out or try to kill me. Not forgive me. I need some space," he said, getting up and walking out of my bedroom.

I listened as he descended the stairs and walked right out of my house.

Adam's sudden departure sent Corey bolting upstairs to check on me.

"You okay? What's going on?"

"I don't wanna talk about it, but I've got to do something."

I hadn't talked that much in weeks. I felt emotionally spent but physically keyed up. I'd been holding onto whatever it was my body produced, some kind of energy, and it was starting to leak out. I needed a release. "How about a run?"

"It's the middle of the day," he whined, already dressed for the day like a normal person. Seeing the smile slip from my face he gave in. "But sure, why not. Who doesn't want to get hot and sweaty on this balmy March day? I'll go tell the others."

"No chance just you and me?" I asked hopefully.

"A, that life is over. We've got permanent bodyguards, I guess for good reason. We've kept you out of the loop, but let's just say we don't want to be left alone."

"I don't even want to know right now."

"Come here," he said, pulling me into a tight hug. "We're going to be okay. You're going to get through this. And whatever you need from me, say the word. Remember, it's still you and me. I don't owe them anything."

"And what about Suzanne?"

"Yeah, well, she's growing on me. Like a fungus. But you're still my best friend and we stick together, okay?"

"I'm worried about Adam."

"What kind of worried? Worried he's, what, on his mom's side or something?"

"No, not really. Thanks a lot, Corey. That never crossed my mind. No, I'm afraid I'm going to lose him too. He's blaming himself."

"I know. He's messed up. I mean, his mom… he hates himself. Echo's worried about him too. He can tell Adam wants to take off, but he hasn't."

"Not yet," I said, despair washing over me.

There was nothing I could do to control Adam. He was stubborn and broken. If he decided he couldn't deal with being around me, then he'd leave. And my heart ached, wondering if I would ever see him again.

Chapter Four

Showered, I sat at the dining room table with Corey as he helped me figure out what to say to my dad.

"You sure about this?" Corey asked, searching the junk drawer for a pen.

"Absolutely. And I've decided how. My dad loves order. I'm going to write an outline and give it to him. Then I'll go through and explain point by point."

It took all afternoon and several drafts. This was what we came up with:

I.   The Four Families
   a. Massacre
   b. General curse and prophecy

II.   Types of gifts/curses/abilities

III.   Length of life

IV.   First and Second Families
   a. Nature: mostly (kinda) good (insane, wretched, nasty, erratic, horrible queen)
   b. Goals: make restitution, bring peace, be free from curse

V.   Third and Fourth Families
   a. Nature: bad
   b. Goals: world domination and immortality

VI.   Me
   a. My biological parents
   b. What I am/my abilities

VII. Today: Us vs. Them

I debated adding more details, such as names, being almost murdered by my mentor, the ghosts, and Gold Manor. But in this case, less was definitely more. My dad was fairly open-minded and uber smart, but not one for the supernatural. Oh well.

"Are you certain about this, Anna? Knowledge is dangerous," Echo cautioned.

"I thought it was ignorance that got you in trouble," I countered.

"Don't you think there's a reason Diane – your Aunt Melinda - didn't tell your parents a thing? By doing this," he said, holding up my outline, "you're saying you know better than her. Really?"

"Leave her alone, man," Corey said, sticking up for me.

"Anna, you know we're trying to look out for you and your dad. I have no problem telling you this is a big mistake. It's better for your dad to stay out of it. I mean, what do you hope to accomplish? You want him to train? Is he going to be on the run? You want him to seek revenge? Call the cops on the queen? I mean, really?" Suzanne added to the argument.

"You guys don't understand. I don't come from the world of lies, cloak and dagger. If my aunt had been straight with my parents, then maybe-"

"You don't know what would've been," Echo said, kindly, but he wasn't stepping down from his position.

"And neither do you. But maybe it would've changed how things turned out. And I refuse to lose my dad due to ignorance. Besides, he deserves to know what really happened to Mom."

"Adam, tell her. Maybe she'll listen to you," Suzanne said to the sound of the garage door opening. My dad was home.

"It's her story to tell as she sees fit. I won't tell her what to do." It was the first thing he'd said since he all but ran out of the house earlier. I agreed with what he said, but the feeling behind it was hollow and disturbing. Like he didn't care what I did.

"Come on, man. This is a bad idea. I mean, Anna, think about it," Echo pleaded.

"What's a bad idea? A little help?" my dad asked, arms full of Indian food, the smell of curry filling the air.

"Let's eat. I'm starved," Corey said, taking a box.

"You're always starved," Suzanne teased.

Automatically we fell into our roles of setting the table, getting drinks, bumping into each other and talking about our day. Usually there wasn't much to report. Today, however, stuff had happened.

"I went to classes today. It was good to be back in the classroom," my dad said, taking another helping of chana masala.

"Excellent, Dad. And I went for a run with Corey and Echo and Suzanne."

"What did you do?" my dad asked, addressing a withdrawn Adam.

"I talked with my bandmates. We have a tour this summer. It starts in a few weeks and there's promo before."

"Does this mean you'll be leaving us?" my dad asked conversationally, ignoring the tension in the air. "Anna, you've really got some static going on. Is it dry in here? Maybe we could get a humidifier."

I used to turn red in the face when I was upset or embarrassed, but lately, if I wasn't paying attention, I'd start levitating or my hair would stand on end. At least big hair was easier to explain.

Adam continued to conspicuously not look at me. "Echo and I are leaving, I'm not certain about –"

"About what?" I challenged, getting up and throwing my napkin on the table.

"All right, kids, calm down. I guess I missed a lot while I was away. Anna, you want to take a seat?"

"No, not really," I said, taking a deep breath, feeling my hair settling back down. "Dad, there seems to be some disagreement as to whether or not to tell you what's really going on."

"You don't mean about today, do you?"

"I'm talking about what started with Aunt Melinda. She thought it better if you stayed out of it. Well, I found my way into it and I'm at a loss. But I know you trusted her. I mean, you really trusted her, and it couldn't have been easy," I said, my anger at Adam for announcing he was leaving me fading, searching my dad for clues as to what I should tell him.

"We had our reasons," my dad said, looking at the remains on his plate.

"Just about everyone here thinks she's still right. I think honesty is the best policy. At least, I did think that. Here," I said, finding a middle way. I handed him my folded-up outline.

"What's this?"

"I think what's fair is for you to decide. If you want to know, if you decide to go against Aunt Melinda's advice, then look at it," I said, pointing at the piece of paper. "It doesn't

25

have all the answers. It's just an outline I wrote for you. But, if you want to talk about it, it's up to you."

"What do you want me to do, Anna?"

"I want what will keep you safe. So, I'm torn. I -"

My dad pounded his fists on the table. "Damn it, Anna. I'm your dad. You're the kid! That's my job, not yours."

"Guys, you mind?" I asked, looking around the table. If my dad was going to lose it, he didn't need an audience.

"Sure. Come on." Echo was the only one of the bunch with manners.

I waited for them to leave and sat back down. "Dad, you do protect me. You always have."

"What? By allowing you to move across the country and take up with them? They seem sincere, but there's something off about them. Even by my standards. And now with your mom gone...."

All the patience I had dried up when he mentioned Mom. "Listen, do you want to know what's really going on or not?"

He reacted to my agitation and yelled back. "You know I do, but I'm old enough to know that sometimes it's better not to know! I'll sleep on it."

"Fine!"

"Now, if you'll excuse me, I've got work to do. Love you!"

"Love you too!" I huffed and stormed off. It was easier to get mad than feel the crushing absence of Mom, who was the peacemaker, who made everything right.

I went up to my room and closed myself in, my new habit, and got online to interact with fans. Most of the notes

26

and tweets were super sweet and supportive. I could read their messages and talk with them. They felt safe. They were distant and uninvolved; unreal in a way. For the first time, when I closed my door, I felt like I was closing my friends downstairs out intentionally.

Coming back from the bathroom after brushing my teeth, ready for bed, my dad stopped me in the hallway.

"Tell me, why do they think I should be kept in the dark?"

"To keep you safe. If you don't know, you can't tell."

"They think I'm a child who can't keep secrets?" he asked, offended.

"Some secrets can be compelled," I answered gravely.

"Oh." That stumped my dad. "Is that it?"

"Also, I guess, they're worried that if you know, you'll feel obligated to get on a horse and charge off to battle."

"Literally or figuratively?"

"Figuratively on the horse, literally for the battle. 'Night, Dad."

I'd settled into bed when there was a tap on my door again.

"What is it, Dad? Can it wait until morning?" I called through the door.

"May I come in?" Adam's muffled voice came through the door.

"Yes," I said, my heart taking off. The sight of him, still, made me turn to mush.

"I thought we could do the inhabitants of the house a favor and go a night without screaming."

"And how do you suggest I go about that? I don't mean to, you know."

"Sleeping with me seems to do the trick. Mind if I sleep with you tonight?"

"Please," I invited.

Adam in my bed was the last thing I expected. I really wouldn't have been surprised to have awoken to a note saying he had to leave early for his tour, not seeing him again until he arrived on the *Ghost House* set deep in the summer.

Adam walked slowly to my bed. It was dark and I could barely make out his silhouette. But his presence filled the room.

"What's going on with you? Why the change? I thought you were leaving me," I said as he lay down next to me on his back, his hands under his head. I snuggled up next to him like I had last night, only this time I wasn't sobbing.

"I was, of course, as you so rightly perceived. But then I went and saw Uncle. He's been in town this entire time. Did you know?"

"Yes. I mean, I thought so."

"I told him I couldn't stay. He called me a coward."

"I'm sorry."

"I'm not. He's right. You are the hardest thing in my life. Harder even than my mother. She I can write off, but you…. And besides, Uncle said it isn't safe for you and me to part. He's had a change of heart on that score. You know he thinks it would've been better, cosmically, if our paths had never crossed. I disagree," he added, kissing the top of my head. "We're in some kind of loop. He doesn't know what will happen if we are physically too far apart for any extended amount of time."

"So we really are stuck together?"

"If that's how you feel," he said, stiffening, "there must be something Uncle can do. No one can compel us to be together."

Adam obviously misunderstood my attempt at humor, so I trailed my hand up the side of his chest, tracing his jaw line.

He grabbed my wrist. "Don't, Anna. It's incredibly difficult to be with you. You have no idea what the sight of you does to me."

"I think of the pair of us, you're the high maintenance one," I said, now inches from his face.

"Of that there is no doubt," he breathed. "But nothing's changed. We still must behave," he said as I started kissing his neck.

"Uh huh," I answered, lost in the scent of him.

"Anna, I really did come here just for a peaceful night of sleep, you know."

"Goodnight," I murmured in between the kisses I trailed down his chest. I was intoxicated by him. I couldn't get enough. And then he was up, at my bedroom door and the bed was cold.

"Anna, I … we have to be careful."

"I don't care," I said desperately, just wanting him back.

"I can tell, love. But I do. And I won't be reckless with you."

"Please come back."

"If I do, you promise to behave?"

I could just barely make out his smirk in the darkness.

"I do sympathize with you, Anna. I am unbelievably sexy. But you've got to try," he said, crawling back in bed with me.

"You're not all that," I lied, but kept my hands to myself out of fear he wouldn't stay otherwise.

"Ha," he said, wrapping his arms around me, my head on his chest. "It's been a month, love."

"I've heard that several times today. What does it mean?"

"We give one month to mourn. That's why Uncle called me in today."

"So he contacted you?"

"I told him you weren't ready."

"Ready for what?"

"Life to resume."

"Oh. I kinda thought the quiet meant it was all over."

Adam rolled onto his side so we were face to face. "Our lot is struggle, those touched by the curse."

"That isn't fair," I whispered.

"I've never known how to keep you safe. I've let you down," he whispered back.

"Have they left you alone too?"

He closed his eyes. Instead of sealing himself off from me, he let down the barrier he usually held, thick and strong, between him and the world. On rare occasion he'd let me feel what he *really* felt.

"My Uncle saw to it. Few know what really happened."

"You're protecting her?" I asked, not judging, but trying to understand. I knew where I stood. I needed to see where he was and why.

"If the Families knew what has become of her, our leader, if the Fourth found out…Anna, it would be chaos and war. The likelihood of us surviving even through the summer, slim. Right now the Fourth picks at us and we retaliate. Back and forth. But if they knew we were worse than leaderless…. We aren't protecting her."

"Maybe it's time for a new leader."

"The way the Families work, the queen would have to die or be gravely ill. It would then fall to Maggie. I see. You think she deserves death," he said, reading me.

"Not death, but punishment. I'm against the death penalty whenever possible. War too. But I recognize there are rare times when both are unavoidable. I'm telling you the truth when I say I don't intend to kill your mother, but I will seek justice for mine."

"I wish you wouldn't," he said softly, fingers tracing my lips.

"And why is that?" I asked, starting to lose interest in anything but the feelings he was bringing out in me.

"Because I want to keep you alive and whole."

"Let's drop it for now, okay?"

Adam sighed and held me close.

Before I fell asleep, Adam produced a very familiar looking vial. "Uncle wants you to start taking these. He knows you're not releasing your energy and thinks it best to take this again. He's been hiding you, but…."

"Month's up?" I asked, taking the vial. I'd expended too much energy today to figure out what I thought about taking the herb, or his uncle, or my next move. But I was convinced I wanted to stay hidden from the Fourth. If they found me, they'd torture and kill me, and probably everyone in the house.

"Fine," I consented, for the time being.

Chapter Five

I awoke bathed in sunlight. I smiled at the commotion outside my bedroom widow: the newly hatched baby birds greedily chirping for their share of the breakfast brought to the nest.

I had the day in front of me, the past behind. I couldn't explain my good mood to myself. Showering, I closed my eyes and reveled in the water cascading and settling around me, pushing me towards the new.

Dressed and out the door, I had a few minutes before I had to be on set for hair and make-up. I found myself driving past the cemetery where my mother was buried. I was surprised to see Aunt Melinda talking to my mom's tombstone.

"You know she's not there," I said, looping my arm in my aunt's, resting my head on her shoulder.

"I know. I came here for you. Will you take me on your day?"

"Today? Well, I've got an event with the cast. A question/answer thing with several different outlets. No big deal," I said, trying to contain my grin.

"No big deal, sheesh. Didn't I teach you better? Own your greatness."

"It is pretty awesome. And I miss my friends. You know, I haven't been out of the house much. Why did you bring her?" I asked, pointing at the green Gold Manor ghost.

"Her sister drives her crazy, just like mine. Old greenie there does as she bids. Looks like she's not the only one following us." My aunt pointed to the bushes. Out walked Mr. Seacrest, brushing the bramble off his tailored suit.

"Are you spying on us?" my aunt accused her uncle, embracing him. They fell into conversation. I backed away and drove off to the studio.

I drove right through the studio gates without being stopped. No one was around. I double checked my texts. Yep. Right time, date, and location, but the lot was empty, a ghost town. It felt like I was on the set of a modern day Western or zombie apocalypse movie. Something wasn't right.

I cautiously got out of my car. The Santa Ana winds whipped up and the sun hid from the brewing storm. I couldn't get on the sound stage fast enough before the heavens opened and drenched me to the bone.

"Hello? Hello?" My voice echoed off the giant metal warehouse.

Nothing. I pressed forward. I knew something was out there, something I had to find. I stopped in the middle of the cavernous building to listen. There was my heart, my breath, my pulse and – a scent. Roses?

I started forward again, trying to follow the fragrance, but it was gone. Dried up. Unlike the drop of blood in front of me. My new trail.

I went in circles, down aisles, past tropical props, out a side door into the rain and back inside, this time finding a blood-smeared handprint on the doorpost of the sound booth.

Locked. A dead end. I pulled on the door, yanked with all my strength, but it wouldn't give way.

I stood looking at the door, wondering what to do next, when I heard a noise, a faint voice coming from the other side. It was muffled and soft. I put my ear to the door.

"Help me," the voice said. It was familiar, someone I knew but couldn't place.

"Please, Anna, please. Help me!"

Chapter Six

I shot straight up, scaring Adam. He jumped up and grabbed my bedside lamp, ready to fight.

I looked at my lap. I was covered in sunrays.

"Anna, what? What is it?"

"Shhh," I demanded, listening for the baby birds. They were there, outside my window, making a racket.

"What's going on?" Adam's eyes were darting back and forth, looking for the danger.

"You can put the lamp down," I said, shivering. "Just a wild dream. Maybe? I mean, wow."

"Just a dream?" He shook his head. "Is there such a thing for you? You shouldn't be dreaming at all."

Putting the lamp back unharmed, he sat on the bed and I told him. Being a dreamer too, he listened intently, asked a few questions, but ultimately was just as stumped as I.

"Sounds like a normal person's dream, Anna."

"I know. But the birds, and this pool of sunlight?" I said, just as there was a knock on my door. I exchanged a look with Adam. Should he be here? Adam didn't seem to mind being seen, and it wasn't like anything had happened or would in the near future.

"Yes?" I called.

"Decent?" Corey called from the other side of the door.

"Always," Adam answered.

"Be nice," I whispered, hitting him on the arm. I could tell Adam's presence in my bedroom threw Corey off since he didn't plow right in. It took him a beat.

"Hey, well, since you were feeling better yesterday, Sylvia wanted to know if you'd be at the question and answer gig down at the TTV studio lot. Some media outlets will be there. Most of us…" he trailed off when I exchanged wide-eyes with Adam. "No worries, though. She'll understand if you're not there."

"Did you know about this?" I asked Adam.

"Not in my contract to do publicity outside of the shooting schedule."

Corey puffed out his chest, upset. "What's going on?"

"I had a weird dream."

"Great. Well, let's hear it," Corey said, relaxing, adding his weight to the bed.

It was a hard day, going back to work and seeing the sad faces, though I appreciated the hugs and kind remarks. I was worried I'd be asked questions about my mom and how I was doing, but the interviewers were told that subject was off limits and thankfully they didn't go there.

I missed Meg, and even Lucy. My dad resumed his life and it felt good to be getting back to mine. Of course I lied all day long. I half-smiled and bobbed my head up and down when people asked how I was. I wasn't better. I wasn't over anything. But everyone wanted me to be. Everyone wanted the same old Anna. I didn't think she'd ever be back.

My covert mission also helped me make it through the day, the constant reminders from the well-intended condolences.

Parts of my dream fit into the day. Parts were coming true, from the morning sunlight and birds and the event at the TTV lot, to passing by the cemetery en route to the studio. Did someone need my help? If so, who?

Being on high alert for the person who'd possibly sent me a secret message in my dream last night was exhausting, but the perfect distraction. In fact, my preoccupation was a lovely distraction from the pain.

At the end of the day I had no leads. The cast seemed fine, in no need of my assistance. I had heard from Lucy that Emma and Dom had been cut from the show.

"They're going to start auditions as soon as it's official!" Lucy said with glee, happy to be the one breaking the news to me.

"Why? Do you know why?"

"They're saying it has to do with contract negotiations."

"But you don't believe that," I said, reading her.

"Not a chance. I overheard Sylvia talking on the phone. Apparently, now get this, Emma thinks she's becoming the star of *Ghost House*! Can you believe it? She's holding out for more money."

"Wow, that's wild. And I thought I had an active imagination."

"I know, I know. But I don't see why that knocks Dom out of the show," she said thoughtfully.

"Tight family? I guess, since they're twins?" I suggested.

"Maybe, though they don't look like it. Still, it's all very weird."

"Are you sure about this?" I would not be sad to see Emma and Dom Vitali go. They were midseason add-ons and I never clicked with either one. I didn't like Emma and Dom gave me the creeps. Adam and the others didn't care for Emma either since she only cared about herself; she was worse than Lucy! But Dom? Everyone loved him. Everyone but me. Having him gone would be a relief.

"Please, who do you think I am? At least their characters weren't very popular. Not like ours, right?"

"Yeah, sure," I said, mulling this change over. Lucy was only half right, because Emma's character did have a growing following.

One full day of activity had shown me what I needed to do. Get on with it.

Whatever 'it' was, I had to get out of the house or I would never do anything. When my dad went back to work, I was shocked and secretly mad that he could go back to his life like nothing had happened. Like his wife hadn't been murdered.

But, maybe that was how it goes with the strong. My dad was strong and courageous. He knew what I didn't: sometimes you've got to do what you don't feel like doing, because if you don't, you waste away. Doing nothing doesn't take the pain away, it allows it to fester. You've got to pretend to live in the land of the living to ever have your heart there again.

And so I resumed my life, or pretended to. A few days later I packed up and hit the road with Adam, Echo ever present in the background. Corey and Suzanne stayed behind since Corey'd gotten a supporting role in a werewolf movie, tentatively titled "Moon Claw Fang."

Corey didn't fight having Suzanne as his bodyguard. Since he'd been marked by the Fourth, he needed protection. It was a working hypothesis that Archie Sawyer, the Fourth who'd killed Kayla and John on set, was the Sweeper who'd threatened Corey. The Fourth didn't do idle threats. They really were a join-or-die group.

Not only did Corey need the protection, he was starting to *like* Suzanne.

The first weeks I hung out in the background, writing in my journal, reading, corresponding with fans online as Adam was in and out of the studio, laying down tracks and doing promo. He took me everywhere with him.

At first I wasn't sure if we were supposed to pretend to not be together. That question was answered right away. Given his mega rock star status and my own budding career, when we were out in public, chances were we'd be photographed. But regardless of whether we were out and about or in the studio or hotel, Adam was sitting by me or holding my hand. In public, he'd never pull away from me, but walked closer.

The only exception was my early morning runs with Echo. Adam was not much for getting up with the new day, and that's when I liked to run. Running with Echo gave me a window into what was really going on with Adam and a way to release some of the energy I was collecting.

The night my mom had died, I'd vowed to keep all my power. But now, months later, if I kept *all* the energy, I wouldn't be fit for public consumption with my levitating and all. Releasing small amounts through exercise, and keeping myself emotionally balanced and centered, I was in control of the rest of the energy, not the other way around.

And then Adam's North American tour began. City after city, crossing the continent on bus. The members of *F&L* were young and wild. At least that's what the fans thought. If only they could've seen what the tour bus was like! It was like traveling with a bunch of old men, because I was. They were all Second, except Adam. Adam was the only one who was the age he looked. The rest were a hundred plus years old.

Mr. Seacrest had made it clear that no one should know I was Fifth, or what had really happened to my mom. The only people who knew for certain about me were Adam and Mr. Seacrest. Echo, Suzanne, and Corey were told once, when Mr. Seacrest suspected I was Fifth, but we'd never revisited that. Never confirmed or denied Mr. Seacrest's suspicion. Echo and Suzanne knew it wasn't their place to ask and Corey didn't understand the significance of the possibility. I just hoped he'd never bring it up. I didn't want to lie to him, but there was no way I was going to burden him with what I really was.

Mr. Seacrest warned me quite harshly to never say a disparaging word against the queen. He claimed everyone was loyal to her and her immediate family. I was to be passed off as Adam's girlfriend who knew something wasn't quite right with him and his friends, but that was all. Mr. Seacrest had Adam order everyone on the tour to leave me alone.

I was already friendly with the way laid-back Ewin, and Kia and Neil were brothers and loyal to Adam. All three were battle-worn and happy for the gig of playing music instead of hunting Fourth. The tour manager and roadies were mostly non-Family people and didn't pay me much attention.

Before bed I took the herbs that dampened my dreams, making it harder for me to be found by anyone looking for dreamers. I wanted to be trained to protect myself, but Mr. Seacrest said it was impractical with the amount of moving around I'd be doing for the next few months. I thought physical proximity was irrelevant for dream training, which made him laugh, though he never explained why. Of course not. I had to settle for his promise to teach me when we began shooting *Ghost House* in the summer.

Keeping me hidden from the outside world used to keep me hidden from myself too, a horrible side effect. At night I felt bottled up. I had no room to think or work out the worries, problems, and puzzles of the day because I felt like I'd been swallowed by oblivion. Maybe my system was getting used to the herb because more and more I was having dreams, disturbing dreams, on a regular basis. And then there were the dreams that were half prophetic, half fantasy.

Most mornings I'd wake with the knowledge of what the inside of the diner we'd be eating at that day looked like. Or particulars about the interior of the venue the band was playing at that night, though I'd never seen either before. That part was fine with me. Amusing even. I'd whisper to Adam some detail of a location before we'd enter and he'd smile back knowingly when we'd both spot it for the first time in the waking world. Though I didn't mind, I could tell it worried Adam because that kind of knowledge wasn't "normal," even for someone like me.

But half the time in my dreams, someone I knew but couldn't place would show up at the end, pleading for help. That was the worst part. It was becoming clear someone needed me. But who?

I wished I could pull Adam into my dreams so he could help me figure out what was going on, but he was taking the herbs too which cut him off from being found, even by me.

The tour progressed without a hitch, for the most part, on the supernatural, scary side. As for the mechanics of the tour, well, equipment failed, GPS flat-out lied several times, there were a few hotels I hoped never to revisit, and our bus broke down in the middle of nowhere South Dakota. But security was Fort Knox tight. No one was getting to us, physically.

Running with Echo helped clear me of the heavy energy during the day, and sleeping next to Adam kept me from screaming at night. Or most nights. And no nights were romantic since Echo was our permanent roommate.

It was near the last leg of the tour when I found I had a new talent. I went to shower after my run and was washing away the sweat and grief. It had been a particularly difficult run because I couldn't get my mom out of my mind. I'd been wanting to talk to her for so long, my desire reached a fever pitch. I cried half of the run, cursing, and talking Echo's ear off when I could breathe. I ran us hard, trying to beat the crushing desire out of me. "Work it out and stuff the rest down," was my motto.

When Echo and I entered the lobby of the hotel I was keyed up, the hair on my arms standing on end. He put his hand on my back and steered me away from the populated lobby to the less used stairwell.

"What is it?" I asked, breathless as he quickly moved us up the stairs.

"Didn't want to wait for the elevator," he evaded nonchalantly. That was code for *you should know by now we don't talk about such things in public.*

"Oh, great idea," I replied, feeling lame and freaked out.

Echo kept his hand on my back for ten flights until we got into our room, and then he dropped it immediately.

Adam still asleep, I mouthed, "What?"

"Your ponytail was rising," he whispered back.

I snorted, shocked. I'd expected something much worse.

"Don't take this lightly. How could you hope to explain it? Think of the havoc one picture could cause."

I shook my head and headed to the shower. I wanted to brush off his warning as that of the overcautious zealot, but he was right. His astuteness was impressed on me when I tried to condition my hair, but it wasn't where I thought it should be. Just to be sure, I stepped out of the shower, wiped off the fogged-up mirror, and stared at my crazy snake-like hair. It was high and dancing about. This wouldn't do.

I was about to dump excess energy down the drain when I decided to try an experiment. When I paid attention, I could feel how much energy I could contain without having this leaking problem. Running naturally allowed me to reach a comfortable set point. Until today. I wondered if there was a way to put my energy somewhere I could retrieve later.

Technically, I wasn't supposed to use any of the stuff flowing through me because it had a way of attracting whomever might be looking.

Lucky for me I was in a hotel, or the shower would've been dumping cold water on me by now. I had one chance to experiment or dump the excess down the drain for the day.

I thought about how I'd do it in a dream. In a dream, I'd see it as something, like a streaming color emanating out of me, or a crystal, and I'd put it in a box only I could see, feel, or open. I thought of the re-runs of *I Dream of Jeanie* I used to watch with my dad. Could I make that happen? Turn extra energy into smoke I could capture in a bottle?

I felt like a dork taking the lid off my shampoo. "Extra energy stuff, go into the bottle," I commanded and decided to believe I could make it happen. Instantly I felt balanced, normal again, the right amount of energy swirling in my veins. To my disappointment there was no smoke, nothing visible. But something had happened, and I felt like something went in the shampoo bottle. I couldn't see what had happened, but I was now in the practice of trusting my intuition first, even over my eyes.

Out of the bathroom, I was greeted by Adam holding a phone in my face. It was a picture of Echo's hand on my back, looking like maybe we were together. "Want to explain this picture? Echo won't say a word. Seems he works for you now."

"I told you I'd let her explain when she got out of the shower," Echo said from the couch, face in a book.

"Did you take a nap in or something? What were you doing in there?"

"Showering?" I smirked, finding his irritation a little funny. I was usually the last to know just about everything, so it felt good to be in the know, even if there wasn't much to share.

"So, love?" Adam asked, waiting.

"My hair. It was standing up and Echo caught it. And someone caught us, apparently. There really are eyes everywhere."

"Oh. Are you okay?" he asked, satisfied that was what was really going on. "Is that what you were doing in there?" he asked, pointing to my white towel turban.

"Uh, something like that," I half lied, which he caught immediately. He was so attuned to me, he barely needed me to talk audibly to know what I was thinking.

"I see," he said, crossing his arms. "Echo, you mind giving us a minute?"

Echo didn't like being put out, but he did what Adam asked, as always. "Will you tell me now?"

I felt nervous. I thought he'd disapprove of what I was attempting and I was worried what he'd do when he found I didn't intend to stop.

"Love, calm down," he said, reacting to my rising anxiety.

"I'm working on something and I need it to be just mine right now. I will tell you, but not yet. Okay?"

"Be careful," was all he said.

I continued to run with Echo, which usually alleviated my excess energy. But some days I had an abundance. I began to notice a correlation between the extra energy and my dreams. On the nights when I had nightmarish dreams about the future, my energy overflowed. Increasingly, I couldn't make it to the shower but had to dump the excess in my water bottle. I got a rush from doing something so powerful, in public, that no one could see. Still, since I really had no idea what I was doing, I had enough sense to know I really ought to do it alone, behind locked doors.

While we were in Toronto, my dad came out to visit. Since I'd left home, we'd talked every day or texted. His texts were just as formal as ever, which was comforting. Dad went to Adam's show, which surprised me a little since he wasn't one to stay up past 9:30 p.m., if he could help it. He was gracious about the music, but Gregorian chant was more his style than the indie rock of *F&L*.

The weekend we were in Toronto was a busy one. The PR team for *Ghost House* flew Jade out as part of a contest and press junket. The people at TTV had been good to me, giving me space. Some days I toyed with not going back to work, backing out of my contract. Some days were bleak.

Being with my dad and hanging out with Jade made for a good weekend. I wasn't at great yet. Nothing felt great. Well, sometimes when Adam held me tight and I could let loose, be myself, my new normal, that was a great feeling. Especially compared to the perpetual fake smile I kept plastered on my face. I wasn't even sure who that smile was for. The band and crew knew my mom had just died and none of them needed me to be happy and normal. I think, actually, the smile was for me. If I pretended, day after day, maybe one day I wouldn't be pretending anymore. One day the smile would be real again.

No one from *Ghost House* had received any scripts for the upcoming season. Apparently, something big was going to happen and we were going to go into the table reads in June cold. TTV sent Jade out to Toronto because at the end of the first season our characters had just gotten together. I'm sure it didn't get past the TV executives that we'd be doing a mini press junket with my TV boyfriend on my right and my real rock star boyfriend on my left.

Jade went to the concert with me and my dad on Friday night, and my dad followed us around on Saturday and Sunday as we answered questions, went to an award show, filmed a few spots, surprised a number of fans who'd won a contest, made radio appearances, and so on. It was a jam-packed weekend.

Jade and my dad hit it off. I guess I shouldn't have been surprised. My dad talked to college kids for a living. Before Jade became a full-time cast member, he'd been going to the local university in Martin. Jade was super smart and easy to talk to. And kind. In fact, he was more at ease with my dad than with me. Adam said it was because Jade liked me. I told Adam to shut it.

Sunday night, Jade flew to California to do more work for the studio. My dad was going back home Monday afternoon, and since *F&L* had a radio appearance in the morning, my dad and I had some time alone. Sorta.

I dreamt the night before of a bakery downtown. In the morning I looked it up, and sure enough, it was within walking distance from the hotel. Adam and his gang went off to do rock-n-roll business; my dad and I went for breakfast. Along with Echo, of course.

"Jade's a nice guy. Have you two become friends?" my dad asked, reaching for napkins.

"Yeah. There's something about him. Right away we clicked. You know how you do that with some people? I feel like we see eye to eye on a lot of things. But he is fairly shy. And, well, it's just that… it feels weird talking about this with you, Dad, and you, Echo."

"You know it goes in one ear," Echo replied.

"Yeah, I know." I could trust Echo to not give my secrets away. Not even to Adam.

"What is it?" my dad asked.

"Well, *Ghost House* did awesome last year, and our ratings are steady for downloads. But I'm worried about this new season. About them pushing the envelope with …"

"Sex?"

"I wasn't going to say that, Dad, but yeah, I guess. I mean, in the new season my character's dating Jade's and I'm sure we'll have to kiss a lot and stuff. I'm worried about that. How it will feel. I tell myself it's just acting. It's not real. But it's still my body and my lips, you know? At the end of last season, when I kissed Jade I was so nervous, and it was awkward, made worse with take after take. I'm more worried about when I'm not feeling nervous or awkward, but normal, maybe?"

"Anna, this is your life. No one else's. You make the choices you can live with. Don't let anyone push you into doing anything that makes you compromise yourself. It's good to feel pushed and stretched, challenged. But not compromised. And you have to decide what that means for you. You may decide this role isn't for you if it involves being romantic with someone you don't want touching you. But, honey, it's for you to decide."

49

"But what about Adam? How will he feel when he sees Jade or someone else all over me?"

"I'm not concerned with him."

"But his feelings matter to me."

"And you, how would you feel if you saw Adam kissing someone, like Lucy's character?" Echo asked.

"Do you know something?" I asked, aghast. I'd hated when Adam had had to pretend to be with Emma for publicity's sake. Would I have to suffer through him being with Lucy now? And on screen?

"How could I?" Echo asked, a twinkle in his eye. That twinkle was there because lately he knew more about a variety of interesting news items than he should.

"Regardless, it's a good question," my dad said, bringing us back on point.

"I would absolutely hate it, of course. But I also know he wouldn't mean it. I mean, the kiss wouldn't mean anything to him. I know how he feels about me."

"Are you so certain? You are, aren't you?" my dad said, answering his own question. "I didn't realize where you stood with Adam."

"I love him, Dad."

The conversation stopped as our pastries arrived at the table. My dad started chuckling to himself mid-bite. So out of character. He took a sip of coffee to right himself. Seeing him working to control the giggles set me smiling. Before I knew it, I was laughing so hard I could barely breathe and the rest of the bakery patrons were giving us looks. Echo was the only one who had it under control.

"What's so funny?" I finally asked. My stomach felt like I'd been doing crunches.

"Sorry, sorry," my dad said, getting it under control. "What's funny? It's more the absurdity that struck me. Here we are, in Canada because you are in love with a famous musician and on a press tour yourself, eating lovely croissants at a fancy bakery, as you open up to me, in public, and in front of another friend of yours. Anna, you're the most private person I know."

"I guess you don't know me anymore," I whispered, sobered up.

"That's why I'm here. We have each other, but only if we decide to." My dad stopped. "Do you have to be here?" he asked Echo.

"Yes, sir."

"Is that because of the massacre?"

Echo looked to me to interpret what my dad meant. It took me a second to figure out why that word would be coming out of his mouth.

"You read what I gave you?" I asked quietly. I immediately fell into my meditation exercises. If I wasn't careful, my emotions would get the best of me and it was anyone's guess what might happen. Why couldn't my dreams give me useful information like this? I would've much rather known about an ambush from my dad than a fantastic place for breakfast.

I closed my eyes and took a deep breath, willing myself to be rooted to the ground, to be hidden from prying eyes and ears, and to be present and honest with my dad.

"The house was broken into last week," he said as I opened my eyes.

"What? Are you okay? Were you there?"

"I was, but I'm fine."

"You've got to be kidding me! You were there?" That was it! He'd have to have a security detail too.

"It was in the middle of the night, it must've been, because when I woke up, I heard something coming from your bedroom. Sirens. One of your windows was slightly ajar. I looked around your room and someone had definitely been in there. I went through the rest of the house and found nothing gone or out of place. From what I could gather, just your room had been disturbed. It could be someone came in through your window and heard something and got scared before they had a chance to go through the rest of the house."

I could feel what my dad was feeling. He didn't believe this assessment, even though he wanted to.

"Later that day I read what you gave me."

"Anna, this should not be talked about here," Echo said over his shoulder, nonchalantly.

"Shall we go back to the hotel?" I suggested.

On the way back, my dad put his arm over my shoulder as we walked. "I didn't come here for an explanation. I just needed to see you and make sure you are okay. Is that his job?"

"Echo is relentless."

"Would it be better or worse for you if I moved to Martin for the filming of season two of *Ghost House*?"

"You'd come for me? What about work?"

"I might be able to get a semester's leave. If not, Martin has a university. I could contact the head of the Philosophy Department," he said, holding open the hotel door for me.

Waiting for the elevator, I hugged him. I loved my dad so much. I knew he loved me too, but to leave his job to be with me? The amazing thing about my dad was he meant it. He'd thought through his offer. He wasn't just saying it on the fly. And so I thought about it as we quietly rode the elevator to our floor.

His plane was scheduled to leave in a few hours, so I helped him pack. I didn't want to shut him out, not when he was making such a grand gesture. But I also knew, for the time being, his safety meant staying put.

"Dad, your offer means more to me than you know. But, really, at least now, I think it's best for both of us if you stay at home. That would be safest."

"Best, maybe, but not as existentially satisfying."

"I'm not sure what that means, but, for me, knowing you are at home and going to work and being with your friends, that's comforting."

"But, dear, how are you going to be able to go back there?"

Unbidden, per usual, the horror scene of my mom's murder ran through my mind.

"I've been back most nights. So, being there in the day won't be nearly as tough."

"I don't want this for you. How can I help?"

"I don't know."

"If you can think of a way, you will let me know. Yes? Can I count on you for that?"

The concierge hailed a cab for my dad. I watched as he rode off. We were closer than ever before. Though he'd read my extremely brief outline, he hadn't asked for any details. For now. But I knew my dad. Someday, soon, we'd be having that hard talk.

Chapter Seven

Adam's tour wrapped the night before we had to be in Martin for table reads. Wow, the difference a year makes! Driving into town was like seeing an old friend. Because of the way Sylvia ran her productions, she kept a barebones crew, which made for a close-knit family feel.

Adam, Echo, and I arrived on location with just enough time for hugs, shooting the breeze, and to see Corey walk in holding hands with Suzanne. We'd talked most days, and I knew he was dating her, but it was still shocking to see them together.

Apparently Lucy had been wrong about Dom and Emma. They were at the table with the rest of us. One of Sylvia's PAs handed out the season opener's top-secret script as she called us to attention.

"Welcome back! Well, we've got a lot on our plates. I know you'll all give me the dedication and level of work you gave last year. The reason you're just now getting the copy is due to last minute changes. I've been working with the writers and they've come up with some amazing story ideas, diverging from where we were originally going to go at the end of season one. I'm excited for the changes, such as the two locations we're introducing. Unfortunately, we're losing two of our cast in the first episode. Emma, you'll be missed."

She said Emma, but not Dom. Shoot! I had gotten my hopes up Dom was leaving. Who was number two?

So Lucy was half right. Looking around the table, it was kind of obvious who already knew what was up and was pretending to be shocked, and those who weren't in the know. That would be just Jade. I'd have to do a better job keeping him in the *Ghost House* loop.

Sylvia didn't give an explanation as to why Emma was leaving, whether she'd been cut or wanted to leave. "That's the only spoiler I'm giving you. Let's get this read underway." We began.

After Meg read the last line of the season opener to a completely silent and stunned room, Sylvia said, "While season one of *Ghost House* centered on Meg and Corey's move to town, making friends along with typical high school angst, and finding out their new home was haunted, season two is going to pick up the pace. And as you now know, we are losing Keith Prater as well as Emma Vitali.

"Our shooting schedule has changed due to the last minute rewrites. I'm also still looking for a few slots to fill. We're close to casting the English teacher and tennis coach."

"Tennis?" Meg asked.

"Ah, caught me. I wasn't going to give anything away, but it's on some of your schedules anyway. Ladies, hope you like hitting the ball around. Your real-life coach arrives on Wednesday. Phil, did you send the link?" Sylvia asked her PA.

"Yes," he nodded. Sylvia's PA's were rarely heard. She ran such a lean operation, they usually weren't afforded the luxury of standing still for more than a few minutes.

"Meg, Lucy, Anna, and Suzanne, if you aren't familiar with the rules of tennis, please follow the link and read up. Scratch that, I want you to even if you think you know the game. I also want you to spend time watching matches. Just go to the link and look around. Now, I'm certain you have many questions. Just know the studio is 100% behind season two of *Ghost House*. Tomorrow we shoot promos. Check your schedule for when you need to be at the manor. Our second annual welcoming party for the entire cast is tonight at the high school gym and I expect everyone to be there. We will be doing some shooting tonight, in case you're wondering what the crew is up to."

"Lucky for you, Meg. You're probably totally up on the game right now," Lucy said to Meg.

"And why is that?" Meg asked.

"Cause of Venus and Serena Williams," she replied. Without blinking Lucy added, "You know, because they're black."

Chairs creaked and groans from every corner could be heard.

"So, you're saying, Meg would naturally be following tennis because their skin matches hers? Not because Venus and Serena are amazingly talented tennis players, or strong role-models, or smart and savvy in business or even just because Meg might happen to like tennis?" Corey challenged.

Lucy looked perplexed as to why Corey was mad at her.

"Come on, Lucy. Geeze. What about me, Sylvia? What's happening to my character?" Suzanne asked, changing the subject. Suzanne's character was now a ghost and she was eager to find her status in season two.

"By the end of episode three you'll be back in your body. And that's the last spoiler. Lucy, behave. Everyone good?" Sylvia asked, looking at Meg.

"Fine. Glad to be back. I'm really looking forward to season two," Meg said with genuine feeling, dispelling any remaining tension.

Phil, who'd left, walked back in and whispered something into Sylvia's ear. "Okay crew, more surprises to come. Here's to a great season. Keep up the hard work."

There was a palpable buzz of excitement in the air. The opener was that good. But I was the elephant in the room. No one wanted to look at me, not even Corey. Adam had his hand on my knee, trying to help me keep it together. I sat immobile as everyone filed out. The only comment I heard came from Lucy.

"Why does she get the juicy parts?" Lucy whined to Meg.

"Shut up!" Meg replied, disgusted. Lucy looked mystified by Meg's response. Lucy was really sticking her foot in it today.

Corey was barely out the door when my phone vibrated with a text.

"Call me ASAP!!!"

"It's from Corey," I said to Adam, looking at my phone.

"Love, I… I don't know what to say," he said, sitting quietly next to me.

"You know, I'd been dreading the reading, wondering if the writers would have me doing stuff with Jade that would make me uncomfortable. I was just…wow… utterly unprepared for that."

"That" was what the writers had in store for my character, Laura Vincent. Near the end of season one, I'd been possessed by a ghost. The writers hadn't done much with that subplot, beyond me waking up and noticing a chunk of time was unaccounted for on a couple of occasions. Not this season. In the opener, I kill both Keith Prater (Corey and Meg's TV dad) and Emma.

The second scene had me pushing Keith to his death from the third floor of Gold Manor. That wasn't so bad. The real kicker was the way I would kill off Emma.

In an extended scene, Meg, Emma, and I get locked in the basement of Gold Manor. By the end of the long scene, the ghost has taken control of my body and plunged a butcher knife into Emma's heart. Meg's bloodcurdling scream snaps me out of the trance. I come to my senses just in time to see Emma's character die, using her last breath to hex me.

"What can I do?" Adam asked, taking my hands.

"What's there to do? I mean, the storyline makes perfect sense. That is, if I can detach myself. You don't seem particularly surprised."

"No, not really. It's a show. The writers aren't concerned with our personal lives."

"This is exactly what I mean! Gahh! Why can't my dreams be helpful? I knew what everyone would be wearing today. I'm fairly certain of the set list the DJ's playing tonight and I know what's being served for snacks."

"At least you've got dreams," Adam said wistfully.

When Adam took the herb he had no dreams. Even when he didn't take the herb, but was around me, he usually didn't dream. There was something about how we reacted to each other. We were both dreamers, but the more time he spent around me, it seemed I siphoned whatever dreaming he was capable of and fed on that energy.

"Double edged sword. My dreams these days are filled with useless information and graves, death, fear, you know, general madness and terror."

"Uncle will be in town in a few days. With him here, hopefully we can get back on track sorting out what's going on with me and you. You ready to tell me what you've been up to?"

I looked around the room. I was about to tell him about my experiment with capturing and saving my extra energy, when I felt a prick in the back of my mind. Something was coming. It felt like my brain was being dipped in ice water.

Adam leaned in and whispered, "Resist but don't react. Kiss me."

The pain grew as the footsteps came closer. I threw myself into the kiss. I focused all my energy on Adam, on the feel of his lips, his warmth. I grabbed his t-shirt, trying to get as close to him as physically possible, letting everything else in the world fall away as if my life depended on it.

I found I was somehow sitting on Adam's lap when my concentration was broken.

"Sorry to interrupt. Guess I missed the read," the guy said.

I didn't look at him, I couldn't. My mind felt like it was fracturing and about to explode. I hid my face in Adam's shoulder, pretending to be embarrassed for being caught making out in public.

"No worries. And you are?"

"Finn. Finn Varga," he laughed, his last name sounding strange when he said it, as though he were not used to using it.

"I'm Adam. New?"

"Just got the gig. I missed the read? GPS doesn't know about this place."

"There's a schedule on the chair over there. Sylvia's around here somewhere."

"Catch you two later," Finn said, walking out.

The further away he walked, the more the pain receded. By the time I heard him exit the building I was back to normal, though trembling.

"What was that?" I whispered, terrified.

Adam shook his head to silence me and pulled out his phone. He began a group text to all Family members in Martin. "Band rehearsal canceled," was his cryptic message.

Chapter Eight

Adam held my face in his hands, taking in my terrified look. "That was embarrassing. Let's go to the manor and drop off our stuff, shall we?"

"I wanted to talk to Corey. I haven't seen him in a few months," I mumbled, trying to act like I wasn't totally freaking out on the inside.

"He's probably there," Adam said casually.

I didn't know what he was doing, but I felt his confidence. He wasn't afraid at all.

We walked out of the building holding hands. I concentrated on feeling nothing but Adam. I wanted to test the area, reach out to see what was out there, but I was too afraid of what I might find or who I might accidentally tip off.

We were met in the Gold Manor parking lot by Suzanne.

"Hey, you two. Need any help?"

"Thanks. You know where Echo is?" Adam asked, popping the trunk carelessly.

"On the third floor. That's where you're staying, Anna. We all have separate rooms this season. I'll help you up," Suzanne said.

"Thanks," I said, trying to match their normalcy.

Just as we came in the house, Lucy walked by on her way to the kitchen.

"Oh, hey, guys. Great to be back!"

"Are you staying at the manor this season?" I asked, surprised.

"Me? Are you kidding?" she dismissed me.

"You want to help us unload their car?" Suzanne asked Lucy, her arms loaded.

"What do I look like? A bellhop?" she scoffed and continued on her way. Lucy was sure growing into herself.

Upstairs, we found Corey and Echo in my new room for the season. Adam locked the door and made a brief explanation. "A chimney sweep. Fourth looking for others like them."

"Did you get caught? What happened?" Echo asked, perplexed.

"I can't explain it all. I don't think that he recognized us for what we are."

"How could he, right, with your protection. You know, what you do so the Fourth can't find you?" Corey asked.

"He wasn't alone," Adam said. "There was another."

"Why are they here? Coincidence?" Suzanne asked, puzzled. "Are they back for Corey so soon?"

"Doubtful. I know who it is. He's making an appearance on the show. It's Finn Varga," Adam announced.

"Finn Varga is a Fourth? He's on our show? You've got to be kidding me! How many of your kind are there? Or is he like me, doesn't know who or what he is?" Corey asked.

Adam shook his head. "Possibly, but unlikely. Finn Varga was the chimney sweep."

As Adam made this pronouncement, I could tell he wasn't completely sure if he was right.

"Wait. This doesn't make any sense. I saw him. I didn't believe my eyes, because why would Finn Varga be in Martin, Tennessee? But I saw him as Suzanne and I were leaving the parking lot," Corey said.

"But why weren't you affected then? Why were you still in the parking lot?" I asked.

Corey went red in the face. "We were still there, okay? But I didn't feel anything. Last time a chimney sweep came around it felt like red hot pokers had been shoved into my brain."

"Finn Varga wasn't the sweeper?" Echo asked, confused.

"I guess not, but he was the only person we saw," Adam said slowly, trying to make sense of what had happened to me. "Maybe the sweeper was in the car, waiting for him."

"But Corey didn't feel anything. What are you not saying?" Echo asked Corey.

What I noticed was Suzanne's remarkable reserve. She was hiding something.

"Didn't you recognize there was another Fourth around?" I asked her.

"Of course she would've. Suzanne, what's going on?" Echo prodded.

Suzanne - strong, assertive, never at a loss for words Suzanne - stood speechless and immobile.

Chapter Nine

"Out with it," Adam commanded.

"Hey, give her some space," I said. I didn't like it when Adam pulled rank. It made me feel uncomfortable.

"Sorry, doesn't work that way, love. Suzanne?"

"Okay, fine. You know I had a life before I was with you. Not a happy life, but a life. And Finn Varga was part of it."

"Are you his sister?" Corey guessed.

"No. Her ex," I said. Judging by the sound of her heart, coupled with her reluctance, Finn Varga was definitely a past love.

"Thanks, Anna, but I can speak for myself. That is very annoying. Yes, I dated Finn a long time ago." Suzanne stopped. She clearly didn't feel like discussing her love life in front of us.

"And?" Echo said.

"That's her business. Lay off," Corey said, coming up behind her.

"Unfortunately, it's not. We don't have those kinds of luxuries, and you know it, Suzanne," Echo pushed.

"I know, I know. Finn was my first love. I'd been living on the streets of L.A. I was a runaway. That's what happens when you have Fourth in you. I was a hard kid to raise. My mom was a single parent. My dad was the one with the Fourth blood. Anyway, I wouldn't listen to my mom's rules because I thought I was so smart and she didn't have a clue. One day I got angry and tore up my bedroom. She told me to clean it or get out. I left and never went back. I was fourteen."

"I'm sorry." I knew she'd had a hard life, but she'd never talked about herself.

"Yeah, well, life sucks for people like me. All this madness running in my veins? About a year later a team of chimney sweeps found me. They told me my options: join them or die. I had nothing to lose and they were offering a direction for my life, and hell, food. So I joined. I was taken to their training facility in Brazil. That's where I met Finn. Everyone else treated me like dirt, but not him. He was a year younger and we bonded almost instantly. Given who he was and who I was, we had to keep our relationship a secret. And that's that."

I didn't know what to say. I was even more surprised that her story came as a shock to Echo and Adam. How did they not know this?

"Finish," Adam said, but this time he spoke as a friend, not her commander.

"Ah, yes. When I met you I'd just been given a particularly nasty assignment, I'm sure I told you. As much as I wanted to stay alive, I couldn't do it. I knew I'd signed my own death sentence by not carrying out my orders, but I felt dead inside anyway. I had lots of anger, but I never had the heart of a killer. Guess there's not enough Fourth in me."

"Suzanne, finish," Adam said once again.

Suzanne crossed her arms and said through tight lips, "I left the Fourth family because I couldn't kill for them anymore. But when I left, I was still with Finn. We'd sworn we'd be together forever. But I knew if I told him I was leaving, he would've come with me. Me they'd let go, but not him. They'd never let him go."

"Why?" I asked, my hand over my heart.

"He's pure Fourth. He's the son of Dane and Lilian."

It felt like a bomb went off in the room. Adam started swearing, Echo had to clutch the windowsill for support, and tears were running down Suzanne's face.

Corey and I looked at each other, completely baffled, waiting to be filled in.

"I can't believe you failed to tell me this," Adam barked, equally pissed and hurt.

"It wasn't relevant before," Suzanne said, defending herself.

"What's going on?" I asked lightly. When I placed my hand on Adam's back, his anxiety was so high it felt like I'd stuck my finger in a socket. Man did it sting.

"Ow, ow, ow," I danced around, clutching my hand.

"Buggar, love. Sorry. Let me see," Adam said, snapping out of his mini rage-fest.

I unclenched my fist. Where I'd touched him, the tips of my fingers were a periwinkle dead-looking color, fading to my normal hue at my wrist. Speechless, as we looked at my hand, a ripple ran from my fingertips through my arm, disappearing under my sleeve.

"Whoa," I said, jerking my hand back. "What was that?"

"What?" Corey asked.

"Didn't you see that thing under my skin? And my fingers?" I asked.

"Looks normal to me," Corey said slowly.

"Echo?" I asked, holding up my hand. It was in the process of returning to its natural state, but anyone could clearly see it still looked wrong.

"What am I looking for?"

"Suzanne?" I asked hopefully.

"Sorry. Looks like a hand."

"How do you feel?" Adam asked, taking my arm and turning it over.

"Startled and confused."

He laughed. "Obviously. I mean, are you in any pain?"

"No, not really."

Adam had switched from studying my arm to rubbing it. "We'll deal with this later. As to Finn Varga, you didn't tell us because you didn't want to alert us to him. Correct?"

"Yes," Suzanne said without apology. "I don't expect you to understand. And I don't think this should throw my allegiance into question. I fight for the First and Second Families. Nothing I have done suggests otherwise."

"Until now," Echo bit back, hurt.

"Finn is my past, as is the Fourth. That's all I have to say. You'd know otherwise."

I felt out, as did Adam, to see if she was telling the truth. What she was leaving out was her terror at seeing Finn again. Her fear was masking its origin. Was she still in love with him? Was she afraid of what Finn would do to her?

"If you can think of anything else, this is the time. I don't like being caught like that, Suzanne. Now to the question, why did Finn's vibe hit Anna and not Corey? What did you feel, Suzanne, in the parking lot?"

"Nothing. Not a thing. I had no idea a Fourth was anywhere close by. What happened to Anna?"

"It's hard to explain, but I felt its filthy presence. That's how I knew to feel out for a sweeper," Adam said, reluctant to tell everyone what really happened to me. I followed his lead and stayed silent.

"Is this something new with the Fourth?" Echo asked.

"Let's hope not. If Finn is the son of Dane and Lilian and living a public life, he's probably doing something to mask his identity," Adam surmised and Suzanne nodded in agreement.

"Like the herbs you take?" I asked, catching on.

"In general, we don't know who is part of the Fourth and they don't know who we are. We know who some of their leaders are and vice versa, but we don't know who the enemy is until we encounter one. And then, only one side walks away."

"Is that why Suzanne says you saved her life?" I asked.

"If it wasn't for Adam and his protection, they would've found me and killed me for leaving. No one gets to leave. On either side."

"Back to Anna," Corey said, looking at me. "Could it be there's something Finn's doing that only affects Anna?"

Looking defeated, Adam called his uncle. Mr. Seacrest had basically told me I was useless to work with while I was mourning the death of my mother, though he had said it nicer than that. Still, the message was the same. I was happy to be rid of him for a while. I knew he was on my side for the time being, but he was as changeable as the wind. If he decided I needed to die, that would be that, no matter what allegiance he had sworn to me.

Adam said I had trust issues. Yeah. No doubt. I wasn't sure if I could ever really trust anyone from the Families again after what had happened to my mom.

"Uncle's looking into it," Adam said, keeping whatever he'd learned from his uncle to himself.

"Did he know about Finn?" I asked. Surely Mr. Seacrest had come across him before.

"No."

"When do we take him out?" Echo asked Adam. The way Echo asked implied the answer was going to be immediately.

"No! This is exactly why I never outed him. Finn is different. Why do you think he went into acting?"

"For money, fame, and power. Sounds like a Fourth to me. When do we kill him?" Echo repeated.

"Stop it! I mean it. Come on. Be smart about this. We aren't them. We don't kill just to kill. You don't know that he's done anything."

"He's a Fourth and that's enough," Echo challenged.

"You want to kill me?" asked Suzanne.

"You're different. It's not the same."

"Give him a chance. Please. When have I ever asked for anything? Just wait and see. No promises. He doesn't know who you are, so we have the upper hand. Please. And besides, there's no way Dane and Lilian's son isn't guarded."

"We can't risk it. How do you know he won't kill you, Suzanne, when he sees you?" Adam asked, starting to lean towards Echo's corner.

This side of Adam scared me. The warrior. He was prepared to leave right now and cut Finn down, kill him. It hit me anew how foreign Adam was to me.

"I don't know, but I'm willing to risk it. Please," she begged.

Adam was distracted when his cell rang.

"Yes? Okay. Not until seven. Yes. Thank you," he said, hanging up. "Uncle has an idea. Echo, I need you to go get a tool, any tool, from one of the boxes we found in the cave."

"I can do it," Suzanne offered.

"No. Echo, go. Take Corey."

I could practically see the hairs on the back of Corey's neck standing on end. "I don't have to listen to you." Corey hated being ordered around.

"Do you want to help Anna?" Adam barked. "I need something that belonged to that Third and I need it fast because Anna needs to fall asleep with it in her hands in the next minute. You're wasting time."

"You could've said so in the first place," Corey retorted, still upset from all the bombshells dropped on him.

"We don't explain. You're expected to trust and obey," Adam said.

"You've mistaken me for someone else, man."

"Wasting time!" Adam yelled.

"You coming?" Echo said, trying to get Corey moving.

Corey wanted to stay and fight. He'd decided he was pissed at Adam, that all this was his fault somehow. But he left. Corey would do whatever he could to help me.

When they were gone, it was just the three of us.

"Anna, Uncle wants to meet you. He thinks he knows how to keep you hidden."

"What do I need to do?"

"I know it's difficult, but you need to fall asleep."

"I've got a splitting headache. I could use a little sleep."

"When you go under, you'll have the Third object in your hands. Decide to take it with you and to meet Uncle in the training room. He'll tell you what to do."

"Will you be joining us?" I asked hopefully.

"No, I've got other business to attend to," he said, looking at Suzanne. "I'll be back soon. Suzanne?" Adam said, opening my bedroom door.

"Wait," I said, throwing my arms around him. "Thank you for saving me and keeping me safe," I breathed into his neck. I wanted nothing more than for the world to melt away and just be with Adam. Just the two of us. I didn't like real life drama, and we'd only been back in Martin for a few hours!

"Go easy on her. Can you feel how torn up she is?" I whispered.

"I'll see you soon," he said, kissing the top of my head.

Alone in the room that was mine for the duration of the shoot, I curled up on the bed, trying to relax. I thought of Suzanne and her desperation and how Adam hadn't responded to my plea on her behalf. I hoped he knew what he was doing.

I was in the middle of my deep breathing exercises when Corey and Echo knocked on my door.

"Yes?"

"We can't find the boxes," Corey said, agitated.

"They're gone," Echo added. He looked sick, like he was about to throw up. He was really worried, but not about me.

"What's going on?" I asked him.

"We told you, the boxes are missing. We put them down in the basement, in the cellar, but they're not there," Corey said, misunderstanding me. "But... hey, I've got an idea. I'll be right back."

Corey ran out leaving Echo with me.

"Echo, what's really wrong?" I'd been through a few harrowing experiences with him and had never seen him this worked up. He shook his head slightly, tight lipped. A wave of his emotion hit me and I saw.

"Oh. I'm sure it'll be okay."

"Then you don't know how we deal with traitors. Why do you think Adam wouldn't let her go look for the tools?"

"There is no way he's going to harm her," I said, losing confidence as soon as the words were out of my mouth. "Would he?"

"He has to. He already spared her life once. Just for being a Fourth. But everyone knows she's under his protection. Anything she screws up means his head. I can't believe she didn't level with him when they met! What an idiot!"

"You mean Adam's going to kill her?"

"Probably already has."

"I've got to stop him," I said, charging for the door. Echo grabbed me by the shoulders and pushed me back on the bed in a rage.

"No. Don't you get it? He has to kill her. And I will hate him forever. She's like my sister. But if for some reason he doesn't? How could I ever respect him?" he shouted.

"You'd get over it," I said, getting up. "Now get out of my way." I barreled into him, trying to get to the door. He pushed me back on the bed just as the door opened. Quick as a wink, Adam shoved him against the wall.

"What's going on here? Don't you ever touch her again!" Adam was a ball of fury and disappointment.

Echo didn't fight back. "Where's Suzanne? What'd you do to her?"

"That is between me and her," Adam said, letting him go. "Now get out of here before I change my mind and send you away. Touch her again and I swear," he let out his warning to Echo's back as he left my room. Adam's intent was crystal clear. If Echo ever got aggressive with me again, bye, bye Echo.

"Are you okay, love? What happened?" he asked, looking me over.

"Echo told me you were going to kill Suzanne because she's a traitor. I wanted to stop you but he wouldn't let me pass."

"Were you afraid?"

"No, just pissed. I was stunned by the whole thing. The thought of you killing anyone, first Finn and then Suzanne, our friend, and then Echo pushing me around. Now I'm mad at myself for letting Echo win. I should've been able to take him."

"You want to fight Echo?"

"No. I love Echo. Don't you?"

"He's… you know it's complicated. He's like a brother, a half-brother of sorts, and Suzanne's like a sister, and they still serve me. We are at constant war. Loyalty is everything."

"But they are loyal."

"Suzanne lied and we all know it. That alone is reason enough to take her life in our courts. In fact, if I don't, I need a damn good reason. If I don't kill her and I let her live, I'll lose Echo. There are few rules we live by, but loyalty in your inner circle is a must or you don't live long. This is a truth proved time and time again."

"I can tell you haven't hurt her. Did you come up with such a reason?"

"You. You are my reason. To protect you, the one I love. Finn's or Suzanne's death could bring Families on both sides to you, and this isn't the time."

"But this isn't the end of it, is it? What is Suzanne going to have to do to get back on your good side?"

"That is between the two of us. I can tell you she'll have to trust me on the Finn issue."

"You mean she has no say? That's cruel. Don't you think she's still in love with him?"

"That doesn't really matter."

"That's really mean! I can't believe you're being so heartless. Especially after all we've been through."

"No, love, you misunderstand. If Finn is a typical Fourth, Suzanne will have to stay away from him regardless of her personal feelings. If, for some reason, he may want to defect…. Well, let's work on getting you fixed up. You're supposed to be with Uncle by now."

"I've got it," Corey said, busting into my room, a huge smile on his face, Echo following behind. "Aren't I so smart? Yes, yes, you're lucky to have the likes of me around in a crisis," he said, thrusting a book into my hand, breathless. "Here."

He'd placed in my hand the binder we'd put together of all the stuff we'd collected and found out about the cave and the Gold Manor massacre.

"Good thinking," Adam said.

"It's not what you asked for, but we did find the newspaper clippings in the cave."

"Thank you. And sorry for before. I was out of line," Adam said to Corey, shocking him.

"No worries, man. It's been one crazy day. You need anything else, Anna?"

"I think I'm fine. Hopefully I'll see you at the cast party tonight and we can hang out, catch up?"

"Sure. Good luck. You know where Suzanne is?"

Adam shook his head.

"Me neither," I added. "Are you okay? Hearing all that about her past?"

"Later, okay?" Adam both asked and gently commanded. I desperately wanted to hug Corey, tell him everything was going to be okay, and listen. I hated to see him leave. But it would have to wait. My mentor was waiting for me.

"Okay, I'm lost. How can I be in the same room with Finn at the cast party tonight? I thought I was going to die." I couldn't imagine how I was supposed to play it cool around Finn Varga when his presence literally made me feel like my head was going to explode.

"There might be an antidote to counter whatever he's doing to your nervous system," Adam explained.

Chapter Ten

I woke up gagging. I tried to make it to the bathroom down the hall but threw up before I reached the door. I dropped to my knees and couldn't stop until it was all out.

After a bout of dry heaving – apparently my body wanted to be certain the elixir Mr. Seacrest gave me was entirely out of my system - I was covered in a bright, milky blue substance. It wasn't sticky, so much as watery, like I'd gulped down a cup of electric blue watercolors and promptly vomited it right back up, with chunks of my lunch here and there.

"Oh. My. Word! Are you okay?" Meg cried, walking out of the bathroom and dropping to her knees. "Anna, your eyes. What happened?"

I squeezed my eyes shut. "No, no, I feel fine. Just gross and wet. Something I ate. What time is it?"

"A little after four. Do you need help?"

"No, thanks. I'm going to take a long hot shower."

"Good luck with that. There's some problem with the plumbing. That's why I'm up here. I'm seriously thinking about moving. Buying a place. You wouldn't believe how cheap real estate is around here."

"Sounds interesting. Mind if we talk about this later?" I really wanted to get into the bathroom and look at my face after Meg's comment about my eyes. That and get the cold ick off my body.

"Sure thing. I'll have house cleaning get this."

"Thanks," I said, using the wall to help me stand. I felt better, no longer sick to my stomach, but weak.

One look at my reflection in the bathroom mirror and I shrieked. The blue was running from my nose, but that was nothing compared to my eyes. The liquid had gotten under my contacts, making the whole of my eyes an eerie cobalt blue. The whites of my eyes were a brighter blue. I looked like an alien, complete with navy tears.

The door thundered. "Anna? Anna?"

It was Adam.

"Are you alone?" I asked through the door.

"Echo is here."

"Will you ask him to bring me my smaller bag? The turquoise and tropical flower duffle bag?"

I heard feet run off but could feel Adam on the other side of the door. I opened the door and pulled him in, my head bent. I slowly raised my head to meet his eyes, feeling his shock run through my body.

"What in the world? What happened? What did Uncle do to you?" he asked, shaking in anger.

"I'm okay. Really. He gave me a dose of an herb, similar to the one we take at night, but specifically for Thirds. He said after this initial heavy dosage I should be able to take a small amount with side effects like the ones we're used to."

"You look absolutely insane."

"That good, huh?" I laughed. I was glad I was back from the meeting with Mr. Seacrest with a relatively painless solution. "I'm incredibly tired. I just need to get cleaned up. If that's even possible." If the blue stained my skin as it looked like it would, it was going to be hard to explain.

"I can't believe Uncle had something for you. I honestly thought it was a fool's errand."

"He didn't want me to tell you, but he knew I would anyway. He went to his library. When you called him, he remembered a story about a Third defector and how someone had come up with an herb to keep her hidden from the other Third and the Fourth. I wish he would've taken me to the library."

"Uncle has a long memory when it suits him."

"I'm glad it suited him to help me. You may also be interested to know he thinks Finn should be spared until thoroughly investigated."

"He does, does he?" Adam asked, deep in thought as he ran a hand towel under the sink and brought it to my face, washing off the grime. "And you? Shall I have your opinion on the subject?"

"You already know what I think. No one should lose his life based solely on affiliation. That's the very essence of injustice."

Adam ran the washcloth under the sink again, this time adding soap, and I took the opportunity to take out my ruined contacts. He stopped and looked at my naked eyes, gently kissing each, and returned to the work of cleaning me up. His soft, careful, meticulous way felt intimate. I thought intimacy was something only found when you were kissing someone or doing something physical of that sort. But Adam's care, despite the fact I smelled like rotten eggs and was covered with a sheen of my own vomit, was reserved for only the closest of relationships.

"See? With a little soap and elbow grease, the blue is coming right off."

There was a knock on the door. "Here's your bag, Anna."

"Thanks," I said, about to open the door. Adam grabbed my hand, stopping me.

"Leave it, mate. I'll see you at the party. I know you've got work to do," Adam said to Echo through the door while studying my eyes.

When Adam was certain Echo had gone, he retrieved my bag.

"You didn't want Echo to see me like this?"

"Images have a way of outing even the most loyal."

"I don't really understand what you mean."

"Suffice it to say, no one should see you as you truly are unless absolutely, life or death, necessary. And I mean specifically your life, Anna. Do you hear me?"

"Got it," I said for his benefit, but knowing in my heart I'd do whatever was needed to save those I loved.

"What a frustrating person you are! Why must everything be a battle with you? You're just like Corey," he said, responding to what I was thinking instead of my words.

"I take that as a compliment. Listen, I am who I am. You are who you are. I don't take orders and neither do you."

"You're wrong there, love. We all take orders. I'm just a lowly foot soldier."

"Yeah, what's up with that? You've said that before, but you've got minions and you're royalty, so I don't buy the whole 'foot soldier' thing."

"I suppose it's true, from your perspective. I've watched American war movies. The military structure in the First and Second Families is much different. First of all, everyone's in the military. It's our life, or part of it. We serve from cradle to grave."

"What do you mean? Like, active duty or reserves?"

"A mixture would be closer to it. As a people we have two missions: stop the Fourth, and live good lives."

"What about breaking the curse put on the Families?"

"Of course. But at this point, for most, that's a fairytale. We look, but without much real hope of finding it, the Fifth, the cure. They don't know what I'm staring at right now. You know they dance?"

"My eyes? They do?"

"It's a universal fact that we don't see ourselves clearly. Trust me, your eyes shine with the fire of stars. It's a wonder those little plastic covers hide the truth so completely."

Adam set the washcloth down and pulled me closer.

"Wait. Your clothes will get all gross."

"I don't care. Anna, have I told you lately how beautiful you are? How stunning? Frustrating and absolutely mind-blowingly … amazing?" he said, one arm around my waist, another tucking a strand of hair behind my ear.

"I feel like you're distracting me," I said, fully diverted from whatever we'd just been talking about. I seemed to remember it was important.

"Is it working?"

"A bit," I answered, and then remembered the question I still wanted an answer to. "So, foot solider, who do you report to?"

Instantly his lips stopped and he slowly dropped his arm from my waist. The atmosphere in the bathroom went from playful to somber in an instant.

"I'd better let you get cleaned up. We still have a few hours till the cast party if you want to nap. Let me know if you need anything."

"What just happened?" My head was spinning. We went from having a sweet moment to me unwittingly hurting him. "What did I say?"

"I'll remain upstairs if you need anything," he said, turning to exit.

"Oh, okay. Thanks."

I could feel him hovering on the other side of the door. As I turned on the shower and ran my hand up the stream testing for the perfect temperature, it hit me. Who did Adam, a prince, report to? His mother.

The reminder of Adam's mom had me crying through my shower. I cried because I hadn't thought much about my mom today, and that made me feel like crap. I cried because Adam's mom, the only person in the entire world I honestly hated, had a hold on Adam, which meant she could still hurt me. And I cried because I was tired and worried the solution Mr. Seacrest had given me wouldn't work.

Numb, I meticulously scrubbed myself free of the blue fluid, wrapped myself in my fluffy robe and forced myself back to my room, where I knew the immediate solution to my problems was the oblivion of sleep.

I felt him before I opened my bedroom door. Adam was waiting for me, stretched out on my bed. I curled up in his arms and dozed off.

Chapter Eleven

The thing about Martin, Tennessee, in the summer was that the weather was absolutely schizo. Truly. I think the town had a weather system unto its own. It wasn't cool in the morning, warm with the sun, and then cool in the night. No. The local weather seemed not to care for the sun and moon. It was often hotter at night than in the middle of the day!

Adam and I decided to walk to the school set from Gold Manor, being fashionably late in case Mr. Seacrest's solution didn't work and I freaked out. When we arrived in Martin, it was around a doable 80 degrees. It was now nine at night and the humidity had decided to come out and play, so it felt like it was closer to 90 degrees. By the time we got to the gym I was a sweaty mess. I was glad I hadn't wasted time doing my hair. What a difference a year made. Last year I had dressed up, hair and make-up perfectly in place. Today my hair was up in a bun.

As soon as we got on the studio property, we could hear the music. The beat was pounding, late party-goers streaming past us in a hurry to get in. My stomach could barely take all the conflicting emotions I was dealing with: excitement to see my friends, eagerness for the new season, the constant suppression of the stabbing sorrow of my mom's death, and the worry of being found out by Finn, a Fourth.

Adam laced his fingers in mine and squeezed. "You ready to do this?"

Whatever was going to happen was going to happen. I wanted to find out if Mr. Seacrest's fix worked. I simply had to prioritize my desires, and for the moment, this had to be dealt with. No hiding. I squared my shoulders and pushed past the security guards, taking Adam along with me.

At the party, Adam was essentially glued to my side. When we'd left the set in the spring, Adam had supposedly been dating Emma. Given how often we'd been photographed together since then, there should've been no doubt in anyone's mind that we were a couple. And if there was any doubt, it was laid to rest when, halfway through Air Supply 's "I'm All Out of Love," Adam pulled my hair out of its messy bun, ran his fingers through it, looked me square in the face and said, "You are the loveliest woman I've ever beheld." Then he kissed me, deeply, setting my body on fire.

The music changed and I barely noticed. I was completely in the moment with him. Adam dropped his arms from my waist to move to the music, sporting a rare grin. Suddenly, I could feel the genuine ease of the moment shift, a slight change in his countenance, and I tensed.

Causally he asked, "How do you feel?"

"Fine, though I'm guessing I shouldn't?"

"You don't feel that?"

I smiled at him, trying to be normal. I pushed out my feelers into the room. All the normal range of human emotions were there. There was a heightened feeling of excitement all around me, but nothing I hadn't felt before.

"Curious. Thirsty?" Adam asked.

"Sure."

Adam had walked off and was ordering me a drink when, out of nowhere, Finn appeared in front of my face. I screamed.

"Sorry. Didn't mean to startle you."

"I'm sorry. I was deep in thought, didn't realize anyone was behind me."

That was a truer statement than he could imagine. I could see Finn. I mean, he was right in front of me. But I felt nothing from him. Nothing. He was completely flat, like a hollow projection of a person. He hadn't actually appeared out of nowhere, I just didn't sense him… but I sensed everyone else around me.

"I'm Anna."

He stuck out his hand. "Finn. I'm playing your brother this season."

"You are, are you?" I asked conversationally as I shook his hand. I'd hoped by touching him I'd get something, but it was almost worse. It felt like I was shaking hands with a cardboard cut-out. Creepy.

"I think we met earlier today, but you were a bit preoccupied with that guy," he said, pointing at Adam.

"Oh, so you're one of those," I said sarcastically.

"One of what?"

"Method actors. Right? You're playing my brother, so you're trying to annoy me already."

"I wasn't the one going for it in public," he said, laughing. His whole demeanor was puzzling. He was a mixture of cocky and silly, but not mean.

Finn Varga was interesting to look at. He wasn't Hollywood handsome, with the square jaw and angular body to match. He wasn't tall and he didn't even have a great head of hair. But he had a quality about him that made you want to watch, to see what he was going to do next.

"No one was around," I countered. "You were the invader. And late. Very unprofessional," I teased, playing it cool.

"You two love the PDA. What was that on the dance floor?" he asked Adam, who'd rejoined us. He handed me my drink with a kiss on the cheek.

"I'm not sure, mate. Sometimes she gets the better of my stoic nature. What's your story? Why are you bothering with *Ghost House*?"

"My agent wants me to diversify," he laughed, rolling his eyes. "No, really, I'm in the process of rehabbing my image. The plight of child stars everywhere. Meg and I go way back. This show has been great for her, and the role of the sexy, mysterious older brother is what I need right now."

Suddenly Finn's smile looked like it'd been smacked off his face. Clearing his throat as his face reddened, he said, "It was nice to officially meet you, sis. See you around." And off he went.

We watched as he quickly slid out the side door of the gym, like he was fleeing. When he was almost out of the door, Adam placed his hand on my back. "Look."

Suzanne was standing on the threshold of the gym.

I noticed two things at the same time: Finn was running from Suzanne, and Suzanne was now as blank to me as Finn.

Chapter Twelve

Adam pulled me closer. "How do you feel?"

"Strange. The strangest. I'll tell you about it later."

"But you're okay?"

"Yeah. Guess all is fine. Well, there is…"

I was in midsentence when I felt a hand on my back and just about jumped out of my shoes.

"Excuse me, Ms. Ellingwood?" a new guy said.

"Can I help you?" I asked, completely thrown off. This guy felt exactly like Finn. A void. Nothingness.

"Hands off," Adam warned. His whole demeanor was a warning. *You mess with her and I'll take you out*, it said.

"Sorry, sorry. I was looking for Finn Varga. I'm Colby Doss, his personal assistant. Ms. Diaz is looking for him."

"Don't know where he is," Adam answered curtly, dismissing Colby like a master dismisses a servant.

Though I couldn't read Colby like I was used to reading people, he clearly felt the sting from Adam's treatment.

"Why were you so rude to him?" I whispered in his ear.

"You know what he is. Do you have any idea what kind of control it took to not take his head off?"

Adam's reaction was visceral and immediate; his animosity caught me entirely off guard. How could a person truly hate someone he'd never met?

"I don't understand at all, but if you don't want to tip your hand, I suggest you keep your loathing to yourself. You already knew Finn wouldn't be alone, right?"

"Love, it's one thing to know, and it's another for the enemy to walk right up and touch …. " But he couldn't finish his sentence, and didn't need to. Even though I couldn't sense anything coming from the Fourth, Adam's feelings were clear. He grabbed my arm and started dragging me towards the exit.

"Ow. Stop it! People are going to think you're possessed!" I said, yanking my arm back.

"No, they think I'm an untouchable rock god. Dangerous. Good, let them think it!"

"Where's Echo?" Something was wrong with Adam. It was like he was fracturing in front of me.

"I told him to stay away," Adam said.

"Is someone doing something to you?" I whispered. Was that it? Maybe one of the Fourth had some kind of power and Adam was reacting to it.

Adam raised his arm to show me his shaking hand. "It's the adrenaline."

"Should we go?" I asked, looking him over.

Abruptly, the music stopped. I looked around to see that everyone's attention was focused on Sylvia up on the stage.

"Welcome back. Ready for another killer season?"

The townies/extras, cast, and crew cheered.

"This season is going to rock it, even harder than our first. And to prove it, please put your hands together to welcome our guest star for a four-episode story arc, Finn Varga!"

Gasps, oohs, and ahhs sounded from the gallery as hands clapped and heads turned, looking for Finn Varga.

"Finn? Finn?" Sylvia called, squinting through the cat-eye glasses she sometimes wore. "He was just here," she said to herself. "Well, when you see Finn Varga, please give him a warm, professional, *Ghost House* welcome. I want to remind everyone associated with this production how important it is to respect and support the privacy of others. Whether you're Meg Sweet or Finn Varga, a boom operator or a local extra, every single member of this operation is to be treated with respect. And that includes respecting privacy when it comes to social media. I have a zero-tolerance policy for violators. I'm sure you know I'm referring to what's been going on at *Kid Palace*. That, people, will not be us. Now, have fun tonight, for tomorrow we hit the ground running."

Announcements over, my duty here was done and I didn't plan to stay one more minute. That's when Lucy came bounding up to me.

"Can you even? I mean, Finn-freaking-Varga on our show?"

Lucy beamed like she was showing off pictures of her baby.

"You didn't know?" I asked skeptically.

"Oh, please. Don't be silly. I've known for weeks. Or at least, I was fairly certain the deal would go through. Unbelievable! Meg Sweet, Adam Lewis, and Finn Varga. This is exactly what I've envisioned for myself. Surround yourself with success and become successful. Just like you're doing with Adam Lewis. Smart move, if you can keep him."

"Lucy, don't be ugly."

"Me? Never. Just realistic. Don't you know what they say about him? Rogue. Player. Don't be played, Anna, be the player," she leaned in and whispered in my ear because Adam was standing right there! Incredible.

"Uh, thanks for the advice. You should write a column," I smirked.

"You're probably right. Do you know how many people look up to me now? I'm actually in the process of developing an entire lifestyle brand. What have you been working on? Where are you living now? Oh right, Gold Manor? Are you ready for training tomorrow? Did you know Finn Varga doesn't have a girlfriend? I think I can help him with that. See you in the morning."

I watched, slack-jawed, as Lucy bounded off, seemingly unaware she'd asked a million questions and hadn't bothered to wait for a single reply. She was a disaster. My feelings for her vacillated between outright dislike, fascination, and pity.

"Unbelievable," I breathed as Adam took my hand. "I'm out. Let's go."

Adam was silent as we walked back to the manor.

"What was going on tonight?" I didn't think he would really answer. He felt closed off and rattled.

Surprising me, he stopped in the middle of the street and exploded in a torrent of emotions. "I'm not ready for this! Anna, I'm in a rock band, I'm young and royal. I haven't made the best use of my life, haven't been serious. I mean, I know how to fight, but not with my own family. And I know nothing about politics in the Fourth. I just know find equals kill. Now I have to figure out how to control the one impulse I *have* honed to perfection!"

I didn't know what to say, so I took his hand and started back down the street. He stopped again.

"How can you be this calm? Are you really so blind to what almost took place in there?" he asked, pointing towards the school.

"There are perks to the way I was raised. I don't think I'm in a war. I don't want to hurt someone because of their family affiliation. I always thought the whole Hatfields vs. McCoys family-feud thing was stupid and juvenile."

"I suppose there are advantages to being raised in ignorance, like not knowing who killed your aunt. She's not the only person I've lost to the Fourth. Maybe I haven't explained sufficiently how evil they are. You want to know what happens to someone they catch? They never upgraded their archaic torture devices. They are well used. Have I ever told you the story of my friend Sam? Sam and his entire family, including his two-year-old sister, were tortured and slaughtered by the Fourth. You know how I know this? They sent a video of it. It opens with the six of them hooded, blood dripping off their naked bodies and – "

"Stop it, stop it! I get it, okay? The Fourth are evil."

"This is not some blind prejudice we hold. We have been given reason upon reason to see them as the vile creatures they are. The only way to deal with terrorists is to kill them. Believe me, other ways have been tried. Reason has always failed. They must be stopped. Warrior 101 is spotting a Fourth and eliminating them. Case closed."

"But that's not true. What about Suzanne?" I asked.

"A rare exception."

"And Corey? Maybe Finn is another exception."

"I know, Anna, I *know* if the situation were reversed, and he knew who you were, you'd be captured and dead by morning. I know this, Anna. You have to believe me."

"I want to always believe you, but sometimes I don't think you see clearly."

"And you think you know more than you do. That will get you killed. Do you want to die, Anna? You have a responsibility not only to yourself. Somehow you are key to breaking the curse. You can't afford to… be irresponsible. I am enormously annoyed with you right now."

Adam texted and listened to music on the way back to the manor as I fumed. It was dark and I didn't care that my hair was standing on end. I was torn between trying to see the world through his eyes, and anger at his outright dismissal of my ability to assess a situation. It was hard to be with him when he tried to pull rank on me. I knew he wanted me to simply submit to his interpretation of the Fourth, but that wasn't going to happen. I couldn't. Sure, maybe most of the Fourth were moral degenerates, but not all. Suzanne was an excellent counterexample to what he'd been saying. Maybe Finn was different like Suzanne, maybe he wasn't. But there was no way in hell I was going to condemn Finn and his entourage to death just because of who his parents were.

We were greeted on the porch by Echo, Suzanne, and Corey. I watched wordlessly as Adam jumped into his car and tore out of the driveway, Echo and Corey in tow.

I turned to Suzanne for an explanation.

"Don't look at me. I'm just here to babysit. Scoot," she said, ushering me inside.

"Do you want to talk about seeing Finn?"

"Definitely not. I'm a fighter, not a drama queen. I don't care to spill my guts to you or anyone. Got it?"

I got why she was being defensive. Earlier in the day she'd been inches away from losing her life for not disclosing her knowledge and past relationship with Finn. That, and she was an intensely private person.

"You know what? You're off the hook. I'm going to bed. 'Night."

Brushing my teeth, I looked into my contact-free eyes, wondering what the swirling patterns meant. How in the world could I be used to break the curse? What a day. I stared in the mirror, trying to see past my reflection and into my soul. Who was I? What was I really about? What was the meaning of life? What was the meaning of my life? Could it be that my purpose was written in the stars even before I was born? I hated that idea. No. I would get to decide what my life meant and what it was for, right?

I walked back to my room, trying to shake the weight of my possible destiny, of putting an end to a generations-long, murderous curse. Was that really me? What did others see when they looked at me?

I got in bed and pulled the covers over my head, wishing to silence my thoughts. If Corey were here, he'd tell me the truth. He always told me the truth. He was my anchor to the real. He was in both worlds, like me, and he knew me. *Corey, Corey, Corey, where are you?* I felt out into the world.

I texted him. No response. I called. Straight to voicemail.

I sat up in bed, and though I knew I shouldn't do what I was about to, I didn't care. I needed to talk to Corey. I opened my make-up bag and found the jar I'd been hiding my extra energy in. I took out the crystal that had been growing and turned it over in my hands, rolling it. It was light pink, hard, but not like a rock. I could pinch a piece off if I wanted to. And lately it had been making an ever so slight sound, a hissing. It reminded me of pop rocks.

Immediately a plan formed in my head. I wanted Corey here, but unnoticed. What if I could conjure a kind of doppelgänger to leave in his place? Then no one would know.

Clearing my mind like I'd done many times in Mr. Seacrest's dreamscape, I envisioned what I wanted.

Nothing happened.

I closed my eyes and tried again. Suddenly, Corey stood in front of me, pizza in hand.

"What the …. Anna? What's going on?" he choked, spitting out his food.

Chapter Thirteen

"Corey, I really needed to talk to you," I said, but the shock of what I'd done snuffed out my temporary crisis.

"Geesh, Anna. You could've called. What did you do? How did you do it? How am I here?"

The rock in my hand had significantly shrunk and was heating up.

"I think I'd better send you back. Will you come see me ASAP?"

"You've clearly blown a gasket."

"Oh, and, don't tell the others, okay?" The look on Corey's face made me feel really bad. If Corey didn't approve of what I'd done, I really must've crossed a line.

"Sure."

The rock was getting harder to hold because of the heat. I concentrated.

Nothing.

"Turn around? The disapproval you're oozing is distracting."

I tried again, saying out loud what I wanted. And then he was gone. A few seconds later my phone buzzed.

"What is wrong with you? I'm coming," his text read.

The whole event caused me to sober up. I wasn't feeling sorry for myself anymore.

Ten minutes later I heard him bounding up the stairs.

"What is going on? How the hell did you do that? They didn't even know I was gone, which is good for you because we were in public at The Looking Glass."

"It's a long story."

I averted my eyes from his hostile stare. Corey was rarely mad at me, and he'd never been this harsh.

He sat on my bed, still pissed. I told him how I'd been channeling my excess energy and saving it. How tonight, I'd been feeling sad about my mom, about Adam, and I'd had this unshakeable urge to see him when an idea popped into my head. I'd been told I could bend reality, the waking world to fit my desires, so I thought I'd try it out.

"That was reckless! Do you know what we were doing? The guys were all hanging out. All of us. Finn was there and his PA too. When I got back, no one batted an eye."

"No harm done, then?" I asked hopefully, wanting his anger to pass.

"You know we don't know that. Every day we find out one of them has this or that power. I don't think we can assume anything. Well, you got your wish, I'm here. What do you need?"

"Forget it."

I crawled back in bed and pulled the covers over my head.

Corey pulled the covers back. "Forget it? I don't think so."

I took the covers back again and hid for a sec before flipping them off and sitting up. I was feeling less emotional and more embarrassed, but I could use a sounding board since he *was* already here.

"Fine. Here's the deal. I'm still sick with grief, it's hard to cope with anything else. Adam's been great. He's really helped me through this whole grieving process. But today, with my head almost exploding from whatever signal Finn Varga was sending out, arguing about Suzanne, meeting with

Mr. Seacrest, and then, you should've seen Adam tonight! He was a crazy person. And we fought on the way home. I'm not a violent person. Or at least, I don't want to be. I believe in justice, not vigilantism, and it bothers me the way Adam thinks he's justified to kill. That he can just kill them."

Corey had cooled off and sat down next to me. He still felt like he always had to me, even though he had Fourth in him too. Maybe his blood was diluted to the point that the new herb I was taking didn't affect the way I saw him.

"Yeah, me too. Adam and Echo, even Suzanne, they seem normal. But if you listen to their conversations, it's like they're mercenaries. Suzanne's told me she's killed people. I know Echo has. I know they don't take it lightly, but still."

"Adam told me some awful stories about the Fourth, trying to get me to see the world the way he does. But all I could see was the way his mother killed mine. The leader of the so-called good guys. She killed my mom like she was squashing an ant. I wish you could've seen her face. Her utter callousness."

"But you know how Adam feels about that."

"I know Adam regrets that day and hates his mom. But will she ever pay for what she did? At first I was saving my energy so I could take my revenge. Now? I want to protect my dad and you and Adam. I want to bring her to justice, but I'm not going to let her ruin my life by basing all of my decisions on finding a way to destroy her."

"Then why that stupid stunt tonight? That could've really gone south. You're smarter than that."

"Sometimes I just need my best friend. I really missed you. Tell me about you and Suzanne. How are you doing with the revelation that she was once with Finn?"

Once I asked the question my suspicions were confirmed. I could tell by his face that he'd already known. "Oh, so you're already that far into the relationship. You've had the talk about past relationships and stuff," I said.

"She told me about Finn Varga. I don't think I'll ever get the whole story, though. She's very private."

"Yeah, I know."

The smile playing on his lips warmed my heart. I was glad to see he was moving on, though Suzanne wasn't what I considered a great choice for him. She was even more messed up than the two of us combined! And then, with my boyfriend almost killing her today... did Corey know, really know how close it had come? That Adam was breaking his own code by sparing Suzanne's life, again?

"Come on, I know you," he said. "I don't need to be a mind reader to know what you're wondering about."

"Spill. I want to hear all about you two. Leave no detail out."

His smile turned to a full-blown grin, showing his now famous dimples, complete with that irresistible twinkle in his eye.

"Please leave some of it out!" I amended when I felt his thoughts.

"You know me. I don't kiss and tell."

"Thank goodness for tender mercies. Tell me all the rest."

He started from the day I'd left with Adam and Echo on F&L's North American tour. Corey was chatty by nature and an awesome story teller. He was just beginning to tell a rather colorful story involving an altercation between Suzanne and a stagehand when Adam knocked on my door. I couldn't see him, of course, but I could feel him. And he was angry.

"I think that's my cue," Corey said, looking at his watch, suddenly nervous. "I'm supposed to meet up with Suzanne in a few minutes anyway."

"What did you do? Did you rat me out?" I couldn't believe it. How had he hidden that from me?

"Excuse me for being worried! You're the one who's convinced me that we need to be careful. It's not just about you, you know. Your actions affect all of us."

"If I can't trust you, Corey – "

"You know it's not like that. My girlfriend could've died today! And you, you just flaunt your crazy-ass abilities like it's no big deal."

"It wasn't like that."

"I didn't realize, okay? I know I shouldn't have told him," Corey yelled at me.

Adam didn't wait for me to let him in. "Step down."

"Don't worry, I'm leaving," Corey said, cooling down. "I am sorry, Anna."

"No you're not, traitor," I yelled. My own anger and anxiety about what was to come with Adam had my stomach tangled up in knots.

"Save your righteous indignation. You would've done the same if it had been me making that kind of stupid move. I'm out."

I stood speechless in my room next to a confused Adam.

"Are you okay?" he asked, worried for me.

"No, not at all," I conceded. I crawled back in bed and pulled the covers over my head again.

Instead of leaving or pulling the covers back, Adam turned off the light and climbed in next to me, pulling his phone out in the sheet tent he'd made, illuminating his concerned face. "You want to tell me about it?"

"You're going to hate it."

"I know you've been hiding something. You'll tell me when you're ready."

"I thought you needed to know everything."

"Love, your stories are yours to tell or keep. It is up to you if and when you share those stories. You are the holder of your life. You get to decide."

"You are killing me with all your understanding," I huffed. "Earlier you were all mean and authoritative, which I hate. And now you're like a basket of kittens."

"Those are two of my sides. What can I say? I'm complex. Don't you love it?"

"And now Mr. Cocky shows up."

I launched into what I'd been up to, leaving out the trick I'd done with Corey. That was the hardest, being fresh.

Catching Adam up on my energy issues was the easy part. Waiting for his reaction was the scary part. "Say something. Please?"

It was rare to render him speechless. He wasn't quite catatonic, but close, and it was frightening me.

"What do you think? Is it bad? Did I totally screw up? Adam?"

He threw the covers off us and sat up, letting his cell fade to black.

It was hard, but I waited. Waited for his pronouncement on my new awful fate.

"No," he whispered and found my mouth first with his fingers and then with his lips. He pulled back and brushed my tears away.

"Is it that bad?" I whispered back.

"I have no earthly idea how what you're describing is even possible. You amaze me. Why didn't you tell me?"

"I ... I didn't want you to tell me to stop. I found this balance where I get to be a semi-normal person by not having the elements react to my moods, *and* I get to have access to the power in case of emergency. I knew you'd tell me to stop and, well, I didn't want to fight with you because I wasn't going to stop."

"Are all women like you?"

"Depends. To what are you referring?"

"You're confident and strong. Wise. You see well."

"I was right? You're going to tell me to stop?"

He didn't answer, but instead asked, "How did you hide this from me?"

"I knew you would know that I was hiding something, so I willed what I was hiding to be undiscoverable. Does that make sense?"

"We both suck at being in a relationship. What's wrong with us?" he groaned.

"I don't think we have the time for a litany of our issues. You're not mad?"

"I am, but I get it. I know my temper can be formidable."

"It's your sense of entitlement. It probably happens to all royals," I said, trying to lighten the mood.

"So what's your excuse?"

"Oh, probably a combination of severe trauma and barely-harnessed super powers."

"I couldn't be with anyone but you. I've never had anyone stand up to me like you do. You're not one bit afraid of me."

"Not anymore. You were quite intimidating, once upon a time," I confessed.

"Oh, the good old ignorant days. You know we need to tell Uncle."

"I don't know." And I really didn't. Logically, I knew the more information his uncle had, the more he could help us. But Mr. Seacrest's reasoning didn't always seem rational to me.

"Do you feel something's wrong? A reason we shouldn't tell him?" Adam asked.

He lay back down and I nuzzled into his side, my arm over his chest. "No, it's just, he makes me feel like a guinea pig. And he's incredibly hard to please. Not to mention he tried to kill me not too long ago. How will he react? Do you think we can wait? At least until I'm done with that stupid blue stuff I have to drink."

"That potion Uncle came up with averted a potential disaster today. But yes, we can wait a bit. Will you refrain from doing that new trick of yours until we speak with him?"

I couldn't hold back my yawns. Adam yawned too. "I'll try my best. I think I need to go to sleep. Is it close to midnight?"

"Just past," he said, playing with my hair.

"Are you going to stay?"

"For a while. Here," he said, handing me the vial of blue liquid.

I propped myself up uncomfortably on my elbows. I drank, half expecting to get sick, even though Mr. Seacrest had said that the heinous side effects would only be for the first huge dosage I'd needed to flood my system.

I lay back down and easily found sleep.

Chapter Fourteen

I didn't have to be on set until 10 a.m. Our tennis coach was driving in from Memphis. Chief on my schedule this week was wardrobe fittings, cheer and tennis practices, and learning my lines.

In the third episode of the season, the tennis coach catches Lucy, Meg, and me trespassing on the school grounds at night. The coach, who is a new teacher this year, says she won't turn us in if we join her team.

At the table read Sylvia gave us info about changes for this season. "We want to shake things up on *Ghost House*. Instead of boys' sports being front and center, we're going to showcase women's sports. In fact, the tennis story arc will be more prominent than the football one. Your coach is running late due to a traffic accident on I-40. She's going to work you until you look like you know what you're doing. Sherrie Hall will continue as our cheerleader choreographer. Once you're ready, Sherrie will work with Coach Maggie to choreograph the tennis scenes. The writers are golden! They've come up with great ideas as to how these scenes will play out."

"What's the tennis coach's back story? Is the part cast?" Meg asked.

Sylvia didn't like being interrupted. "We're close to casting her. The character is fresh out of college, first teaching job. We'll soon find out her association with Gold Manor. And, she used to date Finn Varga's character. She's back because she's looking for something."

"What?" Lucy asked, hating a mystery.

"By season's end, you'll know. All in good time. I like to keep you on your toes," Sylvia added, distracted by her phone.

After the read we headed over to the freshly poured court.

"I love tennis," Suzanne said to me, stretching an arm over her chest. "Played since I could walk. I'm glad I'm no longer a ghost on the show and get to play."

"Really?" I asked, touching my toes. I found it fascinating whenever Suzanne revealed anything about herself, given her private nature.

"It's a popular sport," she replied.

"Not really," I laughed.

"For us it is."

"Interesting. I wonder why?" I felt something shoot through my body and I snapped upright. "Can you feel that?"

"Sorry, no." Suzanne was playing it cool, but she transitioned into protection mode in reaction to my comment. She was ready to fight. "Can you explain? A Fourth?" she asked, arm over head in a deep side bend.

"No. One of us. It feels like Adam, but it's not him," I said, mirroring her stretches.

"What is she doing here?" Suzanne said, a smile in her voice.

"Who?" I asked, not looking, trying to Zen out.

"Coach Maggie…You know any Maggies?"

"No. You?"

"Yes, you do, you just don't know you do. Here she comes, like a hurricane," Suzanne said, looking over my shoulder.

I turned to see and was stunned into silence. Lucy and Meg walked over to us to meet our new instructor.

"Greetings, ladies. I'm Coach Maggie and I'm here to make you look like pros. We don't want postproduction to have all the glory. If you trust me, I'll make you look great for the cameras. For that to happen, you've got to understand the game," she said, looking us up and down. "Lucky for you, Suzanne is a great player."

"You know her?" Lucy asked, miffed someone other than herself had knowledge about anything of consequence on the set.

"Surprised to see you, Maggs. I mean Coach Maggie," Suzanne said, ignoring Lucy's question.

"Duty calls and all that rubbish. Okay, ladies, let's get to work."

Coach Maggie was none other than Maggie Lewis, Adam's sister, whose identical twin I'd grown up believing was my Aunt Melinda. I'd later learned Melinda's real name was Diane. I'd only met Maggie once, and it was in a dream. She looked just like I remembered my aunt, only with a harder edge and a heavy English accent. Much thicker than Adam's. And while Melinda had been in peak physical condition when she'd died, Maggie was pudgy and pale from lack of activity and sunlight.

She didn't acknowledge she knew me, so I pretended I didn't know her either. All morning long I racked my brain, trying to figure out why she was here. And sober. I wanted to call Adam, but I'd left my phone in the dressing room. I decided to accept that as a sign from the universe to chill out. Maggie's presence couldn't be for any good reason, so I decided to give Adam a few more hours of blissful ignorance. He'd find out soon enough.

A tennis court had been built not too far from the football field. Our first lesson almost over for the day, the football team began arriving for their practice and scene blocking. I'd been distracted with the puzzle of Maggie's appearance, I let out a yelp when I realized she was about to face a few Fourths. Would she freak out and go on a killing spree?

Meg, who I was volleying with, gave me a strange look. "You okay?"

"Give me a sec, okay?"

Maggie was not so patiently working on Meg's backhand. "Coach, you have a minute?"

"Thank you," Meg mouthed to me behind Maggie's back.

"You are a mess. It's clear you've never played before. Look at your grip! You're choking up on the racket," Maggie scolded Meg, crossing the court over to me.

Maggie took my racket out of my hands, inspecting it.

"I don't know why you're really here, but we have a situation of the Fourth kind," I whispered, trying to remain calm.

"Why do you think I'm here?" she said, handing me the racket. "Look at my grip."

I tried to hold it like she did.

"No, no, no. At an angle. Not straight on. You know what I do? I was called in to assess this mess."

"You were? By who? Does Adam know you're here? Am I supposed to know you?"

"Later. Ears are everywhere, even where you least suspect," she said curtly under her breath.

Maggie set down her racket and worked my hands into the correct grip. The racket felt unnatural and awkward in my hands, much like her presence.

"So you know there are Fourth here, and you're not going to, you know...."

"What?"

"Hurt anyone," I hissed, feeling frustrated with the whole situation. Just when I'd started feeling in the loop, every stinkin' time, something would knock me right back out.

Maggie laughed and her face lit up as she looked at something behind me.

"Sis, what in the world are you doing here?" Adam said, rushing her with a giant bear hug.

"Duty and all that," she replied, beaming.

"It's been too long."

"Well, now I'm here and can see what you've been up to. You know what I think of the state of affairs right now. I had decided to be an isolationist. Non-involvement," she said, looping her arm in his.

"Had?" I asked, homing in on the key word.

"Why yes, Ms. Perceptive. I'd been hearing nasty rumors, which I tried to ignore. That is, until I got a call in the middle of a most promising date. That was the final straw."

"Why do they think you're here?" Adam asked quietly.

"I'm the tennis pro, of course. You know I own the court."

"I think I could take you," Suzanne said, walking up to us. "Are we free to go for the day, Coach?"

"Yes. Ladies," she called loudly, "circle up. Not a great start to our tennis season, thank goodness for movie magic. I believe we have a three-hour block scheduled in the morning. I've sent you a few instructional videos to watch. Please do so before we meet tomorrow. And maybe tomorrow, baby bro, you can practice with us."

"Sorry, got plans."

Lucy stopped fiddling with her phone. "Wait. Are you related to Adam?"

"He's my baby brother."

"That's unbelievable," Lucy gasped.

"That I should have such a sorry looking brother as him?" Maggie asked, ruffling his hair. "Want to grab some lunch?" she asked Adam.

It was fascinating seeing Adam with Maggie. He wasn't sullen or aloof or acting cool. He was happy and relaxed. The connection he shared with his sister was obvious and enviable.

"Love to, but I've got practice now. Dinner? Where are you staying?"

"The only hotel in town with an indoor pool."

"Naturally," Adam laughed, enjoying an inside joke.

"Where are your manners? Are you at least going to introduce me to your girlfriend?"

"Certainly. Anna, Maggie. Maggie, Anna. I've got to run. Anna, I'll text you when I'm done here," he said, leaving for the football field.

Watching Adam run off to join his "team," I heard the others collecting their rackets and walk off. Except for

Maggie. I could feel her staring at me. I could do this. I could make nice with her.

"Maggie, interested in getting coffee or something?"

"Oh, dearie, let's clear something right up. I don't like you. Not one bit. You have single-handedly managed to nearly get my brother killed, and you've thrown the ranks into chaos. You! Even my uncle is off-kilter. I don't know how, but I'm here to find out and make your life a living hell until you give up and move on. Got it? I knew you didn't love him. If you did, you would've taken my advice and left him. Selfish," she reproached, challenging me.

There was only a little hint of anger in her voice, which was obscured by her confidence. She had not one doubt she could fly out here and set her brother and Mr. Seacrest straight and get rid of me.

I was at a loss. Her mother had killed my mother, and she acted like I was the problem! Not wanting to cause a scene, I held my tears and left.

On the way back to the manor, Suzanne was unusually chatty. Unfortunately, it was all about Maggie. How great Maggie had been when she'd defected. How Maggie was like a second sister to her. Maggie, Maggie, Maggie. The more Suzanne sang her praises, the angrier I got, until I exploded.

"I don't know who you are talking about, but Maggie is one of the meanest people I've ever met!"

"Are you joking? Come on, Anna! You can read anyone. You're not serious."

"I am. She just called me selfish for staying with Adam."

"She's right."

"What?" Suzanne's agreement completely threw me. I thought we were better friends than that!

"Oh, I mean, what do I know? I only left the love of my life because I cared about him so much and wanted him to be safe."

"Not fair. We are not you and Finn."

"I know, but you are selfish to be with him. But really, Adam's to blame. He knew what you didn't, what you couldn't have, and he still went after you."

"If you feel that way then why are you here?" I yelled, livid. In that moment, I hated Suzanne too.

"He doesn't have to live the way I want him to. Loyalty doesn't work that way."

"You don't know everything about us."

"I know that. That's reason number two. I don't know and it's really none of my business, except maybe the part about the constant danger. You know, not everything is about you. I have a life too. And dreams and ambitions."

"By all means, go. Don't let me stop you."

"You don't understand us at all. You are part of my life until you're not. Believe it or not, I like you. I disagree with Maggie. I actually think, in ways, you're good for Adam. But my life will always be tied to Adam's. That's simply the way it is."

"You're not his slave," I spit, my anger at her cooling. She wasn't trying to hurt me like Maggie was.

"You don't understand how it works. I'm not his slave and he's not my master. He's my commander when it comes to Family business. War. But we are always at war. So, we find a balance. All of us train, prepare, fight, and live our everyday lives side by side. We have dreams, goals, careers, families, and non-stop war."

"That's awful."

"It's reality. And we make it work. What are the alternatives? Living in our battle gear or giving up - death."

"I don't know if I'll ever understand the Family system," I said, marveling at her matter-of-fact attitude.

"Give Maggie time," Suzanne advised as she pulled into the manor parking lot. "I bet she'll come around. I did."

And I tried. I tried as hard as I could to change Maggie's mind, but her complete disdain was evident to me and even Adam. At practice she treated me fairly, like all the rest of the cast, but given my abilities, I sensed how she really felt. How it pained her to talk to me civilly and give me pointers and encouragement. *She* was a great actor.

A few days after Maggie arrived, Adam and I were walking through the forest behind Gold Manor. It started off as a lovely, romantic getaway from all the cast and crew, but I ruined the mood with my complaining.

"I know she's your sister, but it's hard to feel all that hatred coming off of her. Especially when she looks identical to my aunt whom I loved and who loved me. It's killing me. I feel like Maggie's trying to steal my memories of Aunt Melinda and rewrite them, turning me against her. And – "

"And what."

"Naw, forget it."

"Are you really going to make me pull it out of you?" he sighed.

"Fine. I mean, it was her mom that…."

"She doesn't know."

I stopped. "She doesn't know? How can she not know?"

"Anna, no one can know. I told you why. Not for my mother's sake. It would cause untold chaos that we're in no position to deal with. And Maggie would be queen if all went according to canon law."

"Who does know?"

"Only Uncle, Corey, you, and me."

"Suzanne and Echo?"

"I'm not certain. After it happened I tried to search their feelings to see if they had picked up on what really went down. As far as I have been able to tell, they don't know. They didn't buy the official story we circulated; they're not daft. If they do know it was my mother, they wouldn't say a word. As for who the queen may have told, we have no way of knowing."

"What does your sister know about me?"

"Thanks to you, she is aware you have an unparalleled dreaming ability. Yet another reason not to show your talents when you don't really know what you're doing, as it might come back to haunt you. But that's all she knows."

"Speaking of haunting...."

I saw the green Gold Manor ghost behind Adam, coming towards us. I hated seeing either one of them, but if I had to pick, at least this one seemed sane.

She walked toward us, twigs snapping under her bare feet as she approached, making her seem solid, corporeal. In the still of the forest, an unearthly wind blew her hair and robes about her preternaturally tall frame.

I wanted to engage her in conversation, which was always my second instinct. My first was to run. Adam and I were polar opposites on this. He was of the mind to stay put, immobile, when one of the ghosts appeared, responding or engaging only if necessary.

As she came closer, we could see her eyes, which were looking past us.

"Lovely day," I commented, trying not to shake as she approached.

She flew towards us, startling me, bridging the distance instantly, inches away from my face.

"Go to the tomb. The Fifth from the Third. Go and find or she will die and all is lost," the ghost whispered, repeating her mantra. This was the first time I'd seen one of the Gold Manor ghosts since I'd learned I was Fifth, my mom with Second blood and my biological father a Third.

"I am her. Do you mean me? Do you know who I am? What I'm supposed to do?"

"The tomb beneath the ground. The tomb of storm and sea. You are not, you are other. Finder, seer, server, binder."

I was mesmerized by her movements as she swayed in the still of the noonday sun. Her words were as addictive as they were puzzling. When she reached out to touch me, I leaned into her fingertips. I wanted to know what she was made of. I needed to know her. But Adam pulled me back, putting himself in between the two of us. Before I could protest, the green ghost shrieked and disappeared, leaving me hollowed out.

"Why did you do that?" I cried. "I was so close!"

"To what? Anna, they can't be trusted. Those kind are notorious for their deceit. Look up. Where is the sun? Where should it be?"

It should've been overhead, but it was setting. "More time passed than I realized. So?"

"What if she did it on purpose? How would you know? They mess with our minds."

"Did you hear what she said?" I asked, relieved and sad, though I wasn't sure why. I was confused by my own reaction. I hadn't wanted the burden of being a people's sole means of liberation or damnation, depending on who won. But when it came to it and the ghost confirmed what I'd truly believed, that I wasn't the one who could allow the Families to finally rest in peace, I was sad.

Adam felt my disappointment. "I don't believe anything she or her sister has said, though it's clear they want us to find something for them. For what purpose, who knows?"

"But did you hear that phrase? She said, 'storm and sea.' That's from the prophecy about the Fifth. 'Eyes that shine in the desert, hungered for and rejected. The storm of the sea and the murky ropes tossed.'" I would never forget those words. "How could she know that? What does it mean?"

"Ghosts play by different rules. You think you and I come from different worlds? They are absolutely otherworldly. Our kind don't even speak of them, are loath to acknowledge their existence."

"Out of fear? Is that it?" I asked.

"Prudence. Any time one of us has engaged a creature such as that, it has ended badly. They are devious, tricky, downright mad. They're akin to imps from your mythology. Would you trust an imp or a sprite?"

"I can honestly say I've never asked myself that question."

"Okay, smarty pants, but you get my point. Where do you think that krim came from that nearly killed me?"

"I guess I figured it was from the Fourth."

"Unlikely."

"But they led us to Samuel's bunker. Why?"

"Why indeed."

Chapter Fifteen

F&L had a festival gig in California the weekend before we began shooting. I had several reasons to get out of town with Adam, not the least of which was his infuriating sister. In fact, it gave me great joy going since I knew it would piss her off.

My dad met us at LAX. The moment I saw him I immediately relaxed. There was something about my dad that made me feel whole. I wished I'd been selfish and took him up on his offer to be with me in Martin while we shot *Ghost House*. But I knew I couldn't be careless with him. For the foreseeable future, we'd only have short bursts of time together.

"Anna," he called, grinning from ear to ear, waving to get my attention. This was completely unnecessary since I'd felt him before I exited the plane. My ability to "feel" people was increasing, but spotty.

I rode up front with him on the way out to Joshua Tree to meet up with the rest of the band. Given our shooting schedule, we were only out for a short weekend, flying back on Sunday. I made it a point to check in with my dad at least every other day. Since Mom died, our relationship had changed. For the better. Before, she was our go between. She'd fill him in on my life and vice versa. With her gone, as soon as the initial shock wore off, we'd made an unspoken agreement to change our habits.

We chatted the entire drive because we actually had stuff to talk about. He knew what was going on with me. I told him all I could, like the silly and petty happenings on set, and he'd talk about his book project, students, and colleagues. I told him my worries, as best I could, and he told me his. We were both determined to not have the mysterious parts of my life define or lessen our relationship.

Since my dad didn't really care for what he called "pop music," he was going to drop Adam and me off at the festival and wait for us at the hotel. When we finally found the *F&L* bus, navigating through the horrendous traffic, we were greeted with scary news.

"Sorry, mate, you've got to stay with us," Ewin said to my dad, who had just put his car in reverse.

"What's up?" Adam asked, scanning the bus area.

"Remember what we were up against at that gig in Bakersfield? The favor for Andrew? I've been told it's the same problem many times over."

"Anna, we're leaving," Adam said, taking my elbow and steering me back toward my dad's sedan, Echo following in his wake.

"Relax," Ewin called, chasing after us. "I've been told it'll be taken care of."

"Why chance it? What are they to us?" Adam asked.

"You know my history with Andrew. He gave me a friendly warning but said it'll be okay. I believe him. He can't lie. He's not lying. And besides, you'd be a real ass to pull out now. I know you've got your jerk persona to keep up, but this is a charity event for clean drinking water. Sometimes you've got to keep your word."

"I don't owe anyone anything."

"Whatever. But we're doing this. And so are you. Just keep pops with you and he'll be fine. Anna too. Echo will stay with them."

Echo nodded, already on alert.

Adam wavered, his hand on the car door. I had been present when a fight broke out between Ewin's friends and something else. At the time I didn't know what they were, but they didn't feel right. Not human. Adam had never explained what they were, but I could feel their presence in the air all around me now. Stifling. Did that mean there were more of them this time, or that I'd honed the skill of testing my surroundings?

Adam looked at me and said, "There are more."

"Come on. I'm not letting you go, so it's best to make it easier on yourself and the onlookers who are taking pictures of you and posting them online as we speak," Ewin warned, calling our attention to the loitering people. We were in the dusty parking lot designated for the bands who were playing and the famous who came for the concert.

"Fine," Adam consented. There were few people who talked to Adam like that. Like a peer. Actually, Ewin seemed more like an uncle or grandpa. Which made sense because he was hundreds of years old, his young body not matching his age.

I'd planned to go out in the audience and watch the battle of the bands preceding *F&L*, but now that plan was nixed.

Though my dad and I were working on sharing, we'd run out of things to talk about. He didn't put up a fuss about being ordered to stay put and excused himself to the back of the bus to read. My dad always had a book with him. I did, too, since I always had my phone with me. But my dad was a purist. He only wanted to read books in the flesh, so to speak. Sure, he'd read articles online. But when it came to books, he wanted a physical copy. If you asked him why, you'd be in for an hour long philosophical lecture on what it means to be an embodied creature. In other words, ask at your own peril.

Adam was talking to Kia, the lead singer, about their set. I took out my phone and watched a tennis video Maggie had sent. There was no Wi-Fi and it went against my frugal nature to watch videos on my data plan. Given my salary, the cost for watching video was trivial. But it's hard to shake ingrained habits.

Adam broke away from his band conversation to be with me. I looked up as someone knocked on the bus door.

"Welcome, Andrew," Ewin said, ushering in a massively large guy and a girl half hidden behind him.

"Wanted to let you know everything's taken care of," Andrew said to Ewin.

"Entirely?" Adam asked for clarification.

"Yes," Andrew replied.

"They know about the wrai-" the girl behind Andrew blurted out in surprise. He cut her off, whispering to her for so long it bordered on rude.

Duly ashamed, the girl's face and neck flared up with big blotches of red. She nodded and apologized to Andrew. Andrew didn't seem mad as much as one hundred percent sure about what he'd said to her.

Being an excellent reader of body language, plus my other special skills, I could usually guess not only the tone of a conversation but the content too. With these two, I gathered she had been about to say something that was a secret she'd vowed to take to her grave, and that she'd renewed her vow. I also knew she wasn't from one of the Four Families. She was a normal human girl.

"This is Katie Torres," Andrew said, introducing all of us by name to her. I was surprised he remembered me.

"How've you been, friend?" Ewin asked, falling into conversation with Andrew and Katie while I tried unsuccessfully to tune them out and watch my video. There was something about Andrew I couldn't put my finger on. Not natural.

"He's changed. Radically," Adam whispered in my ear.

"I don't understand him. He's not from the Families, he's human, but feels really... old and ... confused?" I whispered, trying to talk out what I felt coming off of him.

"Old, yes. It's almost as if that's not Andrew. I've known him my entire life and he feels like a completely different person. Alien," he whispered in my ear, pushing my hair behind my shoulder.

Adam looked over to Ewin and asked the question we wanted answered. "Is he okay? Don't mean to be rude."

Ewin looked to Andrew. "I haven't seen Andrew in a while."

Andrew remained silent, the girl by his side fidgeting. You could tell she was a doer and was pained to quietly sit by and wait for Andrew to defend himself.

Andrew's answer was cryptic. "I did change, for the worse. I am as you are."

"I vouch for him," Ewin said, ending the exchange.

Adam relaxed and had just begun rubbing my back when one of the festival organizers announced it was time for *F&L* to go on stage and give the Battle of the Bands award. Disappointment rushed through me as Adam got up and kissed me on the head.

"Don't worry. Echo is staying with you. Come out when we go on, if you'd like."

"Miss you already," I said, kissing him goodbye.

The tour bus now held just Echo, Andrew, Katie, my napping dad, and me. Andrew seemed the silent type and Echo was quiet in a group unless Suzanne was around. It was up to me to break the awkwardness. Or so I thought.

Katie perked up and opened with, "Tell me about yourselves?"

This brought a smile to Andrew's face.

"That's quite broad," I laughed. "Why don't you tell us about yourself," I countered. And so she did.

She began telling us about her mom, whom she loved, but she thought was really lonely. She moved on to her friendship with a boy named Will.

I interjected. "Did I meet him at the Battle of the Bands in Bakersfield?"

"Yes! He's one of my very best friends. He's here. Their band played tonight. He and I and a few of our friends all went to school out in New York, but I'm not going back in the fall. I'm living in New York City right now. I'm an actress too. Not successful like you, yet. How long have you been acting?"

"Actually, *Ghost House* was my first real job."

"You're kidding! How lucky you are!" she exclaimed at the very moment she remembered the gossip she'd heard about me.

I could tell she was thinking about my mom's murder by the way her easy smile seemed to freeze. I think Andrew noticed too because he gently squeezed her hand. She flushed again, for a very different reason this time. Either these two were a couple or they wanted to be. Feeling mischievous, I asked, "Are you guys together?"

Katie's eyes involuntarily slid to Andrew and back to mine. "It's complicated."

"Always," I smiled back, feeling bad for asking. "Are you acting right now?"

"I'm in a musical. In the chorus. Off, off, *off* Broadway. You know the bit. It's never-ending. I get up, go to casting calls when I'm not waiting tables or rehearsing. It's hard to eat right and exercise when I'm constantly running from thing to thing. But if I don't exercise I go crazy. Can you tell I'm a little hyper-active?"

"What do you do?"

"I love dancing and aerobics, but right now I can't afford a gym membership, so I usually end up hitting balls at the park two blocks down from my building. I like cardio, but the downstairs neighbors don't approve of me jumping on their ceiling."

"You play tennis?" I asked.

"They were the only lessons my mom could afford - because she gave them. I played in high school. I never took it too serious. You know, with all the different rackets and gear. Why? You play?"

"No. And that's the problem. I'm not sure if I should be saying this, so please don't repeat it, but I'm going to be on the tennis team this season on *Ghost House*."

"Cool. Are you being coached?"

"Yes," I said, rolling my eyes, which she caught.

"It sucks to learn when you don't like your coach."

"It's not that I don't like her. She doesn't like me."

"Ouch," she commiserated.

"At least I like the game."

"What do you like the most?" Katie asked me.

"Hitting the ball. I like having something socially acceptable to hit. I'm just not good at it."

"Yet," Katie added very graciously.

I liked Katie. Her words matched her body language. I constantly read between the lines with people, but chatting with Katie was effortless. Andrew, on the other hand, was a complete mystery to me. I'd never met a soul like him. He was fascinating, though not for his stellar conversation – he barely said a word. But the vibe he sent off, it was thick and blinding. It was hard for me to look at him since my "talent" for reading people wasn't something that came with an off switch. Sitting across from him was starting to give me a headache.

"We've still got a bit," Adam explained as he came back in the trailer. But really, he was checking in on us. He was on edge, still thinking about grabbing me and taking off.

I took his hand and continued my conversation with Katie.

Katie asked me questions about myself, and I deflected them back to her while the stoic men sat silently by our sides. While she was telling me about her first year of college, clearly censoring what had really taken place, I had the greatest idea.

"Stop right there. Are you interested in television?" I asked, excited at my brilliant idea.

"I mean, sure, yeah. Who isn't?"

"Sylvia Diaz, that's our producer, director, and all around show dictator – in a good way, usually – is holding auditions for parts on *Ghost House*. I know playing tennis would be a bonus. Interested?"

Andrew finally, unfortunately, joined the conversation. "You don't want to go there," he warned her.

Ah. He knew. Andrew knew what Ewin was and what was going on at *Ghost House*, but Katie didn't. Who was he? *What* was he? Katie was a normal girl caught up in something supernatural, that much was clear. But what?

And then Adam jumped in. "Katie seems sound enough to think for herself."

"She is none of your business," Andrew snapped at Adam.

"Didn't know you owned her," Adam shot back.

The tension between the two of them was intense. It was like watching a train wreck.

Andrew sprung off the couch, showing his full, immense stature. I loved Adam and knew he was an awesomely trained fighter, but this guy, Andrew, had a crazy body. He was built like a Greek god. And he was pissed. Adam could take him if Andrew didn't know how to fight, but Andrew looked like he'd been fighting his entire life. Echo put his book down, ready to join Adam.

"I don't know who you think you are, playing mind games with Anna and telling people what to do, but I don't bow to bullies," Adam lashed out.

"You will bow down to me," Andrew promised as he lunged for Adam's throat. Only his hand didn't make contact. Just as quickly as Andrew's arm shot out, it was back by his side and he slumped to the ground, like he'd imploded.

The entire macho escalation took less than sixty seconds, leaving all the words – *Hey! Stop! Calm down!* - caught in my throat. Katie looked just as baffled.

Adam towered over Andrew, wondering what to do next. I put my arms around him, whispering in his ear, "It's okay. You're okay. Let's sit."

Wordlessly, Adam followed my lead. "Are you okay, Katie?" I asked her, knowing she wasn't.

She shook her head, taking a moment to compose herself. "I don't understand what just happened."

"I think these two have tempers."

"Well it's highly unattractive. You hear that?" Katie said to Andrew, gingerly placing her hand on his back. She wasn't used to touching him. Andrew relaxed slightly at her touch.

"Ditto, Adam. Chill out," I said, putting my hand on his knee.

"What happened to you?" Adam asked, completely shocked.

Andrew lifted his head. "I am the man I am now. I'm trying, but it's hard to be good. I'm sorry, Katie, for being rude and possessive. I had no right. In my defense, I know what being on *Ghost House* entails and I do not wish that for you. But it doesn't matter, it is your life. Please forgive me."

Katie was confused. She was the only one not in the know, and her head was spinning.

"I'm just telling you, we can't hang out if you scare me. I mean it. I know you'll get it together, eventually, but …." Katie stopped, leaving out that piece of the puzzle that would tell me what Andrew was.

"All I was going to say, Katie, was if you're interested, I'll mention you to Sylvia. Last I heard, she has two females yet to cast. I don't want to get into whatever's going on with you two, but I'll leave it up to you," I said.

Just then Ewin came back in the trailer. "Show time!" he exclaimed, all smiles, until he looked around at our dour faces. "What's happened? Adam? Andrew?"

"You can do what you'd like, but I have an obligation to tell Katie the truth. If you insist on dragging her into that mess of yours, be certain I will tell her what she's getting into."

"Are you threatening us? Why don't you mind your own business." I snapped at him. I didn't like the way Andrew was looking at Adam.

"Whoa, whoa. Let's step off the crazy train," Ewin said, super confused.

"What's wrong with him?" Adam asked Ewin, as if Andrew wasn't sitting right there.

"Listen, man, you don't want to mess with Andrew."

"Whose side are you on?" Adam demanded.

"Oh, no you don't. I've known Andrew forever. You're my bandmate and, well, you know what else. Anyway, we don't have time for this. Let's get on stage."

"I'm not leaving Anna with him."

"Echo's right there, mate. And believe me, Anna can take care of herself. Right, Anna?" Ewin said.

"You know the way to a girl's heart," I replied. Ewin was my favorite non-Adam band member.

"Come on, we've got to go," Ewin pleaded with Adam.

Poor Ewin. He was completely baffled. All messed up inside, like what he was seeing didn't make sense. I didn't know what it was that he was seeing, but I was curious enough to plan on getting him alone later and making him talk.

Most of the tension left the bus with Adam. Echo went back to his book and Katie and I chatted, while Andrew said nothing. His aura was different now, not as blinding. He eventually fell asleep, head slightly slumped over.

"Sorry about him. We've had an intense day, over the top. He was just looking out for me," Katie whispered.

"Seems we're a bunch with big secrets. The world keeps on getting stranger, right?"

"For me too. I thought he and… were the only…." She trailed off, not sure what to say.

"I know the feeling," I said, smiling. Katie was caught in a paranormal world of her own. I got the feeling she was okay and not in danger or in need of my help in that regard, but I could use hers.

"Can I ask you something?"

"Sure," she replied slowly.

"Don't worry, it's not about secrets. It's just, I've noticed your boyfriend is possessive and hotheaded like mine."

"He's not my boyfriend," she said too quickly.

"But you are together, right?" They both liked each other and it didn't take a reader to see they had a history.

"It's complicated," she said again, smiling. I could feel her turning over the idea of what it would be like to let loose and go for it with this guy she was falling for.

"It always seems to be," I sighed, thinking of my own entanglements with Adam.

"Andrew is working through some heavy issues. I know he likes me, but I'm worried I'd never be enough for him."

"Why?" I pried. I shouldn't have, but her honesty and vulnerability had put me at ease.

"Two main reasons. I'm not sure which is the most important. First, the love of his life broke his heart."

"The wretch!" I said, applying the universal code of vilifying past girlfriends.

Katie stopped. "The opposite, actually. Lizzy is the best person in the world. I mean it, literally. The best. I love her. Like a sister."

I had never seen anyone's honor so fiercely defended.

"I'm sorry," I apologized. "It's usually good form to demonize the person who broke the heart of the one you love and want to be with."

"Like I said, it's complicated."

"I guess so. If that's reason number one, what's number two?"

"He's lost his entire family and way of life."

"But they're not dead," I guessed.

"How did you know?" she asked, looking at me in a new way, past the person she'd see on her TV screen.

"I'm good at reading people."

She accepted my vague answer with a raised eyebrow, but continued. "So you see, Andrew is adrift. He's broken, but still worth so much. I really care for him, but – "

"He's a bit of a loose cannon? And even though you don't want to be scared of him, you are."

"Yes," Katie replied.

"Has he ever hurt you?"

"It's complicated," she repeated, averting her eyes.

"No it's not," I said, raising my voice, drawing Echo's attention.

"Everything okay?" he asked.

"Fine. Go back to your novel."

"But it is complicated," Katie insisted. "He's always been a perfect gentleman, except for one time. Someone drugged him and he'd been drinking. The combination made him violent."

"Oh."

"And it gets even worse. I don't know why I'm telling you this, but, I'm the one that drugged him. Probably didn't expect that, did you?"

I couldn't help the look of shock on my face. "No. I don't get surprised often. Tonight has been full of exceptions."

"So you see, he probably would've never lifted a finger against me if I hadn't done what I did. But I did it, and I've had to face the consequences of my actions. And he's still paying, because it nearly broke him. He's not that guy."

"And tonight? What do you think happened between him and Adam?"

"Beats me. Andrew has never told me what to do before. Ever. He's not like that. What about Adam Lewis?"

"Adam? What can I say. He knows I can take care of myself. It's not like he goes around threatening every guy he perceives as rude to me. I think it was just a reaction to Andrew. He sends off a really intense vibe. Kind of overwhelming. Maybe that was it."

"And maybe guys are just idiots sometimes," she said, smiling.

Chapter Sixteen

We'd blocked our first episode. I pushed through, embracing my character, Laura Vincent, and her new murdering, possessed alter-ego. I told everyone to back off and give me space. I could not do my job while fretting about Finn Varga. Ghosts. My dead mother.

And I was left alone, in the waking world. In fact, no one wanted to deal with me, except Adam and Corey. It was heartless in the extreme to have my character become a murderer months after my own mother was murdered, and in such a hands-on fashion. People were watching, anticipating me falling to pieces. Sylvia had given me the best pep talk she was capable of, which gave me a small amount of peace, because it was genuine. She also told me my character wouldn't be killing anyone for a few months – probably.

Dreaming was different. The nightmares continued. Someone needed my help and I was powerless. I didn't understand why I could manipulate the real world, but couldn't get peace at night. Mr. Seacrest had no idea how someone was getting around him, which served to make everyone even more on edge. There were Fourth on set, and someone was hunting me at night. Neither of which we could remedy.

But I still had running, sort of. Martin was a small town, and I had to avoid many places for my psychological well-being. The side of town where I'd lived last season, where my mom had died, was off limits to me. Places I'd eaten with her, where we'd shopped. This made planning a route hard. Echo never complained, but when Corey joined us for morning runs, he'd whine about making the same loop over and over and over again.

He called it boring.

I called it survival.

I'd been getting overwhelmingly positive support from my fans about my decision to return to *Ghost House*, to continue to shoot in Martin.

One fan told me she was a runner too. She told me her tragic tale. Said for a long time she couldn't run anywhere near where it happened, but she eventually found a way, and assured me I would too.

I messaged her back for the secret to her success. She responded immediately. She said she began by mapping, specifically, the areas she didn't want to run. She made a detailed route and ran on the outskirts of her no-zone for a while, until she felt comfortable. Then she'd take a look at the area to see if any spot could be shrunk, if any place on the outskirts gave way so she could move closer to the spots she psychologically needed to avoid. This, then, became her new route until she was at ease. Once secure, she'd reevaluate her map, looking to further shrink the area. Over and over, bit by bit, until the day she was finally able to run by the spot where her boyfriend had been senselessly mugged and killed in front of her.

Pain. It was everywhere. None of us were immune to the misery of life. I was no different. I wasn't the first and I certainly wouldn't be the last to suffer the death of someone I loved. So what was the point? What was the point of the pain?

My eyes glassed over, my heart trying to hold itself together, I heard my two favorite people. I was splayed out on the couch in the second floor sitting room, widely recognized as the best spot in the whole of the mansion for its comfiness, as they came up stairs… both laughing. These two, who agreed on almost nothing save their mutual dislike for each other, looked like friends.

"What's so funny?" I asked, putting down my laptop, momentarily forgetting my despair.

"It's nothing," Corey said, straightening up, trying to hold back his smile.

"Nothing? I find that hard to believe. Adam?"

"Not mine to tell, love. You'll have to ask her."

"Who's her?"

Meg had come up the stairs behind the guys. She was laughing too.

"Meg? Are they laughing at you?"

"It's Lucy. And it's really not that funny, you guys."

"Yes it is. I got schooled in the meanings of diva and alpha," Corey snickered.

"Come on. What happened?" I whined.

"In the second episode Lucy starts working at the gas station, the one Finn Varga works at," Corey said.

"I know. She's been bragging about it."

"I doubt she'll be bragging now. We were there when she had her costume fitting," Corey continued.

"In Lucy's defense, the outfit is really ridiculous and does add some extra poundage to the middle region," Meg said.

"Yeah, well, maybe Drake would've listened to her and made some changes if she hadn't totally flipped out."

Meg countered. "It wasn't just that. You know the new girl, Katie? She's in the scene and was being fitted too. Let's just say she wasn't wearing any schlumpy polyester. There was a change to the script where Katie catches Finn Varga's eye, not Lucy. Needless to say, Lucy freaked."

"Sylvia was there. Meg, you're the star. I've never seen you go crazy like that," Corey said. I think he was trying to pay her a compliment but it sounded kind of condescending.

"Whatever. See you guys later," Meg said, walking off to her room.

"What did I say?" Corey asked, mystified.

Adam understood as well as I that Corey had offended Meg.

"You can be really dense sometimes. You know how often Meg gets called a diva, difficult to work with, a bitch? Is any of it true?"

"No," Corey said, slowly.

"Of course not. I think she expected more from you. That you'd know her by now, and that she isn't that way and wouldn't act unprofessionally or mean, even though she's supposedly entitled to because she's famous. Get it?"

"Not really. Do I need to apologize?"

"Wouldn't hurt," I said.

Corey cut his eyes in the direction of Meg's bedroom, walking towards it without further comment.

"What happened with Lucy?" I asked, scooting over to make room for Adam.

"Sylvia put her in her place. Reminded her, sternly, and all the lookers-on, that no one's irreplaceable."

"Katie's on set? Did she bring that guy with her?"

"No, though Ewin said Andrew's likely to make an appearance."

"And you still don't know what Andrew is?"

"Ewin said he's sworn to secrecy about his oldest friend. He did say, enigmatically, that Andrew isn't what he once was, which has really bummed Ewin out. To the extreme. I've never seen Ewin so shaken. I can't imagine how someone else's change could affect him greatly, but it has. Ewin has always completely trusted Andrew and his judgments, and so have I. But now, apparently, Andrew is to be taken with a grain of salt."

"Is that all you got? Is it wise to have Andrew here with the other new additions?" I wondered how Andrew would react to the presence of the Fourth around his girlfriend. "What does she know? You think he followed through on his threat?" I whispered. I knew we shouldn't talk about this here, but the couch was comfy that I couldn't imagine moving just yet.

"Ah, love, that's just what I wanted to talk to you about. Feel like going on a mission?"

Chapter Seventeen

Duplicity was not my thing. I'd leave the scheming to people like Lucy. I already liked Katie and hated the idea of using her for information. And yet, we *really* needed to know what she knew about the Families. What had her strange and unnatural boyfriend told her?

Adam and others from the Families played people out of necessity. I got that. But that wasn't me. My dad's advice about my acting career echoed in my head: I was in control of what I said "yes" to. There were always consequences to choices, less dire in my career than missteps when it came to Family business.

When the coffee date I made with Katie drew closer, I increasingly felt nervous and wrong for what I was about to do. I changed course.

It was late in the morning and the regulars at The Looking Glass, the local eatery and coffee house, were gone. My anxiety gave way to peace as I saw Katie sitting, waiting for me.

We chatted about her first night in Martin and I asked about the scene Lucy had caused. Tough as Katie was, her feelings had been hurt. More than that though, she was pissed. Katie had spirit like Suzanne, but unlike Suzanne, she wasn't jaded or closed off from the world.

"Katie, I want to be up front with you. I wanted to meet with you for two reasons this morning. First, I wanted to see how you were settling in and give you a few pointers that I wish someone had given me last year when I was new. But I'm also curious what Andrew told you about us."

"I'm sure," Katie said, looking down at her mocha. "Well, let me ask you. Do you know what Andrew is?"

"No. I mean, it's obvious he's not normal, usual. I do know he's older than he looks. But that's it."

"Are you telling me the truth?"

"I am. I try to be honest, which is harder than I ever imagined. At one point in my life I thought there was never an excuse for lies."

"And now?"

"I still hate them. I guess, when I wrestle with my conscience, I see a ladder of good things. Sometimes all the good things can't be had at the same time."

"What do you mean?"

"I want to keep people safe. Sometimes the best way to do that is for them not to know everything."

"But isn't it always best to be honest? To trust that people can handle the truth?"

"Not everyone can be trusted," I said, looking at her, willing her to trust me.

"You think I can be trusted?"

"I do. And so does Ewin, because Andrew said you could be. For Ewin, anything Andrew says is gospel. Or at least it used to be, I gather. Something's changed in their relationship. It's rather murky to me."

"Anna, I don't want to start off on the wrong foot with you."

I could feel her nervousness and sincerity. It was mean to blast her with all this stress when she'd barely been in town 24 hours. But there was just no helping it.

"Let me tell you something about myself, Katie. I can read people. No, I'm not a mind reader."

"You just read my mind!"

"It doesn't work that way. It's reading body language mixed with predicting what's likely."

"You predict the future?"

"Not really. Sometimes. Fine – I'm a complicated mess. You're not the only one. You have deep secrets, which is clear to me. What they are I can guess at and come close to figuring out. But no - see I caught that - I can't read your mind. That thing, that thing you don't want me or anyone to ever know, when you hide it like that I can see it's there, but not what it is. You'd have to do something to show your hand."

"He told me you could read people. I had no idea."

"I could tell he told you. He also told you," I said, lowering my voice to a hush though there were no other patrons in the cafe, "about the Families."

Katie nodded.

"He told you we're on the good side?"

"Andrew said it wasn't that easy. That the sides aren't divided as neatly as the Families try to pretend."

I was taken aback. Even though I'd expected Katie to agree that we were good and 'they' were bad, I knew it didn't work that way. I saw the lines in the sand as arbitrary too. Sweeping generalizations are usually wrong. Still, what were we going to do with her if she knew about all of it and didn't side with us? What would Adam do to her?

My second thought was the one I verbalized. "Wait. You knew all this complete insanity and still came out here? Are you out of your mind?"

"It was too good of an offer to pass up," she shrugged. "But what about you? Andrew said you were different. You didn't grow up with the others but you stayed around once you found out. Right?"

"Yes, but for a different reason."

"Really? I'm here because I want to be an actress. That's all I want. Please tell whoever sent you that I won't get in the way. I'm on no one's side. I just want to do my job, that's all."

"I wish it were that simple. Did Andrew tell you about the ghosts?"

Her eyes bulged.

"Oh, he didn't."

"Ghosts are real?" she whispered.

"I suppose. My advice is to leave them alone. If you see one at the manor, or want to talk about it or anything, you can always come talk to me. You may not want to tell Andrew. Apparently ghosts freak everyone out."

"No problem there. He barely let me come with you crazy cursed people! One more supernatural issue and he'd, I don't know, do something. He begged me not to come. And I appreciate his concern, but this is my life. He had his," she said, and then all of a sudden became flustered, feeling like she'd given something away. "I mean, well, I just couldn't say no to this role."

"I don't need to know your secrets. Adam has this great mantra about people's stories belonging to them. They aren't ours to tell. It seems whatever info you're holding has nothing to do with what's going on with us."

"Can you really tell? Just like that?"

"I know that's what you believe and Andrew's not here. He is a much different read."

"Can you read him?"

"Somewhat. Did you want to know something?" I asked, smiling at this lighter turn to the conversation.

"Can you tell what he thinks of me?"

"I can tell you already know. That's easy to read."

"Maybe for you. He used to be in love with someone else. I thought he'd never get over her. And if he did, not this quickly."

"I'm not going to pretend to know Andrew, Katie. But I could see his genuine affection for you. And it wasn't brotherly."

"Can I ask you something else?"

"Shoot."

"What's up with Lucy Moore?" she asked, a bit of vitriol in her voice.

She caught me off guard. My laugh was, shall I say, unrefined.

Chapter Eighteen

Finn Varga didn't hang around Martin after his first spectacular entrance. He reappeared weeks later when we did the table read for his episode. I knew he was going to be there. I got on set early and sat opposite the door so I wouldn't jump out of my skin when he appeared.

I'd resumed my training with Mr. Seacrest at night. He still didn't know about what I'd been doing with my excess energy or my bad behavior with transporting Corey in the waking world. Mr. Seacrest knew a lot, but he wasn't as omniscient as I'd once thought. He was, however, a very smart and powerful man, and much of my fear of him had changed to respect.

Due to our fresh problems of Finn and his kind in Martin, coupled with someone actively stalking me in my dreams, Mr. Seacrest had decided to change the direction of my training. For the time being he dropped the business of working with me to switch dreamscapes, opting for what he thought could be of immediate use instead.

His direction proved extremely helpful. Still under the impression I was dumping my excess energy, he made a suggestion. "Anna, tomorrow I want you to keep the extra energy and send it out into the world, right around you, to gain an understanding and awareness of your surroundings."

"I thought I wasn't supposed to try and pry into people's minds."

"Yes, indeed. That is not what I'm proposing. Let me reiterate that point. Do not try and get in anyone's head. Not only is it highly dangerous, it is a gross violation of privacy.

No, I'm suggesting you feel out to gauge the environment. What is the chemistry of a place, given those present? With each person the environment shifts, and shifts can take place even though the inhabitants remain the same. You must stay out of minds, but not pulses, scents, movements, etc. You see where I'm going?"

"I'm exhausted thinking about it. Sounds impossible."

"This kind of knowledge embodies the contradiction of being mentally present and attentive to each individual and the whole. This is indeed a rare art. It could be a good use for your excess, if you think you're strong enough to try."

"To what end?" Adam asked.

I was lost in thought, trying to imagine what it was Mr. Seacrest envisioned.

"Control for Anna, information for us."

"It sounds dangerous. Why waste the herbs, only to give herself away?"

Mr. Seacrest laughed. "You misunderstand me, Adam. I'm not suggesting she go out in the morning and let loose on the general public. Of course not. We will train here in the dreamscape. When she's ready, she'll move on to you, Echo, Suzanne, maybe even Corey, in the waking. No rush. Anna, tomorrow first try in empty rooms. Soon you can try with people."

Something Adam said made me remember a question I'd had for a while. "What do you mean about wasting herbs? Are they expensive?"

Adam closed his eyes, tight-lipped. I looked to Mr. Seacrest for an answer. "Well, what's the deal?"

"They are not expensive," he said, not lying, but not telling me the truth.

"Then what are they?"

"They cannot be bought. There is a finite amount of the herb. It is tightly controlled. That's all I'm saying on the subject right now. Let's get back to your training."

Chapter Nineteen

I awoke from the familiar dream of terror. I was being buried, or trapped, held down while someone frantically called for me. I wouldn't have thought it possible, but her pleas were growing in intensity, just like the knowledge that if I didn't figure out what the dreams meant, someone was going to suffer.

It was 5 a.m. and I couldn't get back to sleep. I tried reading, but what I really needed was release. A run.

I tip-toed down the stairs and was out the kitchen door. Free, by myself, in the comforting darkness of the pre-dawn world. I crossed the train tracks, noting the progress the city was making in the new housing development, and turned to run alongside the field under construction.

Half a mile past the field, I came across a subdivision I hadn't run through before. From the looks of it, the tract housing was from the 1980's, and most of the ranch style homes were very well kept. I slowed down to watch the dawn sweep the dark away.

"Lookin' good, sweetie. Need a break?"

I was completely startled by a man leaning on his car. I hadn't noticed him. At all.

Instinct took over and I started running.

"Hey, sugar, don't be like that. It doesn't have to be like that," he called out.

I couldn't feel him, but I could hear him running after me.

I pulled out my phone as it rang.

"Anna, where are you?" Echo reprimanded.

"I need your help. I'm being chased. Fourth, I think. I don't know. I can't tell. Where are you?"

"I'm out in the car looking for you. Where are you?"

I'd just run through an intersection and gave him the street names.

"Calm yourself. You can take whoever it is. You're strong. He has no idea who he's messing with."

Echo's words helped a little, but the fear was overwhelming. And the stranger was gaining on me. In a minute, I'd be fighting.

"You're going to regret running from me," the man called out. "Lucky for you, I like to take it slow."

In seconds he'd overtake me. I could do this. I'd been trained. Echo was right, this guy was in for a surprise.

I stopped in the middle of the street and faced him. He slowed, his face glowing with excitement. He was in his element and enjoying it.

This was it. I couldn't outrun him, I'd have to fight him.

He scanned me from head to toe. "You gonna fight me? Bring it, baby."

He took out a knife and grinned.

My relief was immediate as I heard the car tearing up the street. The headlights washed over me and I felt Echo running towards us. Him, I could feel. Echo didn't slow down. He rammed himself into the man, taking him down.

In one swift move he took the man's own knife and plunged it into his heart without hesitation.

Dead.

My cell buzzed again.

"He's dead," I said numbly to Adam as I answered.

"Who? What? Are you okay? What's going on? Where are you?" I heard a door slam and a car coming to life from Adam's end.

"Sun's almost up. I gotta move this guy," Echo said, lifting the Fourth and throwing him over his shoulder.

"Anna! Where are you?" Adam shouted.

At the same time, Echo said, "That must be Adam. Tell him where you are. You should be safe, but run back to the main street and meet him there. I've gotta go." He threw the body in the trunk.

"You know the new housing development, about three miles past the set?" I answered Adam, out of breath.

"I'm on my way. Stay on the phone."

"How did you know something was wrong? Weren't you asleep?"

"You were in my dreams. I actually had a dream."

"I'm glad for you. That's good. Or is it bad?" Adam's dreaming abilities had been seriously damaged since I'd been around. But he wasn't supposed to dream when he took the herbs.

"I'm just around the corner."

I could feel him, his presence a mixture of relief and dark thoughts. He somehow knew the real danger I'd been in.

Adam barely stopped before I jumped in the car. He took off and kept driving down the road, turning onto the two-lane, taking us right out of town.

We drove under miles of open sky before Adam asked, "You want to tell me what happened?"

"Echo killed someone. I can't believe it. He murdered him. I… I don't understand. We could've done something else."

"No. Echo was right."

"How do you know? You don't even know what happened." I was too stunned to be angry or self-righteous.

"That guy was Fourth."

That's when I lost it. I felt my mind breaking, the sea coming to swallow me. It started with a small tremor in my hand. I watched, detached, as the shivers began to shake my body. I hugged my knees to my chest to try to get a grip, but my legs didn't feel solid, more like a jelly.

"Adam?" I said, poking a finger into my leg, watching it unnaturally bounce back.

Adam took a sharp turn onto on a dirt service road in the middle of a field.

He pulled me out of the car, swearing as he did. "Come on, hold it together." He helped me into the field, a trail of water flowing behind us.

I wanted to hide where no one, not even Adam, could find me. I wanted to disappear. If he only understood, he'd let me go, escape. Adam loosened his viselike grip on my hand and I thought he'd understood what I wanted. But instead of being glad, I felt abandoned.

He was talking to me, yelling maybe, but all I knew was death. The death of that man. Of my mom. Me.

I was slipping away and didn't have the strength to do anything about it. I couldn't keep doing the same things over and over. Fighting to forget and failing, my mom's death always of the edge of my thoughts.

I looked out to see a helpless Adam, at his end, not knowing how to reach me. There wasn't a way. I was already gone.

Chapter Twenty

"No you're not. I won't let you," Adam spoke to my mind, breaking through.

I'd tuned everything out but my own misery. His clear, determined voice shocked me, but not as much as his full body tackle, bursting the bubble of water encasing me.

His weight on top of me, the reality of his presence snapped me out of my trance.

Adam rolled off me and sat up. "Anna?" My name came out as a question, full of his confusion and pain.

I pushed up, mud oozing between my fingers, drenched. "I have no idea what just happened to me, I was almost killed today, and I saw my would-be torturer cut down without so much as a word from Echo. He didn't get to say his bit. The cops didn't come and arrest him. Echo took the guy's own knife and ripped his heart out. And then you tell me he was Fourth? I WAS JUST OUT FOR A RUN!" I screamed into the morning sky.

"By yourself," Adam said quietly. "Why? You aren't stupid. Why would you take such a risk? Don't you know how important you are?"

"You all got along just fine before I showed up."

"I didn't. Anna, how do you think I would've fared if that Fourth had gotten his filthy hands on you? And forget about me. Don't you care about the rest? Echo, Suzanne, Corey? They would've hunted with me and many would've died. What about your dad?"

"I just wanted to go for a stupid run by myself. Is that too much to ask? Does that make me selfish?"

"Under normal circumstances, no. But these are not normal circumstances."

"I know," I said to the ground.

"Do you want to die?" Adam asked softly.

"Sometimes," I answered honestly. "But only because it would be easier, not better. When I started dreaming as a child, I learned to control the chaos of reality bleeding into my dreams by having a strict regimen. Discipline. I... I sought control and gained it, along with my sanity. And I fought hard."

"I know you did."

"I did. I'm not afraid of the hard work, it's the being out of control. I can't control myself. I didn't plan whatever that was that happened with the water. Sometimes my emotions take over and I get lost. That's the downside of the extra power. Sometimes I'm at its mercy. And it just wants to run rampant without constraint. It's hard to explain."

"I think I understand."

If anyone could, it would be Adam.

"I can't be a hostage. I should be able to go out by myself."

"Do you think the PM or president should be able to go for a run alone?"

"But I didn't run for president."

"Okay, fine. What about the kids of a president or head of state. Should they do whatever they want?"

"In an ideal world," I retorted, already knowing I'd lost. This was not an ideal world.

"Exactly. Damn it, Anna! When are you going to get it through that thick head of yours? I can't believe how reckless you are sometimes. You are rather bright, usually. Why won't you follow orders?"

"And when will you learn to never say things like 'Anna, follow my orders' to me if you want me to be on board? I hate that side of you."

"You still think I tell people what to do because I'm arrogant? That I have ego issues?"

"No, I know it's not that. But you've got to learn there's an art to leadership, and if you need people to follow you, you've got to figure out the right way to get them on board."

"You're not listening to me. You're doing something else. I know how to lead just fine. I tell people what to do and they do it, or else. It's the same for me. I know who my superiors are."

"And?"

"I don't need you to follow me."

"Good, because even though I love you, I don't work that way. I don't see myself ever being a good little soldier."

"I believe I'm having an epiphany," he said, crossing his ankles and lying back in the dirt.

"Do share."

He turned his head towards me. "You are from the land of the Freers and we are the Cursed. Ever heard that before?"

"I think I've heard the reference."

"You grew up one way and I another."

"Medieval comes to mind," I smiled.

"Naïve is the word that comes to mind for your lot. And you. Be that as it may, we can't work together if we are always acting like two school kids yelling at each other from opposite sides of the street as to which way is the best. We've got to drop it and do something different."

"You mean team up? For reals? You and me as equals?"

I liked the idea, but my mind immediately went to the secret I'd been keeping from him. If we tried something new, did this mean I didn't get to keep this secret to myself? Any secret?

"You know I know you're still keeping something from me. And, why yes, it's driving me mad. But it's yours. True partnership means trust. You know, I've got secrets too. Deep, dark, interesting, and extremely sexy secrets that I don't feel at liberty to share with you presently," he joked.

"But really, you and I are one step away from reading each other's minds. It's impractical to keep much to ourselves," I argued.

"Don't worry. I'm not worried. Raging curiosity, sure. But I'll probably survive."

"Stop it," I laughed, glad for the person he was. Someone I could completely trust. "How will this partnership work? We both know we aren't always going to agree on stuff."

"True."

"Who will win?"

"I guess it will depend on the circumstances. What I'm most concerned with is keeping you safe. What I went through this morning when I felt your fear –"

"Is that why you called?"

"I was dead asleep and I felt you. I also felt what you didn't. A filthy Fourth and his mal intent. He was going to kill you after causing you to suffer. Do you understand? I need you to clearly see what we're up against."

Adam let his wall down, allowing me to feel what he'd gone through this morning, letting me experience a portion of what it was like for him.

He looked apologetic for being cruel. This was the part he regularly held back when he could. And maybe this was why I routinely underestimated the dangers of the Fourth and the war he insisted he – we – were a part of.

To feel his fear and abject helplessness was crippling. What if it was reversed? What if he was being chased unaware by a monster and only I knew he was in serious trouble, but not why it was happening or where he was to send help?

I instantly felt ashamed of my thoughtless behavior. I hugged him, apologizing.

"We move forward, yes?" he said, kissing my muddy hair.

"Yes. And I've got to get my sight back when it comes to the Fourth."

"Uncle said it should happen soon. We stick together. And maybe, one day, we can live the free life you envision. Though I really do think you've picked the wrong profession if freedom is what you crave."

"You never know what you have until it's gone. I never realized how much I prized being by myself, going here and there unaccompanied, until it was taken from me."

"A luxury I've seldom known. And, Anna, I think you need help."

"Don't we all!"

"I'm specifically referring to your almost watery grave. We have to tell Uncle."

"Only him, no one else. Okay?" I conceded, embarrassed by my irrational reaction.

"Of course," he said, helping me up.

Chapter Twenty-One

After such an emotional morning, I was able to get out of tennis practice, thanks to Adam. Maggie was clear in her anti-Anna, pro-Adam stance. She supported him in everything except his relationship with me. But he batted his absurdly dark eyelashes and told his sis in just the right way that she wouldn't make a scene when I didn't show at 9 a.m. for practice. I sent Sylvia a text assuring her I'd be on set for hair and make-up as scheduled at noon.

I wasn't surprised when she came around a half-hour later.

"Do you need medical attention?" Sylvia asked, feeling my head for a fever.

"I had a horrible night's sleep and a bad run this morning. I didn't want to miss practice, but I thought it best if I rested up and was ready this afternoon instead of needlessly wearing myself out."

"Smart decision. Yes. Is Gold Manor not agreeing with you? Meg and some others are buying property. My idea of shooting on location isn't working as I'd anticipated."

"I'm not ready to think about finding a different place to stay," I said. Strange, but Gold Manor felt like the right place to be.

"If you change your mind and need help finding another place, let me know. There are still plenty of people filling up the manor. You're not alone here."

Those words were truer than she knew.

I went back to bed and thankfully fell into a dead sleep. No nightmares, just oblivion. Up with my alarm, I showered and grabbed a quick lunch as I went downstairs for hair and make-up. I tried not to think about what I had planned for the day.

I was shooting a few short scenes at the manor with Meg and Lucy, and then over to my new TV house to block a scene with Finn. He'd arrived in town sometime yesterday and we'd be rehearsing together for the first time this afternoon.

Because of the blue stuff in my system, Finn was impossible for me to read. Impossible. Talking to him was like talking to an animated cardboard cutout. He moved, he talked, but he felt empty, like no one was there.

I didn't know how to act around him because, not only could I not feel him, I knew a lot about him that he didn't know I knew. Looking at him made me blush, and my fear that he would think I was blushing because I liked him just made me blush more.

As I left hair and make-up, thinking about how awkward it was going to be today, I jumped when he called my name.

"Sorry, Anna. I always catch you deep in thought. You a deep thinker?" Finn asked, smiling, his PA next to him.

Suddenly, I felt a panic coming on. I knew Echo was one flight up, on the first floor, but I'd just promised Adam I wouldn't go places alone. And here I was, just a few hours later, basically cornered in the basement by two Fourths.

"Sometimes," I croaked, my face flushing.

Finn took my response in stride. He was used to girls reacting like that to him. He'd been on TV and in movies since he was small.

"I was thinking, want to grab dinner tonight after we block our scene? Since you're my sis, I think it's high time we got to know each other. You free?"

"Sure," I said, startled.

"Great. See you later," he said, turning into the hair and make-up room, his PA lingering long enough to give me a disapproving once-over.

I hurried to the first floor and found a chair. I was in the process of calming down, slowing my heart rate, when I saw Mr. Seacrest.

"Ms. Ellingwood, good to see you," he said as he walked right by.

I had to start the calming process all over. What was he doing here? It had been a few nights since he'd met me in my dreams and he hadn't mentioned he was coming to town. Was something wrong?

I couldn't think that way every time I saw him, or anything out of the ordinary. If I did, I'd be in a constant state of alert and my hair would perpetually stand on end.

I stood up to look in the gothic mirror behind me, wondering if my hair was doing a crazy dance. It wasn't. It was as smooth and coiffed as if I'd just left the stylist, probably because I'd expended all my built up energy turning watery this morning.

I made a mental note to heed Adam's advice and talk to Mr. Seacrest about that unfortunate reaction of mine. It had happened twice now. I wanted to avoid a third time.

"You look fine. They want us outside," Lucy sniped, catching me looking at my reflection.

Lucy and I weren't BFF's, but she'd never used that tone with me. Her bitchy voice was usually reserved for anyone she considered "underlings."

"What's wrong with you?" I asked.

"Maybe my eyes wouldn't be so puffy if I'd gotten more sleep too. I don't see why you got out of practice today. I'm just as important to this show. Seems like favoritism, just saying."

"I wasn't feeling well," I said, defending myself.

"Sure, whatever." She was already done with her mini-grievance with me and on to the next person to torture.

We shot several exterior scenes on the driveway and porch. I had one quick walk-through in the kitchen. Satisfied, Sylvia dismissed me so I could hurry up and change, making it to rehearsal on time at the new location.

My first scene with Finn was an exterior shot at our house. Last year I'd stayed in the Pritchett's home because Sylvia planned for my character's mom to play a part in the show. But it never happened. Scenes were rewritten and my character's home interior never made it on screen.

It turned out my mom and I had lived with the Pritchetts for no reason. The only exterior shot was in the street, the house never in frame.

This season, with Finn playing my big brother home from a year backpacking around the world, our house was in a new location.

On the drive to the house in a neighboring town, Dresden, I told Adam about my run in with Finn.

"I'm at a loss. Do you expect me to literally always have someone with me at all times? I mean, Echo was on the first floor and I was just getting ready for the shoot. I want to be smart, but not crazy."

"Too late, love. I love your crazy," he said, smiling but troubled. "Just be smart and don't take unnecessary risks. Be aware."

I was glad he gave such a reasonable response. Maybe he was being generous because nothing had happened and he could tell I was genuinely mortified by my basement encounter.

"I hate that he thinks I like him."

"Maybe that's good. It's what he's used to."

"Is that what you're used to?"

"Who wouldn't want me?" he laughed. Some thought changed his bravado to sincerity. "You love me for who I am. No one ever has. It's always been what I can do for them, and recently the fame or even my amazing abs. They think they want me. But they don't know. They don't know what I've done. What I'm capable of. What I'll have to do. But you, Anna," he said, staring stiffly ahead at the road, "you amaze me. You're making me rethink it all."

I wanted desperately to ask what he meant, but that would ruin the loveliness of the moment. Instead I took his hand and kissed it.

When we arrived, there was a lot of activity at the farm house the production had purchased. The scene being blocked involved Finn's character, Jonathan Vincent, coming home for a surprise visit. My character is cleaning mold off

159

the siding of our house when a mysterious guy pulls up on a motorcycle, who turns out to be my brother. We reunite, he asks after mom, and I tell him she'd been deployed sooner than we anticipated.

We ran through the scene several times, which was nerve-racking. Not because Adam was there watching, but because I was acting opposite a person I couldn't feel, but I could feel how I was really stinking it up.

It was clear I was having trouble, and Finn was being nice about it, but I felt awful. My problem was that, because I felt nothing from Finn, I reacted by closing myself off. All I could see was my own numbness and awkwardness. I needed to loosen up!

Chad, Sylvia's newest assistant director, said, "Let's try this. Anna, you notice the obnoxiously loud motorcycle coming down the street and watch as the rider stops and gets off. This time, when he comes up and startles you, the ladder shakes. Finn, you steady it. Okay? Let's try it again."

"I'm going to take the bike around the corner and ride in," Finn said.

"Great," Chad affirmed, two thumbs up.

I climbed the ladder, Chad handing me the bucket of suds once I was in place.

Given my cue, I willed myself to let loose, to let go of the anxiety I felt when I even thought of Finn, let alone saw him. As I washed the green grime off the white siding, I felt out, noting all the people in their proper places, their own worries and issues mixing into a background noise. Adam's was the strongest, always.

I knew this was just a rehearsal, but when we shot in a few days, whatever I managed to come up with would be put down on film forever. Talk about a decent motivator.

The scene began and I turned toward the loud noise coming up the dusty road. I watched the rider dismount and walk up to my rickety ladder.

I didn't need to fake surprise when Finn removed his helmet. How I wished I could've blamed Zeus and his bolts of lightning or the San Andreas Fault for what happened next.

I was attempting to be completely open and present in the scene with Finn so I didn't look like a fool. Too bad so sad for me.

Mr. Seacrest had said the side effect of the blue pills blocking me from feeling the Fourth was temporary. When Finn took off his helmet, I felt like I'd been kicked in the gut. It was involuntary. I vomited my lunch all over Finn Varga and fell from the ladder, knocking him flat and landing on top of him.

My shame was instant. The small crew, led by Adam, descended, helping me up, checking for injuries.

I pushed Adam away and stumbled to the house stoop, putting my head between my legs. I was covered in goosebumps, feeling for the first time what it was like to be in the presence of a full-blooded Fourth. I still had to remind myself Suzanne was on our side because her Fourth blood sang a different story. But she was diluted. Her mother wasn't related to the Families, and I could now tell her father must've been only distantly related, because her bad Fourth vibe was a whisper compared to the force that was Finn. I could feel viciousness pulsating through him. He was no longer blank to me.

Every move he made reverberated through me. I'd never been in the presence of evil. How could Adam stand nonchalantly by him?

"I'm sorry," I stammered to Finn. "Will you please take me home?" I asked Adam.

"Of course," Adam said, helping me up.

"Feel better, Anna," Finn said, taking off his nasty vomit-covered shirt. "I'm off to the showers. We'll catch up when you're feeling better."

I was about to apologize again, but instead I dropped to my knees and dry-heaved my heart out.

On the ride back to the manor Adam confirmed what I was pretty certain had happened. The temporary side effect had worn off.

"That was rough to watch. You okay?"

"My pride is wounded more than anything. I looked like such an idiot. But…. I mean, how do you do it? I could smell it on him, like at any moment his smile would turn sadistic and he'd go ballistic."

"Maybe my behavior on the night of the cast party makes a little more sense?"

"You said it. And yet…."

"And yet. Yes. The kicker. He's obviously not pure evil. He seems to genuinely be concerned for you, which shows good taste."

"But it's hard to push past the cloud of hate he's sitting in. You know what I mean? It makes it seem like his smile is a lie, but I can feel it's not a lie. Could one person be more confusing?" I asked. "I thought he was doing something to mask what he is. So why can I feel him so strongly?"

"He is hidden, to others. But because of our gifts, it's almost impossible for someone of Family descent as pure as he is to hide. How are you feeling now?"

"Hungry, actually. But, how can you be so cool and collected around him?" I asked again.

"There's a reason acting is as natural as breathing for our lot, especially when you're like me," Adam said.

"You mean being pure-blooded?"

"I think you've got it upside down, love. I'm full First, which means I'm completely cursed. Anything but pure."

"That's not true. Your blood doesn't make you who you are. Your actions do," I said.

"Tell that to the supernatural curse we're under. That's what you're reading off Finn. Think on that. You're reading what his parents did, and more than likely still do. I've been told my entire life that the ends justify the means. That if you have a great good you're trying to achieve you can do whatever you need to bring it about. In fact, you must. That's why Uncle tried to kill you. Not because he's bad, because he can only see the end of suffering. But causing suffering to an innocent to end the suffering of others, well, it's getting harder for me to rationalize. That's the real reason Suzanne is still alive. I believe in the goal of my people, but not their old methods."

"And that's why you're not going to kill Finn. You're going to let him write his own fate."

"I was, until one of his tried to kill you today."

"But he didn't know who I was."

"And that matters?" he spat. "I'm sorry. This mess is so vast, it's hard to see what the right course is."

"Adam Lewis, what have you been taking?" I exclaimed.

"What do you mean?" he asked, startled, turning into the side lot at Gold Manor.

"Such much wisdom for a boy who claims to be lost."

"I am not lost, not anymore. But I'm certainly not wise. Let's get you inside."

Chapter Twenty-Two

Sylvia insisted I see a doctor and take the rest of the day off. I didn't argue, though I felt fine. And feeling fine after my weird behavior would've been too hard to explain. I grabbed a book and fell into Orwell's dystopian world.

"Sorry to disappoint, but I know you're there," I called out to Suzanne. She was standing silently on the other side of the door, no doubt planning to scare me, still under the impression I couldn't sense her.

"Rats," she said, pushing the door open. "Mind if I have a seat?"

I motioned to the bed.

"You okay?" she asked sincerely, her voice softer than usual.

"Have you seen Adam? Did he tell you what happened?"

"Yeah. But I mean this morning. The run," she said, laying her hand on my foot.

I knew she was getting at what neither Echo nor Adam had the guts to address: what that guy would've done to me before he killed me if given the chance.

"I'm beyond mad at myself for being so stupid. For thinking this is all some kind of game."

"You've never thought that," she said, looking at me squarely.

"But I don't think I ever understood, not really. I thought there was some kind of mistake and that the Fourth were just misunderstood. But that guy wasn't just bad, he was a psychopath."

"That's why I got out. Not all of them are like that, but when you spend your formative years as an assassin and killing at will, you tend to lose compassion and start to see people as objects to be used. Or worse."

"Thank you."

"For what?" she asked, puzzled, getting up to let me get back to my book.

"Checking in on me."

"No sweat. It's my job, remember?" she winked, hand on the door.

"Wait," I yelled involuntarily.

Suzanne pushed the door shut and locked it. "What is it?" she whispered.

"He's here. I can feel him. On the first floor, I think."

"Who?" she asked, searching my eyes.

"Finn."

The pain in her eyes was immediate, in tune with her racing heart.

"Wait with me, please," I asked.

"Absolutely," she said, standing like a centurion.

In the safety of my bedroom I felt out. I allowed myself to feel the aura around him, to think about what I was sensing. It was counterintuitive, because what I wanted more than anything was to pull away and plug my nose.

But then I thought about Suzanne. How did I deal with constantly being around her? She was different because I trusted her, but there was still a mind trick I constantly employed when we were together.

As I thought about Suzanne, who was standing so close to me I could reach out and touch her, Finn was getting closer. He was now on the floor below us.

Suddenly I had an image of Finn as an unnatural, raging fire. And I was made of water. Compared to Finn's fire, Suzanne was a lit match. What did I do with the match? I'd tried to blow it out countless times, to no avail. Instead I'd use it to light a candle. That's what I did automatically when I was around her.

But Finn was too big, too unwieldy. I couldn't hope to set him aside.

It wasn't that I felt in casual conversation he was literally going to consume me or burn me alive, but the malice radiating from him was incredibly unnerving and distracting. It was easier when he felt like a walking corpse.

That was it! What was it I had to do with Suzanne? Set my feelings aside. I'd spent so much time with her that it'd become rote, I barely recognized I was doing it. I would do the same with Finn.

Whereas I envisioned Suzanne as a candle, Finn would be a bonfire. I'd still probably feel him, but he wouldn't be as noxious.

"Why are you smiling? Is he leaving?" Suzanne asked, a mixture of relief and sadness at the thought of Finn taking off.

"No. I'm going to try something," I said, concentrating.

The pain and maliciousness below, swirling about me, I commanded the fire I visualized to collect and settle, pushing it to the farthest corner I could to minimize the distraction.

"What's going on?" Suzanne was anxious.

"Shhhh," I said, trying to breathe. I sat on my bed, feeling his movements below. I couldn't know for certain, but it felt as if he was moving around the room. I was fairly certain he was leaving.

The further he got from me, the smaller the fire became until it went out.

"Suzanne, will you go see if he's gone? Maybe find out why he was here too?"

"Sure," she said, turning red, which she knew I caught. "I really hate that."

"I don't mean to. But please know, if you want to talk about him or anything, I'm here."

"Thanks," she replied, but meant it would be a cold day in hell before she discussed her complicated love life with me.

"Got it. Well, let me know what you find out."

Chapter Twenty-Three

Turned out Finn had come to check on me. He'd brought me flowers.

Why couldn't he be a jerk?

Why was life hard to navigate?

Since the doctor found nothing wrong with me besides exhaustion, Sylvia let up on early morning tennis practice. It was no longer mandatory, and now a health care professional would be on site to make certain we stayed hydrated and weren't overworked.

Maggie thought it was all kinds of ridiculousness, adding to the long list of reasons why she didn't like me.

Knowing my ability to feel Fourths was back, I was careful to keep my reading of others as minimal as possible. Most of it I couldn't help. It came as natural as breathing. But Mr. Seacrest had taught me techniques for pushing, feeling out for others even when they weren't in front of me.

I was nervous about seeing Finn, but this time I'd finally be myself. I also had a tested plan to deal with him. After my morning run with Echo, I held on to the little bit of energy I had for an extra kick.

Adam's shooting schedule was such that he couldn't go with me this time to the set in Dresden, but Echo was assigned to the lighting crew for the scene. Though we all saw the looming problem. What about the time that would undoubtedly come when everyone would be scheduled to be somewhere else and I was left alone with Finn? How would we make it work without someone noticing something was weird?

Before I parked the car, I knew Finn and his bodyguards were already on site.

"He's here. You ready? Can you feel that?" I asked, talking about the stifling negative energy.

"I know some kind of Fourth is around here, that's all," Echo answered.

"Really? I can smell him."

"Literally?"

"Kinda."

Echo smiled at me. It felt comforting when he found me funny. "You ready?"

"Yeah," I said, taking Finn's aura in and starting to gather it in the space I'd carved out.

I was barely out of the car when he approached. "How you feeling today?"

I had mentally rehearsed how I was going to play this. But like every other encounter I'd had with Finn, I was caught off guard. I was prepared to act my way through being around him, like I was holding my nose against a foul odor. But it wasn't there. No stench.

There was the spine curdling cry of the Fourth I was pushing past, and expected the man, Finn, to match his curse. He didn't. There was a complexity to him I didn't have time to sort out as he stood there, waiting for my reply to his simple question.

"Much better, thank you. I'm really sorry for yesterday. I'm beyond mortified."

"I had to burn my favorite jacket," he joked. "No worries, though. You're sure you're okay today? I happen to be fond of these shoes."

"Ha. I think I'll manage to pull through."

"If we make it through this harrowing scene in one piece, would you like to grab dinner afterwards?"

I couldn't explain the immediate affinity I felt toward Finn. Once I'd pushed his heritage aside, we clicked. There was an ease about him that was appealing. "Better not push our luck. Let's see if I can make it through a scene without falling apart."

"And then dinner?" he pressed. He responded to the suspicious look in my eyes by adding, "We're shooting tomorrow, and for my own character development and research, I want to get to know you and what you think about your character. Just so you know I'm on the up and up, feel free to bring your boyfriend."

"Okay. Dinner it is, if all goes according to plan."

It did. Actually, much better. We had a noticeable compatibility with each other, so much so that Sylvia commented on it. How incredibly odd. It wasn't that I was attracted to him, but after spending one afternoon with him, I got why Suzanne put her life on the line to save his.

Finn got his wish. Adam and I met up with him at Snappy's Pizza. We sat in the private party room in the back usually reserved for birthday parties or little league end-of-season celebrations, separating us from the other patrons with an accordion door.

I could still go into most restaurants without being recognized. In most small towns, Adam would be fine too. But not in Martin. And then there was Finn, who'd been a star for years and was highly recognizable to young and old alike. So that we were actually free to eat and have a get-to-know-you-conversation, we went through the back door and had our food brought to us, even though Snappy's was mainly a pizza buffet.

Finn's PA was none too happy about being exiled from the party room, but I was glad he was gone. He was Fourth and as creepy as his blood felt. It seemed to me he had about the same amount of Fourth blood as Suzanne, but his chemistry felt nasty.

"Dude, you know what your problem is around here?" Finn said in his chill way.

"You don't like Martin? Just wait. It'll grow on you," I said, sipping my water.

"No, it's the vibe on the set. Too heavy."

"You do read, don't you?" Adam retorted, and I swatted his arm. "Seriously. Did you take a look at our track record before you signed on?"

"Let's just say I took last year off. I was off the grid. When I came back around my agent told me about this role."

"You mean really off the grid, like no media? Phone, internet, papers?" I asked, shocked. I knew I could use a day or two off, but a year? Sounded like a jail sentence. Maybe it was. Maybe it hadn't been voluntary.

"What was it like?" I asked, imagining extreme boredom.

"I spent seven years growing up on a set. Then there were the movies after," he began.

"Your last one was *Ice King*, right? I loved it. Aren't they making the others in the series?" I asked.

"That's one of the reasons I left. Things fell apart," he said, suddenly finding his drink super interesting. "Hey, wait a minute, Anna. I called this dinner to interrogate you. She always this way?" he laughed, clearing away whatever unhappy thought had come over him.

"Pretty much, mate. I've found giving her what she wants is the best way," Adam answered, leaning back in the black pleather and wrought iron chair, putting his arm around my shoulder.

"Too bad. The notes I got from Chad, the assistant director, say I'm supposed to be a pain in your ass."

"Don't tell me you're a method actor," I groaned.

"You think we should start our 'brother and sister' relationship out with a lie? I'm gonna be unbearable," he grinned wickedly.

I was thankful I'd worked on being in his presence and seeing past his threatening physical aura, or those words might've freaked me out. But I was in control. I held my emotions in, testing the area around me using my built-in meter to feel him out. While he wasn't harmless, he wasn't a monster.

"Just remember, turnabout is fair game. You may not want to travel down that road," I joked.

"Okay, fine. Now down to business. I want to know about you, the real you, and then about how you've been playing Laura Vincent."

"Have you even watched the first season of *Ghost House*?" I asked.

"Yes, but I want to know what *you* know about her. What you think about Laura. First, what about you? What should I know about you?"

"What do you want to know?" I asked, not feeling as comfortable. My past was difficult before I came on set last year, and now my story was impossible to tell.

"Do you have any siblings?"

"No, just me," I answered, glad for the softball question. "But I really don't like talking about myself. You understand."

"Tell me about it. Just a few more then," he said, artfully going on even though I'd politely told him to back off.

"What about your parents?"

Adam's mouth fell open as all the merriment vanished from the room.

"Did I say something wrong? You know what the problem is around here? I could tell instantly. Way too serious. We really do need to ramp up the practical jokes, maybe even schedule parties?" Finn laughed.

"You really should've read the news before coming," Adam said, disgusted.

"He doesn't know," I breathed, trying to calm my heart and keep Adam from decking Finn.

"What?" Finn asked, confused.

Before Adam could say or do something we'd regret, I caught Finn up on a few *Ghost House* details. "The shooting had wrapped for the season and my mom came to surprise me, to help me pack up and spend time with me. She was murdered," I whispered, tears running down my face. I couldn't help adding, "The last time I was at Snappy's was with her."

Finn went very still, his olive skin turning pasty. He dropped his head to the table and Adam took my hand. We all sat in silence, letting the food get cold.

I could feel his PA coming toward us, but I still jumped out of my seat when Colby tore open the flimsy accordion door that separated us from the rest of the restaurant.

Finn threw him a furious look. "Stand down," he growled at Colby.

The poor dividing partition was mangled and off its track, and our privacy was compromised, so I said, "I think we'd better go."

Finn followed us back to the manor. He jumped out of his car to catch us. "Anna, please believe me, Adam," he said, looking between the two of us, "I had no idea. Truly. I can't believe I wasn't told."

"I believe you. You're okay. And now we're even. I threw up on you and you didn't know about what happened. Neither were really our faults in the first place. Maybe we secretly really are family," I joked, my tears gone.

"Thanks, sis," he said, hugging me, startling me.

"Oh, you're not a hugger. Surprised. Well, seems we really do need to get to know each other."

"Why would you assume you know me?" I asked.

"I watched the first season of *Ghost House* at least three times through, and your scenes even more. You're very different from Laura Vincent. But there's something else. Right, Adam? You know what I mean?"

"I'm utterly biased because I'm in love with her."

"Exactly! That's what I'm getting at. Anna, you've got this cool rock star eating out of your hands even though, and don't take this the wrong way, you're...different."

"I'm assuming you mean that as a compliment."

"Obviously. I'm not a complete jerk. I mean even that comment, the way you talk to me," he said, turning pensive. "I don't think it's you. It's me. I had a wild upbringing and then I was thrust right in front of the camera. I'm not used to being treated as a regular guy."

"Get used to it. Anna's not intimidated by anyone. Not even my uncle."

"I've not met Mr. Seacrest, but I heard you're related. He's as scary as they say?"

"Yeah, even for me. But she treats him like anyone else."

"I'm right here, you know," I said, rolling my eyes involuntarily.

"I really would like to chat more, Anna, but it'll have to be some other time. I'm leaving tomorrow or the next day. Need to visit my parents and I have a few appearances. I'm also not sure how long I'll be a part of this project."

"What's your contract for?" The prospect of him visiting his parents sobered me right up. He was not a regular guy.

"Four episodes."

"Really? I'm shocked. Sylvia's been acting like you'll be around longer."

"I'm only obligated to be in four, but I've been given the option to sign on for as many episodes as I'd like. It's complicated because of the writers, but, not to brag, TeenTV just about lost its shit when I said I was interested in a guest appearance."

"All of this for a few episodes?" Adam asked skeptically.

"It's how I roll. If I agree to do something, I dive in. What other way is there?"

There was something authentic about Finn. I wasn't ready for him to leave yet, so I invited him on to the porch and told him the litany of tragic events that plagued our set, from the fall of Mac Allen, the guy Corey had replaced, to the stringing up of Jade, and the unsolved murders of Kayla Locke and John Thompson.

He was stunned.

"While we all love the show, the show hasn't loved us. Maybe the tension on the set makes a little more sense now," I said, ending my explanation. Adam was his usual silent self.

"Why isn't there a fence?" Finn asked, looking around the Gold Manor property.

"Excuse me?"

"There was a double homicide, where's the security?"

"They installed a state-of-the-art security system in the manor afterwards. And we do have signs posted at the entrance to the property."

"Signs? Maybe that's why I'm here. Fate has brought me to your show. Believe me, I know a thing or two about security. I'm talking to Sylvia before I leave."

"There are security guards," I protested weakly.

Finn gagged. "Ha! They only get the gawkers, not the real crazies or murderers."

He pulled out his phone and sighed. "I've gotta take off. I really am sorry about earlier. Are we good?"

"Yes. Do you run?" I asked.

"Do you?" he retorted.

"I'll be running tomorrow, 6 a.m. I run with a friend, Echo. You can come with us."

"You don't?" he asked Adam.

"Too early."

"My bodyguard won't like it," Finn shook his head.

"Echo's my friend but also like a bodyguard. I'm happy to share."

"Is he on the lighting crew?"

"Yeah. How'd you know?"

"I did a little bit of homework before I came. Apparently I focused on the wrong things."

Chapter Twenty-Four

"He's waiting for us on the porch, isn't he?" I asked Echo as I exited my room in my running gear.

Echo nodded.

"Let's do this. Ready?" I asked, heading down the stairs, not able to look him in the eye.

"No need to worry. I'll keep you safe. Anna, *I'm* safe. You know that, right?"

I stopped and turned around. I hadn't talked to Echo about what had happened with the guy he killed.

"I only did what was necessary. You can feel that about me. I didn't get any pleasure out of what I did. You can trust me."

I laid my hand on his arm. "You misunderstand. I'm not mad at you. I'm sick at myself. You totally saved me. You did what you did for me. But if I hadn't been so utterly careless, you wouldn't have needed to do it. Yesterday is all my fault."

"No it's not."

"But it is. And I'm sorry. Doing *that* has got to take a piece of your soul, even if the other person is like that guy. I'll never forgive myself for putting you in that position. Thank you," I said, pulling him into a hug.

Echo hugged me back stiffly, not used to such emotion.

Just then Finn Varga walked into the manor. "You two ready for a run? Everything okay?"

"Yeah. Just a show of affection. Echo's a great friend."

Finn smiled, but I could feel something just underneath the surface. Jealousy. He was jealous he didn't have true friends.

"You mind if I lead the way again? I'm trying a new route and there are some places in town I can't go yet. Too hard, you know?"

"Lead the way, little sis!" Finn joked.

We ran, more like trotted, through the streets. Finn really had dissected my portrayal of Laura Vincent. He asked why I'd made certain choices, what I was thinking during different scenes. He was thorough.

"Given your understanding of Laura Vincent, what do you think she thinks of her brother?"

"I think they have a good relationship, that she misses him. I bet, given they were raised by a single mom who was military, that they spent a lot of time together growing up. Best friends, maybe? I'm not sure about that. But close. That's what I think, anyway."

"You think Jonathan will notice Laura is possessed?"

"Not right away."

"Really? If they are as close as you say, wouldn't he see it right away? A massive personality change?"

"If the writers wrote the possession that way, sure. But it's way more subtle. Laura is herself, but sometimes whatever is in her takes over. Right now it happens so seldom, and I guess her brother would have to be around when it happens to know."

"I think you're wrong there. If a person is possessed in some way, even if the spirit only came out to play every once in a while, the unconscious mind would know something was wrong and act out. Somehow."

"I never thought about it that way. Do you believe in demons in real life?" I asked.

"Demon possession? No, not really. But Laura is possessed by a ghost. And yes, I think ghosts exist."

"Really?"

"You don't?" Finn asked, surprised.

"I don't see how they could. A ghost makes no sense to me. I think when you die, you leave this world and go on to the next, whatever that is." At least, that's what I used to think. I liked pretending to be the old me, where nasty ghosts were only scary make-believe stories.

"No, believe me. Ghosts are real," he said, slowing down.

"You are so sure? Have you seen one?" I asked as we came to a halt. He didn't need to answer for me to know he had.

"Most people think ghost talk is crazy. Like talking about aliens." He was trying to gauge what kind of person I was before telling me what he'd seen.

"I have no problem with the possibility of aliens."

"Really? Aliens but no ghosts?" he said, taking us from walking back to trotting.

"To clarify, I think aliens are possible, not that they *actually* exist. As for ghosts, I am in the paradoxical position of thinking they don't make sense, yet… I've seen one." It was an on-the-spot self-disclosure that shocked my trotting partners.

"Anna!" Echo blurted out in reprimand, making Finn's eyes grow bigger.

"Let me get this straight," he laughed. "You don't believe in ghosts and yet you've seen one? And I gather Echo has too?"

"They don't call it Ghost House for nothing," I retorted as I picked up the pace.

We ran for almost a minute in silence before Finn stopped me.

"Are you serious? There are ghosts here?"

Finn's pleasant, easy-going demeanor was replaced with the warrior expression I knew all too well from when Adam heard disturbing Family news.

"Yep," I responded lightly.

"Anna, Echo, let me give you a friendly warning. I've been around and I've seen some crazy things. Dangerous things. But ghosts are…a whole different horror show. The best advice I will ever give you is to stay away from them. This show makes them a joke, plays with the idea of the supernatural. That's a mistake."

I'm not sure what he was reading from us. I tried my best to look blank.

"I don't care if you think I'm crazy, but you gotta listen to me," he said, grabbing my hand, which made Echo flinch. "Ghosts, once engaged, are like a stench you can't wash off. They will follow you until they get what they want. And believe me, you don't want that."

"I'm sorry, Finn. I didn't mean to make light of ghosts. I didn't know how you felt."

"Most people either don't believe in ghosts or have a romantic notion of what they are. I don't mean to be this intense, especially since we barely know each other. But I'm leaving town tomorrow. Please promise me to not go looking for them."

"Sure. It freaked me out anyway. I wasn't sure what I'd seen, but I certainly didn't like it. Right, Echo?"

"Don't have to tell me twice. Thanks for the warning, though."

Finn stood firmly planted on the sidewalk for a few moments longer, looking between the two of us, wanting to impress on us again, with his posture and demeanor, the seriousness of what he was talking about.

"I'm close to my hotel. I'm leaving tomorrow morning, but have time for a run if you don't mind me tagging along again."

"Sure," I said.

"Take care," Finn said as he took the road to the right and we continued straight.

"Why did you do that?" Echo asked. He was more confused than mad.

"It's hard to explain. I could feel something inside of Finn and being open with him felt right."

"Did you catch what he said? What he gave away."

"Yes. He referred to the one ghost I said I saw as them."

"You think he knows about the Gold Ghosts?"

"I'm fairly certain he heard about them and we confirmed his suspicions."

"Maybe it's a good thing we didn't kill him when he came to town," Echo laughed.

I didn't find that funny at all.

Finn ran with us the next morning, before he left town.

More comfortable than he'd been the day before, he talked the entire time. I learned he had a large family. His parents weren't married, hadn't been for a while. He told me he had lots of full, half, and step siblings. When he was two, he was carted off to live with his father, and then with a cousin, and then shuttled around. He said he wasn't interested in the family business and wasn't very good at it anyway, so he was left to find his own way.

"But you've been acting since you were, what, nine?"

"Ten. The family business starts as soon as you can walk. It's hard to explain. Part of the agreement with my parents is I leave them alone and they leave me alone. Mostly. I still have to check in."

"And you don't see them regularly?"

"There was one summer I tried. It was a disaster."

"Sorry to hear it," I said.

"Yeah, well, it helped me to find myself."

"Was it last year?"

"Why do you ask?" he said, disturbed by my question.

"You said you were in self-imposed exile."

"No, this was a few years back. You see, there was a girl. We fell in love, but because of my family it could never work out. She left. It sucked."

"You still love her?"

"I don't think it matters. I need to move on," he said, trying to convince himself.

"But you can't?" I pushed.

"You are incredibly perceptive. Ever think of studying psychology in college?"

"I haven't thought too much about college lately."

"Really? Huh. Not to be rude, but you know this won't last." Finn's easy going demeanor had turned reflective. Thoughtful.

"To what are you referring?"

"The show. The fame. It's nice while you have it, but it will go and you'll have to ask yourself what kind of life you want. What do you want to do? Who do you want to be?"

"Those sound like separate issues," I said, chewing on this new food for thought.

"Not to break up your meaning-of-life conversation, but I've got to head back," Echo cut in.

We'd been out for a long time. We were halfway between Finn's place and the manor. "You two head back, I'm fine," Finn said.

"You certain?" Echo asked. How odd it was that Echo seemed concerned with Finn's safety when not too long ago he'd been ready to kill him.

"Yeah. See ya," he said, taking off before anything else could be said.

Running home, I could feel Echo's mind reeling.

"I know. He's Fourth and a nice guy," I said to Echo.

"I didn't think it possible. There's Suzanne, but I'd convinced myself she was the exception."

"She's not. Need I remind you of Corey?"

"I liked life better when everything was clear. When there was the good side and the bad side."

"That hasn't changed," I answered.

Echo was being made to reconsider the world as he knew it. "True. But blood no longer draws the line. It's harder when it's person to person. How are we supposed to fight a war when we fight individuals and not the conglomerate of evil that is the Fourth?"

"Yeah. Enlightenment's inconvenient."

Chapter Twenty-Five

I watched the news for reports of my dead attacker. Nothing. Adam wasn't surprised, but I was. In this day and age of cameras on every corner and forensic evidence? Not only did Echo artfully get rid of the body, but no one reported the guy missing.

Finn and company had left town. It was a weird feeling. I'd gotten so used to having him and Colby around that I hadn't noticed the pressure on my chest until it was lifted. With the Fourth about, I hadn't had excess energy. I had diverted it, using it to help me be normal around them. As they rode out of town, I felt a burst. I felt light and buoyant.

That night I met Mr. Seacrest in my dreamscape for lessons. It had been a while. I explained what I did to be able to be around Finn and Colby. He offered some suggestions that might not take such attention. He thought exposure would also lessen the symptoms, just as it had with Suzanne.

Since my mom's death, for the most part, Mr. Seacrest had been unavailable. Beyond his full business schedule, he'd been working in the Family library to put together what he'd – we'd – uncovered about me. He was puzzling through what I was meant to do, how I was supposed to end the curse.

"You aren't being honest with us," I challenged him after hearing what he'd pieced together so far.

"Anna," Adam chided. "Restraint."

"We are not all equals, child. You'd do well to remember that. I am on your side, obviously. But I will not send you off half-cocked with my broken narrative."

"What did you find in the library? About the prophecy of a Fifth born from a Second and Third?" I asked.

"Not what I'd hoped," he answered, side-stepping something important.

"If you'd let me in, I'm happy to look. Please? I want to help. I need to know."

"No," he replied emphatically.

"Not good enough. I deserve to know the truth about this. What aren't you telling me?" It pissed me off Mr. Seacrest had info that might really make a difference to me, but stubbornly refused to share!

"I know I've sworn to help you, but keep your place!" His anger got the best of him.

"He can't, Anna," Adam said. "He burned that section of the library."

By the look on Mr. Seacrest's face, Adam had guessed correctly. Whatever documents had been there were now lost to time.

"But you do want us to do something. What is it?" I asked Mr. Seacrest, his demeanor impossible for me to figure out.

"Trust me. Focus on training your mind. I can still break in, which is problematic for us all. To that end, why don't you focus on those nightmares. That is one point I can clarify for you; whoever is trying to get your attention is not Family related."

"I kinda thought as much. Is that good or bad?"

"Depends, of course. Someone is reaching out to you. Find out why."

"You've got to be kidding me, Uncle. That's crap advice. Even I think that's foolhardy," Adam protested.

Disapproving of being challenged by his nephew, Mr. Seacrest rolled his eyes at me for encouraging Adam's insubordinate behavior.

"Now you're being a bad influence on me!" Mr. Seacrest said, pointing his finger at me, fighting back a smile. "Enough. I've got to go, but Adam, tell Anna to try 4 a.m. Understand?"

Adam looked like he was trying hard to remember the reference, but nodded.

"It's settled then. You work on the dream intruder and I'll continue to puzzle you out, Anna. I've searched my whole life for you, though never giving real thought to what to do if you were found. You are pure myth."

In the morning, over breakfast, Adam quietly explained what his uncle meant.

"There's something about the early morning hour that stands between days."

"Midnight?"

"No, not technically. It's ... an experience. It's that time between days, when one is dying and another beginning, or something like that. I never think about it because it's a place I never go. 4 a.m. Have you been there?"

Of all the questions I'd been asked, that was up there as the oddest.

"Do you mean, have I been awake at 4 in the morning?"

Surely I had been. I was certain I'd been awake at 4 a.m. and searched my mind for recent examples.

"It's more than just the time of day. It's not about simply being awake at that time; it has to do with how you came to be there. Why you're there and what you're doing."

"Do you know what your uncle meant then?"

"In passing, as part of training once, we had some kind of mindfulness lesson I blew off. Turns out I should've paid more attention in school. But I've got the gist. We'll do it tomorrow."

"I'm still not sure what the *it* is."

I was at the part in my nightmare when the winds were blowing overhead and I was buried far below the surface, my face alone exposed, when Adam woke me.

He put his finger to his lips and motioned for me to come with him. It took me a moment to get my bearings. I was in my nice, soft bed, not buried in the layers of dirt, rock, and time.

I slipped on my shoes and grabbed a sweater, following Adam out of the manor. We crossed the back patio and walked into the expanse beyond the wooden white fence outlining the kept part of the Gold Manor property.

It was dark, damp, and still, but not creepy. The darkness of night no longer had that scary quality since all of creation knew it only had an hour left to hide before the sun would undo the shadows.

Adam laid out the quilt he'd brought. "Let's sit."

I sat facing him, wondering what I was in for.

"No, no. Relax. The point of being at 4 a.m. is to listen."

I lay down and looked into the stars, giving the world my full attention. What was there? Corey and Suzanne.

Suzanne and Finn. Finn's broken heart. Finn rejected by his family. My dad. My mom. The guy who'd tried to hurt me. Being possessed on set. Lucy getting under my skin. Those tweets I couldn't let go of. Uncle Seacrest hiding something important. Having puffy eyes for shooting today. Maggie's hatred of me. Missing Aunt Melinda. Loving Adam. Not knowing what I want. The mystery of the meaning of life.

"Enough already!" Adam laughed, sitting up.

"What?"

"We're not here for you to get in touch with your inner self, while you clearly need that. You're supposed to listen to the universe."

"Now the universe has to throw her two cents in as well? Great!"

"That's not what I mean, as you well know. If you can settle down long enough, then you can hear others. That's the point. But there's a small window and we've already lost time."

I settled down and tried to clear my mind, but I was distracted when Adam laid his hand on my arm. "We aren't alone."

I looked up to see the sister ghosts a stone's throw off. Neither were paying us any mind. Their attention was focused on the heavens. The night was still, but they swayed, flowing in the phantom waters or winds that always accompanied them.

I watched as they considered the stars. Even the crazy sister looked devout, like she was praying, finding a modicum of peace.

As for me, I was done for. The ghosts were too distracting. I gave up on the universe and gave myself over to my raging curiosity about them.

I'd always supposed ghosts were categorically impossible creatures. But then so were curses and all the strange powers I seemed to possess. And that was my problem. I needed to let go and find what was true instead of what I wanted the truth to be.

Adam and his kind said ghosts were unstable and should be avoided. I had no reason to doubt Adam, and all the evidence I'd gathered supported this stance.

And yet.

I knew there was something I needed to do for them. Or at least one of them. Somehow, I was supposed to help them and they were going to help me too. Somehow. Maybe?

The thing was, I couldn't read them the way I read others. Nothing extra came through besides what was obvious: they were terrifying, dangerous, duplicitous, broken, lonely, and wanted something.

The darkness passed into more darkness, but I could feel the progression towards light. Did they feel the light coming too? What did they feel? Were they stuck here forever?

Before I could catch myself, the truly scary ghost was right in my face. Adam reacted by grabbing my hand and squeezing it tight. My body told me to bat it off, get up and run away; but Adam was telling me the safest response. Nothingness. Stillness.

The gold ghost looked me in the eyes, forcing me to take in her despair and the depths of her desperation. Just when I thought she would crush me, her sister, the green ghost, flew in and carried her away. Surprisingly, the gold ghost went quietly.

"Are you okay? You handled that brilliantly. Anna?"

I was stunned. Absolutely stunned. I was grateful it was only me and Adam in the dark because I couldn't have pretended to be okay. I wasn't.

"Love, tell me. What is it?"

I was trying to find the words. I knew he got the feeling. He knew I was terrified.

"I want to cry... but I can't. Adam, I have never seen such despair and vengefulness. She'll burn down the world to get what she wants. All of it. You, me, anyone. She sees nothing else."

"What does she want?"

"I have no idea, but she really is...." I couldn't put it into words. "She scares me."

"That's saying something. You know you have a problem with being properly frightened."

"Isn't dealing with the Fourth and the acting and this awful recurring dream enough? Why the ghosts?" I moaned.

"Why indeed. Look at that." Adam pointed at the sky, distracting me.

"To which of the million stars are you referring?"

"That's the point. Life is full, but not always with what we want. As they say, it is what it is."

"Mystery, yeah, fine, whatever. But are you saying I should give up on trying to make sense of it?"

"Never."

"When I bring up questions like this, my father talks about a principle of reasoning that goes something like there is a sufficient reason for everything. He says we might not know the reason, but that doesn't mean there isn't one."

"I've always liked your father."

"I'm glad. But I think that's a difference between us. You are okay with not knowing the reason, but I want to know. I need to make sense of it all. Is that so wrong?"

"I think it's an impossible task, but far be it from me to stop your pursuit of truth. Just so you know, I'm fine with all the surprises in the universe. You and I, for one. I never would've thought there was a you out there. And because of you, there's an us."

"I wish you questioned more. How do you know what you've learned is true? I mean, you've got two good examples that go against all you've learned. Suzanne and Finn."

"Suzanne, yes. Jury's still out on the other. But you're right. According to our code and training, I should've killed him that first night. Time will tell if I made the right move."

The experiment was over because the magic of the hour had passed, the world was coming to life.

"What are you two doing out here? You're not shooting, too?" Meg asked as she approached.

"No, no. Just enjoying nature," I said.

"Lucky you. I'm shooting all day. All morning in the cave, afternoon in the courts with you, and manor shots tonight."

"The price of being the star," I said, teasing her.

"I know, I know. What a hard life," she said, smiling. "Oh, before I forget, I saw the dailies of you and Finn. Great work. Way to pull it back from the brink of embarrassment, not that I'm all that surprised."

"Thanks. Hey, I never thought to ask, but do you know Finn?"

All I usually needed to do was suggest a topic to someone to see the general truth of an issue.

"Sure. I mean, we're not best buds, and this is the first time we've officially worked together, but we've been at a lot of award shows and parties together."

"He's nice," I offered, to see what she thought of my concise character assessment.

"He is now," she laughed. "See you on the court. Better watch out. I think Adam's big sis is out for a little blood." Meg's body language gave nothing away. She wasn't sure what to think of Finn Varga.

We walked back to the manor.

"I wonder what she meant," Adam asked, taking the back stairs.

"I don't know. Why is she extra mad at me?" I asked out loud, making Adam laugh.

"No, Anna, there's no mystery when it comes to Maggie. She thinks she's protecting me and the Families from you. I was talking about Finn."

"But what's wrong with me?" I said too loudly in the echoing staircase.

"Shhh. Let's not wake the dead." Adam stopped and the sweetest mischievous expression settled on his face. "Poor choice of words," he said, putting his arms around my waist, pulling me up to the stair he was on.

Being normal with him, our relationship out in the open, and doing regular couple stuff was invigorating.

Committing to the moment, enjoying his solidity, his presence, I felt an emotion that rarely emerged these days. Joy.

"I feel it too, when I'm with you," he said, pulling me into a long kiss.

I was thankful for the gothic railing in the stairwell. His kisses left me dizzy.

"We'd best get back. A big day. Plus you'll be under the watchful eye of my monster sister. She'll be harsh. She doesn't want to look the fool. She'll expect top performances."

"Thanks for the pep talk."

"No worries, love."

Chapter Twenty-Six

I got to tennis practice early to warm up. I didn't want to chance being late, though being on time and playing flawless tennis would've probably just added to reasons why Maggie didn't like me. I could do no right in her eyes. Meg and Lucy chalked it up to me dating her little brother, which was true. But it was more than that because of all the supernatural stuff.

Or was it? Maybe that really was it. No one would be good enough for Adam in her eyes.

Great. I could feel the hostility rolling off her as she approached.

Standing over me as I stretched out, Maggie laid into me in front of Lucy, Katie, and Suzanne.

"How come you always seem to find an out? When's the last time you stayed for a full practice? I'm actually here to save your neck. You want to look out of your league on TV? If so, by all means keep on skipping practice."

"I don't know what you're talking about," I replied, taken aback by her unmasked contempt. It was evident to everyone by now that she didn't like me, but she'd never let her hatred show. Until now.

"Do you mean to tell me you don't know where you're supposed to be right now?"

I was lost "My schedule has me down as practicing from 8 to 10 this morning."

"You should be professional enough to check with the set manager for changes. You and Meg are going to the L.A.

studio today. Leaving in a half hour. Bye-bye," she waved at me as I scampered to gather my things and head out.

Was Maggie right? Surely not. How could I go anywhere without a guard? I got to my locker as fast as I could and pulled out my phone. Sixteen unread texts.

I quickly scrolled through and called Adam.

"Anna, morning," he said, half-awake. He'd gone right back to bed after our early morning experiment.

"Guess what?" I didn't wait for a reply. "Sylvia is sending Meg, Corey, Jade, and me to the studio today, like, right now, for a press event."

"Slow down, calm down. Let me make a few calls. Meet me at the manor."

"That's where I'm headed right now, to pack apparently. Geesh!"

"Be safe."

I was about to make a sarcastic remark about what could possibly happen to me on the short ride home when the Fourth attacker's face flew into my mind. "I'll be right there," I said, shivers running down my spine.

The non-explanatory text came from Sylvia, calling the four of us to a meeting at the manor at 8:30 a.m., telling us to pack an overnight bag.

I got to the manor with minutes to spare. My plan was to sneak in, find Adam, and figure out what I was supposed to do. Unfortunately, Sylvia pulled up to the manor right before me and I had to walk in with her. No easy way to make my getaway.

Sylvia's PA ushered us into the dining room where the others were already assembled.

I took a seat and she began.

"I'm sorry for the short notice, but in the wee hours of the morning I was contacted by Mrs. Haven's assistant. Tonight, TeenTV is airing a fundraiser for refugee relief as part of their What I Can Do campaign. The cast of *Chloe & Cason* are billed to attend, but they can't."

"Don't they film on the studio lot?" Meg asked.

"They do, but due to a miscommunication someone's getting fired over, they are shooting in New Zealand right now."

"I'm shocked. I can't believe the studio went to the expense," Corey said.

"This is the Fifth Season for *Chloe & Cason* and the biggest hit TeenTV has. Given our success, which in part is owed to shooting on location, *Chloe & Cason* want to be certain to stay relevant. Smart move.

"That being said, the hiccup in the scheduling has made it impractical for their principal players to get out to L.A. by tonight. We are doing this as a favor to our studio, with the added bonus of publicity for our show."

"Are we taking their place on the telethon tonight?" Corey asked.

"Your flight is leaving at 11 a.m., out of Paducah. Drake has packed clothes for the event for each of you. We'll use their hair and make-up people. I've sent you the schedule for the day," Sylvia said, the tone of her voice making it clear she expected no resistance.

"Why us? Why isn't Adam coming?" I asked, feeling anxious.

"Has to do with contracts and season two storylines."

"I should hire his agent," Meg laughed, drawing all eyes. "What? I don't enjoy being summoned and ordered around, expected to drop everything at a moment's notice."

"I apologize, Meg. If this is going to cause a real problem for you, of course you don't have to go. It's not mandatory for anyone."

"Like hell it's not. Don't lie to these guys. They're all newbies. Not doing what the studio wants is a good way to get blacklisted," Meg said.

Sylvia didn't reply to Meg's super cynical comments. Instead, she said, "Please be ready in 15 minutes. See you tomorrow."

I rushed up to my room where Adam was waiting for me.

"How is this going to work?" I was in a full-blown panic. My hands were shaking and I could feel the ends of my hair defying gravity.

"Fortunately my uncle is going too. Sylvia asked if we could use his private jet."

"He has a private jet?"

"Recently acquired. He'd been using his company's or renting one. Given what's been going on lately, he decided he needed his own."

"Must be nice."

"You be nice. This solves the problem. Uncle will keep you safe."

"But I want you to come."

"Me too, love. But you'll be fine."

"I thought your uncle was worried what would happen if we were too far apart from each other."

"He said it would only be for a day. He doesn't anticipate anything. But, I thought it was telling when he said if something happens, he'd be there and then he unconsciously touched his chest where his amulet is."

"You really trust your uncle that much, even with everything that's happened?"

When I asked him, his real feelings leaked out. His fear, which shamed him.

"It doesn't matter what I want. I want to take you out of here and far away where no one will ever find us."

"Then why don't we?" I asked, wanting his vision to be reality.

"Because it's a lie. It's not possible. There is nowhere we can go and not be found. No place. And we aren't cowards. You and I are going to find a way to rid the world of the Fourth. That is worth staying and dying for."

"You mean living for, right?"

"Right," he said, kissing the top of my head, wishing for the impossible – that the world could be a place where our friends and family were not hunted and slaughtered by the Fourth, or any Family member.

I threw my overnight bag together and was the last one to get into the limo, detained slightly by the long goodbye kiss Adam gave me.

Though I was sad to be away from Adam, I was glad to be getting out of town, and to spend time with some of my favorite cast members.

It was no secret on set that Corey and Suzanne were seeing each other, so I finally had hours of Corey's undivided attention to grill him on all things Suzanne.

"She's really cool. We have fun together."

"Do you love her? Like, in love with her?" I asked.

"I don't think so. Not yet. I do like her, and that's enough for right now."

"But you don't want to be with anyone else."

"Not anyone who's available," he said, looking at me completely exposed. "I don't know if I'll ever be over you, Anna. And well, I don't know if she'll ever be over him, so I guess we make a good pair."

"Varga?" I whispered.

"Don't pretend. I can tell she's still into him."

"Why do you think so?"

"Ever since he showed up she's been on edge, quiet. I wouldn't be surprised if she breaks up with me."

"Huh," I said, thoughtfully turning over his words.

"Don't give me that look. You already read or intuited this stuff, or whatever you do."

"I don't see it that way. We've both been busy," I said, looking around the plane. Mr. Seacrest was reading, Meg was absorbed in her phone, listening to music with headphones on, and Jade was pretending to sleep.

"They're not paying attention to us," Corey whispered.

I shook my head in disagreement and pointed at Jade. "He's not sleeping," I whispered back.

Corey sat back, his voice at normal volume. "Enough about my love life. How are you and what's-his-face?"

"Ha, ha. Well, thank you very much."

"So, he's not pissed at you for the other night?"

"Oh, he was… though I haven't really copped to all of it yet. He was pissed for something else I did that was even dumber, if you can believe it."

"Yes I can!" He laughed, quickly glancing at Jade. "Out yet?" he mouthed.

"Close," I answered back. "I'll tell you, since I said I'd tell you whatever I could. I didn't tell you sooner because it was so awful and I still can't believe it. I'm about to tell you and I'm drawing this explanation out because the sound of our voices is lulling him to sleep."

"Is anyone else paying attention to us? What's Meg doing?"

"She's listening to music, working on blog interview questions. You know, that's why she was mad about this impromptu trip. She had already made a commitment to be interviewed by an entertainment blogger. And you know how she hates to break her word and look unprofessional."

"Isn't the beauty of online media and interviews that you don't have to be in any certain location?" Corey asked, confused.

"Surprise, surprise, the blogger lives in L.A., so she got her tickets to the event tonight and they're going to do the interview there."

"What about Mr. Seacrest, is he listening to us?"

"I'm not sure if he knows, but this isn't really a secret from him. He'll find out sooner or later, if he hasn't already. But I don't think he's paying attention to us."

"The suspense is killing me. Is Jade out yet?"

"Yep," I said, suddenly nervous. Corey was going to flip out. "I need you to remain calm. What happened was really bad, but you know the end. I'm fine. We all are."

"Anna, you're scaring me."

"You know how I like to run alone, right? And how I haven't been able to in forever?"

"Yes, and..."

"A few weeks ago I woke up early. Nightmares."

"You still having the same one?"

"On repeat, most nights. Anyway, I was up early in the morning and I couldn't go back to sleep. I didn't want to wake anyone and I really wanted to run by myself. You know the feeling of being alone with your thoughts, out in the cool of the morning, seeing the sunrise on your way back home?"

"Yeah, and...."

"It was stupid. I see that now. I mean, really see it."

"Just spill it."

"Fine. I took a new route and, well, long story short, I was attacked. Or nearly attacked."

"You got in a fight? Some guy came after you?" Corey's hands were balled into fists, skin tightly stretched over bone.

"I didn't sense him at all because – "

"You've got to pay attention when you're out, Anna. Always. Come on, you know better than that."

"You don't understand. I didn't sense him because I'd taken something to help me deal with being around Finn Varga and his assistant, remember? Remember how it worked so well I couldn't feel Suzanne either?"

"You've got to be joking. Another Fourth? In town?"

"Of course Finn Varga wouldn't be alone, unprotected."

"What happened?" he asked in his normal speaking voice.

I leaned closer and whispered. "He startled me. He had no idea who or what I was, just some girl he was going to hurt. Lucky for me, Echo was out looking for me. He found me just in time and killed that man right in front of me. Not one moment of hesitation. He didn't ask the guy a single question or look him in the face. He just parked his car and ran towards us, passed me, and took the guy's knife out of his hand and killed him. Then he picked him up and threw him in the trunk. The end."

Corey slumped back in his seat and closed his eyes. He sat there for a long time, taking deep breaths. I used the silence to center and calm myself too.

He sat back up and took my hands. "How are you doing?"

"Honestly, even with everything that's happened, I don't ever remember being so scared. If Echo hadn't come, that man was going to do awful things to me before he murdered me. It all happened so fast and my senses were all off. I'm still in shock and honestly, I haven't felt safe ever since."

"I'm sorry that happened to you, but maybe it was for the best. I mean, if you finally get it. This isn't a game."

"Don't you think I know that?" I cut back, momentarily breaking Jade out of REM sleep. "My mom is dead," I spit. "She's never coming back. I was nearly raped and murdered. I saw Echo kill someone, just like that," I snapped.

"Then why did you run alone?"

"Because... because...." But I didn't have an answer, besides my own stupidity. And I was saved answering by Mr. Seacrest's approach.

"This is not the place to have a conversation such as this," he chided the two of us.

"No one is paying attention," I said.

"This time, maybe. Don't overestimate your own wisdom. Always take precautions. Did you stop to think this airline might be equipped with cameras and microphones? One of your fellow cast mates could be recording what's going on around them as they sleep or are otherwise engaged. Always take full stock of your environment, not just the obvious threats."

"Point taken," Corey said thoughtfully. He was seriously trying to understand what he needed to do to be smart, given our harsh reality. I liked this new, maturing Corey.

"Were we being watched? Were you listening?" I asked.

"You know that I was. Your friends were not recording you. The plane, on the other hand, I will see to."

"Are you mad?" I asked Mr. Seacrest.

"I am pleased to hear of Echo's high standard of behavior. I hope this incident has shown you what we're dealing with. What I've fought against for centuries. I'm glad you came to no harm."

Chapter Twenty-Seven

We flew into the Burbank airport and were whisked away right into L.A. traffic. Though the studio lot was less than 20 minutes from the airport, it took us over an hour to reach our destination. Rural Tennessee traffic - or lack thereof - was definitely a selling point of small-town life.

"I don't think I'll ever get used to all these people," Jade said, looking out his window.

"Yeah, what's up with that? I mean, are you just staying in Martin because of the show?" Corey asked.

"That's rude! Maybe he likes his home town," I said, defending Jade.

"You've got to be kidding me!" Corey scoffed. "No offense, man, but Martin has, what, ten thousand people and it's in the middle of nowhere, hours away from a decent-sized city?"

"I don't expect you to get it, but I hope I never leave."

"Look around, man. You're gone. You're in the big leagues now. Famous. You won't stay," Corey said.

"I wouldn't be so sure," Jade said firmly, turning his attention back out the window.

"Real nice, Corey," Meg chided. "Way to be a jerk. I'm from a small town in Virginia. Want to make fun of it too?"

"Whoa, wait. I wasn't making fun of anyone." Corey was starting to get upset, his teeth clenching.

I threw him a sympathetic smile.

He took a beat and a few calming breaths. "Sorry. Guess I never considered people actually wanted to live in small towns."

"Why do you think people live in rural areas then?" Jade asked.

Corey answered honestly. "Trapped? Couldn't afford city life?"

"No," Jade said, shaking his head.

"Guess I was wrong. As for me, I really miss L.A. I miss the traffic and noise and people everywhere. I miss all the choices of places to eat and go. I miss the beach. Don't you, Anna?"

"My favorite place. But it's probably different for me. I wasn't raised here. You've lived in the L.A. basin your entire life."

"And that's something hard for me to understand. After being in the clean air and peacefulness of Tennessee, you'd rather be here with the smog, trash, crime, and bumper-to-bumper traffic? Now that's what I call weird," Jade said, still looking out the limo window.

"Perspective. We see what we want to," Meg added.

I looked up in time to see our driver miss the exit. "Weren't we supposed to get off there?" I asked, a little worried.

Meg looked out the window. "Oh, you're thinking of the main studio lot. No. We're going to the back lot off the 5, just past where the 405 merges into it. You ever been there?"

"No, have you?"

"That's where we shot *The Life and Times of Kelee Klark*, my show, for six years."

"You like shooting *Ghost House* the way we do with so many locations?"

"Yes and no. The end product is better, I think. Not that we didn't have great sets. But we also had a studio

208

audience, which made some things easier and others harder. Trades. Life was easier shooting on TeenTV's back lot. I had a more normal life."

"But is that just because you were younger?" Corey asked.

"Partly, I guess. I know this is all new to you, but Sylvia runs her production like no one I've ever heard of. She's a control freak."

"Aren't all good producers?"

"Not like her. She's a total micromanager with the crew. She overworks everyone."

"Then why do they stay? Her crew seems loyal," Corey said.

"Two reasons. First, she pays really well. Second, if you stay with Sylvia for a few years, you can get on pretty much any set. And, we're here."

As we pulled into the lot a chill ran up my spine. I'd been here before. Many times. In my nightmares.

Chapter Twenty-Eight

Passing through the studio gates, I grabbed Corey's hand. Loud enough for Mr. Seacrest to hear, I said, "Wow. I'm having a strong case of déjà vu."

"Yeah? I kinda feel like I'm at home," Meg said, her voice hitched slightly at the end.

"Still going. Oh – so weird. That ever happen to you, Jade?" I asked to distract myself from the strong sense of foreboding coming to me in waves. I was not expecting the raw emotion my simple question brought out in him.

"Sometimes," he said quietly.

Right then Corey took his cap off and put it on my head. "Looks like it's about to rain," he explained, smiling at me.

"That was nice," Meg sighed.

"Mr. Seacrest, what will you be doing tonight?" I hoped he heard the desperation in my voice. I felt like I was walking into a trap. I didn't want to be left alone, without any protection. Certainly he wouldn't leave me. Would he?

"Meetings, mostly. I plan to watch the event backstage."

Though the guard gate and studio entrance were right out of my dream, the level of activity wasn't. There were people and vehicles everywhere.

We were ushered right onto the set to block our part of the main event. Meg was tagged to do all the talking, naturally. My job was to stand behind her and look supportive. We all had pre and post show duties, including rocking the red carpet, signing autographs and taking pictures, doing mini-interviews, and hanging out with fans who'd won radio and internet contests. For Meg this was nothing new, but I was excited. So excited I wasn't thinking about being in my dream landscape until an assistant ushered us onto a soundstage set up for overflow hair, make-up, and wardrobe.

Upon crossing the threshold, a wave of nausea hit me. I looked behind me, and the sunny Southern California skies had clouded up, bringing rain.

"Come on, everyone, inside. The rain shouldn't last long," the studio assistant assured us. "We have enough chairs for everyone. Right this way, please."

I knew I needed to sit. I wasn't confident I could go five more feet.

"I'll catch up. Feeling a little sick," I said, waving the others on.

"I'll stay with her. Which way are we going?" Corey asked our guide.

"You see that sound studio? We're set up right behind. I'll walk them over and be right back," she said, her voice fading.

"Stay with me," I said to Corey, terrified.

I felt pulled, dragged. I couldn't keep my eyes open, they'd become heavy with sleep.

"Anna, Anna. I'm here. What do you want me to do?"

I heard the panic in Corey's voice but I couldn't respond, I was too tired. I had to go to sleep.

I opened my eyes. I was in the same spot, in the same clothes, on the same sound studio with the sound of rain beating down on the roof. But now I was alone. The rain was the only sound.

I wasn't sure if I was in a dream, or if I'd been drugged and woken up after everyone had packed up and headed home.

I slowly stood up. "Hello? Anyone here?" I called out in the cold, hollow building.

In front of me was a trail of blood and the smell of fresh, blossoming roses. By instinct, I lurched forward as I'd done countless times in my nightmares. But then I stopped. I was overcome with the knowledge that I was in control of myself in this place for once. I had the upper hand.

I felt out. For the first time I saw a visual manifestation of my ability. Hundreds of thread-thin tendrils shot out from me, testing the environment and bringing me instant information. This place was not a dream, but it wasn't the waking world. It was a midway state, a trance of some sort. I got the sense that whoever brought me here had done so unintentionally. This wasn't supposed to happen because I wasn't supposed to be a possibility. I was a myth.

But I wasn't.

And I wasn't alone.

My body sprang to attention as I snapped my abilities off, feeling exposed. I wanted to call for help. But who could reach me here? Where was I?

I allowed myself to panic for the space of three long seconds.

"Enough," I called out into the dim space. "Show yourself."

A light next to the sound booth popped on.

I followed the fresh blood trail to the booth. I tried the door, willing it to open.

I pushed the heavy metal door, ready for what was on the other side.

But how could I have been prepared to see Emma Vitali standing before me, drenched in blood with a krim buried deep in her belly?

Chapter Twenty-Nine

I came to, hearing Corey's voice. "You okay? You kinda turned transparent for a sec. That or I'm seeing things. I hope I'm seeing things."

It was as if no time had passed. Corey helped me to my feet, waiting for my response. I could imagine what my face must've looked like. I was utterly speechless. I wanted to explain, but I had no earthly idea what had just happened.

"I mean it, Anna, you okay? You look really weird. I'd say you look like you saw a ghost, but we both know that's not funny."

"Will you follow me?" our guide asked, coming back for us. "I brought you some water. Can I get you anything else?"

I croaked out a thank you. I felt disconnected from my moving feet. Had I just imagined it all? Was it an hallucination? What about Emma? Was she dead or alive?

I tried to bring myself back to reality. The last time I'd seen her in the real world was the night after we shot the first episode of season two. I remembered saying good-bye to her and the funny smirk she gave in reply.

Since then I hadn't given her a thought. I did notice that Dom didn't seem to care she was gone. Her brother – her twin no less – never talked about her.

My stomach dropped as we passed the sound booth from my dreams. I stopped following our guide and turned the doorknob of the booth, slowly pushing it open. And just as I had dreamt or imagined, Emma was standing there, krim firmly in her belly, eyes closed. I turned to Corey, who was right behind me.

"Do you see her?" I whispered, my lips numb.

"There's nothing there, Anna," he said, peering into the booth, just on the edge of panic.

"I'm sorry, Ms. Ellingwood. They're waiting for you and I'm afraid we have a tight schedule," the page said, coming back for us.

"Anna's just a little dizzy. Give us a few minutes. I swear we'll be right there."

Our guide looked sympathetic, but stood right there, not taking the hint.

"Mind giving her some privacy?"

"Certainly, Mr. Edwards."

As she walked off, Corey whispered in my ear, "What do you see?"

I stepped inside the booth and Corey followed, closing the door behind us.

Still not believing what was before my very eyes I told him. "Right there, about ten feet in front of us is Emma Vitali. She has a krim in her stomach, it killed her. She's covered in blood."

Corey went from concerned to totally freaked. "Killed? She's dead?"

"I don't know. I'm just telling you what I'm seeing, okay?"

"Uh, okay. Just so you know, I see nothing. Is she saying something? Does she want something?"

"She's just standing there."

"She's not a ghost, is she?"

"This is so over my head, you don't even understand." Was I having a psychotic break?

"Wait," he said, grabbing my wrist, "do you feel in danger? I mean, is she going to wake up and stab you?"

"I don't think so, but thanks for that awful image."

"What should we do? We can't stay here much longer."

I pulled out my phone to call Adam.

"Adam?" I asked, feeling an immediate sense of relief at his voice. I looked up, about to explain the situation to him, but the scene had slightly changed. Her eyes were open. "Oh crap," I gasped, jumping back, knocking into Corey and scaring him half to death.

"Geeze," Corey cried as Adam called out, trying to get my attention.

"Just a second. I'm trying to restart my heart," I said breathlessly into the phone.

"Who's with you? Are you safe?" he demanded, not one for patience.

"I'm with Corey, and I think so."

"Where the hell is my uncle?"

"He's somewhere on the studio lot," I replied.

Corey said over my shoulder, "Tell him what's going on. What you're seeing. We don't have much time. She'll be back any second."

"Okay, okay," I shushed Corey.

"Anna?" Adam growled.

"I'm having a hard time processing what's going on, so I'll tell you what I'm seeing. Corey and I are currently standing in the sound booth that's been in my nightmare."

"But that's not all," Adam surmised.

"Right. Okay, I can't even explain everything that just happened. I mean I literally have no idea how, but right now Emma Vitali is standing in front of me, a krim in her stomach. She's dead and I'm the only one who can see her. Corey can't see her at all. What do we do?"

"Is she really there? What I mean is, is she actually there and cloaked in some way from Corey's view?"

"I don't know."

"What do you think? Do you think you're having a vision or waking dream or do you think she is actually there?"

"I don't think she is really here, and that's what's scaring me."

"Have Corey walk over to where you see her and have him pass his hand through the space where she should be. But as a precaution, make sure he goes nowhere near the krim."

"What is he saying?" Corey asked, his heart back to its normal rhythm.

"Go over there, by the green chair. But be careful!" I warned as his big body just about ran into Emma.

"What do you want me to do, exactly?" Corey asked, looking at the chair.

"She's to the left a little, right by the chair. I want you to stay right there and put your foot out a little."

"What? You mean you, like, want me to kick her? That's sick!"

"Stop it," I said, an inappropriate giggle escaping. "No. Not kick her. Nudge. Think nudge."

"What's going on?" Adam asked in my ear.

"Just a sec," I replied.

"What do you want me to wait for?" Corey asked, his foot hovering inches from where the dead and bloody Emma stood, her eyes still wickedly wide open, staring at me. My freak-o-meter was off the chart.

"No, not you, I was talking to Adam. Just go on, she's right there."

Corey looked where I was looking and gently moved his foot right through her.

"Did it work, what did you see?" Corey asked.

"What happened? You're killing me!" Adam's voice was stressed.

"His foot passed right through her," I said to Adam, catching him up. "Did you feel anything? Any resistance? Did it feel cold there?"

"Nothing," Corey said.

"Nothing," I told Adam.

"Let me try something," I said to them both, slowly walking up to dead Emma and living Corey.

"Careful, love," Adam warned.

I reached out to touch her arm, fully expecting my fingers to fall right through her as Corey's foot had.

The instant I touched her she grabbed my arm and screamed.

My phone went flying out of my hand as I yanked my arm back as fast as I could and screamed my head off in response.

The door to the sound booth flew open and Mr. Seacrest rushed in, piercing me with a glance that told me to pull it together.

Seconds later a whole team of people were at the doorway, those ready to help and the curious. Mr. Seacrest seemed to disappoint them all when he announced loudly, "It was just a mouse. Ms. Ellingwood saw a mouse and it startled her."

I heard one of the crew laugh and say to another there was plenty of wildlife in these buildings, to which there was a reply about prima donnas.

I felt like my veins were crackling with electricity. I didn't know what to do.

"Aren't you two supposed to be getting ready?" Mr. Seacrest asked me, the crowd already dispersing, no longer paying attention to us.

I was nodding when Corey said, "Anna, your arm!"

The skin on my arm was a faint periwinkle where the phantom Emma had grabbed it. As I turned it over for us to see, the veins beneath were throbbing, but not to the rhythm of my heart.

I looked up, but I already knew she was gone. If she had ever really been there, she wasn't now. I just couldn't bring myself to explain it to Mr. Seacrest.

"Are you all right? Does it hurt?" he asked in a rare show of compassion.

If Mr. Seacrest was being fatherly to me, something was really super wrong.

He picked up my arm gently and felt the area around my seizing veins.

"How did you know we needed you?"

"I honestly didn't, which is disturbing. I was checking up on you, and you weren't where you should've been. Imagine my surprise when I started looking around and realized this place looks exactly as you'd described. I expect a full rundown tonight. I'll find you."

"Let's just go to hair and make-up," Corey said, trying to help me normalize.

I was about out the door when I remembered my phone. Adam was still on.

"Sorry about that."

"As long as you're safe. Sounds like you can't talk right now," Adam said, rattled.

"I'll call you tonight."

Mr. Seacrest walked the short distance to the open chairs waiting for us. "I've been talking to some of the heads about product placement this season."

Such a radical change in conversation made me laugh. "Sounds real exciting."

Mr. Seacrest walked off without another word, but his message to me was loud and clear: don't go wandering off. Of that there was no need to worry. Today you couldn't get me alone for a million bucks.

"What was that all about?" Meg asked, her hair getting worked on.

"I saw a rat."

"I thought it was a mouse," she said.

"Mouse, rat, same difference."

"You've been acting really weird since we landed," she said.

"Uh, thanks? Never claimed to be normal."

"What was Mr. Seacrest saying about product placement?"

"Nothing really. I mean, no details," I said, trying to act normal. Unfortunately Meg saw the thin bruises on my arm, then looked down to my tapping foot.

"Anna, if we don't stick together…. You can talk to me," she said quietly.

Her offer felt one hundred percent genuine. "Thanks, but I can't really talk about it."

"Do I need to be worried for you?"

"No," I said, and felt her automatically pulling back. She'd been trying to reach out to me and she felt rebuffed. "You know when I hung out with you and Corey late last year, at the mansion? When Corey called me over to chat in the middle of the night?"

It took a sec for Meg to realize I was referring to her ghost sighting.

"Oh, really?" she asked, her heart rate picking up. "I was hoping that was in the past."

"No, not really. Not for me. But I'm okay."

"You sure you are?" she asked, looking at my arm, not buying what I was selling. "Well, if it was just about anything else, I'd be of great help, I'm sure," she laughed.

"For sure," I agreed.

"But not with this," she added soberly.

"Yeah, please don't worry. I know it doesn't seem like it, but I've got it under control. And I'm not alone," I said, glancing at Corey.

Meg looked his way too. Corey looked up from his phone to see the two of us staring at him. "Yes? Can I help you ladies?"

Meg turned to me, ignoring him. "Corey's got his issues, but he's a good guy. He's a good friend to you. I really can't believe you pulled that one out. You've got mad skills."

"Are you referring to my selfish ability to have Adam and not lose Corey's friendship? It hasn't been easy, but I think things are getting back to normal. Or a new normal. It helps that he has Suzanne."

"I'm sorry, I know she's your friend too. In fact, I think you're friends with everyone. Anyway, I don't trust her. There's something about her that's off-putting."

"There's lots about Suzanne that's off. But underneath her rough exterior, she's a good person. And I hope we're friends, but she's really hard to get to know."

"You mean like you?" Meg joked.

"Are you looking in a mirror?" I laughed back.

"What? I'm an open book. Got a question about me? Just ask Google."

"Ha ha," I said, and turned quiet.

Was it true? Was I hard to get to know? My life *was* a labyrinth of secrets. These days I felt I could hardly talk about the weather without revealing something I was supposed to take to the grave.

"What do you think, Jade? You're 'dating' her now. Do you feel like you know her?" Meg asked.

Jade was sitting on the other side of Meg, no doubt trying to mind his own business.

"Well, Anna and I have an understanding," he said in his sweet Southern way, both deferential and authoritative.

"Awesome response," Meg nodded in appreciation of Jade's way of being.

"Please hold still," the guy said who'd been working on Meg's hair, ending our conversation.

Chapter Thirty

The evening was a blur of activity. I was paired with Jade because we were dating on the show. Corey was with Meg since they were brother and sister and best friends.

Mr. Seacrest arranged for special security, the detail peppered with First and Second Family members. I'd met none of them before but could now pick Family out of a crowd, provided they had a sufficient amount of Family blood running in their veins.

From the moment we stepped onto the red carpet, Jade impressed me. He was usually quiet on set, allowing the dominant cast and crew personalities to have their way. I'd expected I'd have to do the heavy lifting for the two of us. Not so. While still being his laidback self, his ease at answering questions, taking pictures, signing autographs, and all around talking and hanging out with fans, impressed me. He was less steady with the reporters, but there was really just no hiding his innate sweetness and charm.

Watching him shine was completely unexpected. The nice surprise kept my mind off the horrid surprises midday had brought. By the end of the night, back in the limo, I could honestly say I was glad I'd come.

While we were all consulted on our ride to the Paducah airport this morning, it was really up to Meg. Did she want to stay the night in L.A. or fly back after the event?

"If it's all the same to you, I'd like to get back. I have friends coming into town on Monday. But, if someone really wants to stay, that's fine with me. Anna, were you going to see your dad?"

"No. As luck would have it, he's out of town at a conference."

I loved L.A. at night, lit by streetlight. As we rode to the airport, I was extremely glad for that decision to return to Martin tonight. Thinking of my temporary home, the pain in my arm flared. The powdery blue bruise was deepening in color and I noticed fingernail marks I could've sworn weren't there before.

Looking at my arm, I had the feeling I was watching a ticking clock – I only had so long. Until what ... I couldn't say. I just had the feeling I needed to get back to Martin as soon as possible.

While Corey had been chatty on the plane ride to L.A., he and everyone else were zoned out for the return trip. I played around on social media and listened to music, Corey in the seat next to me. Every time I started drifting off, Emma's dead, accusing eyes woke me up. Hours from home, thousands of feet in the sky and oblivious to the world around me, I felt Corey nudge my arm.

His alarm was stifling. I looked down to see blood coming through my sweater. Quietly I pushed up my dampening sleeve, revealing that those once–thin, wispy, white lines were now full-blown gashes in my skin.

I quickly pulled my sweater back down, unbuckled myself, and made a beeline for the bathroom. Alone, I yanked off my sweater to get a better look.

My arm was covered in angry cuts, like a witch with wicked, razor-sharp fingernails had sliced it open.

Corey knocked and I let him in.

"What the hell, Anna. What's going on?"

"It's where she grabbed me. It's getting worse."

"No shit! What do we do?"

Our attention was immediately diverted because one of the scratches started actively bleeding, trickling down my arm. A steady little stream.

"I'm getting Mr. Seacrest. Stay right here," he said as he let himself out of the tiny space.

As if I'd go anywhere, I laughed to myself, too horrified to think about what was happening.

Mr. Seacrest didn't bother to knock and I didn't say anything in greeting. I just stuck out my arm in evidence of the trouble. Another scratch began to bleed uncontrollably.

"Just a minute," was all he said, returning in moments with a medical kit.

The kit made me grin.

"What did you expect? Magic herbs?"

"Yeah, I guess so. Not Walgreen Band-Aids."

"We need to stop the bleeding. How much blood do you think you've lost?"

"Not much. I have been trying to bleed responsibly, into the sink, so there's not a big mess."

"That's very thoughtful of you," he responded, all business-like, masking his alarm.

My phone rang.

"Should I get that?" I asked him.

"By all means."

"Adam?" I said into the phone.

"Wanted to check in. Corey thought you might want to talk."

"Corey called you?"

"Texted."

"Anna, your arm," Mr. Seacrest said. He'd been getting gauze and other paraphernalia out to bandage me up.

"What's going on?" Adam asked, anxious. "I swear, Anna, I can't stand this. Not twice today."

"Let me call you back," I said, hanging up before he could respond.

My arm had stopped bleeding. In fact, it was looking better.

"What a lucky turn of events," Mr. Seacrest said, gingerly examining my torn, but no longer bleeding, arm.

"What happened?" I asked Mr. Seacrest.

"Maybe it was infected and the infection had to run its course? For now, let me clean out the wounds and bandage you up."

"I guess I'll just have to tell the others that flying twice in one day really doesn't agree with me. Think they'll buy it?"

"No, but they will accept it. And that's the important thing. This kit is missing antiseptic. Be right back."

Minutes later Mr. Seacrest reappeared with the medicine he was looking for, phone to his ear. He locked the door behind him, and I was starting to feel better, but then the main tear in my arm opened on its own and began pouring blood.

"Guess whatever it is isn't over yet," I said, defeated. I knew it was too good to be true.

Mr. Seacrest pursed his lips, nodding his head, saying to the person on the other line, "Why don't you talk to her."

"Don't hang up on me," Adam said, super pissed. "Please," he added.

"I can't handle any drama from you right now. I might be dying."

"No you're not. Calm down. How would you feel if you were in my place? If you knew something was really wrong with me and I was cryptic and freaking out and wouldn't call back and was bleeding? Damn right I'm pissed. But not at you. At me. I should've gone with you."

"It's not your fault."

"I don't care."

"It stopped again," Mr. Seacrest said. "Put Adam on speaker. I have a theory. I sure hope I'm wrong, though."

"Let's hear it," Adam said, his voice full of impatience.

"There's a reason I haven't kept you two apart, even though all signs point to mayhem if you and Anna stay together."

"You sound like my sister."

"Yes, but others have given the same counsel. To date, however, only your sister has taken a real interest in Anna."

"That's not true," I cut in, unable to contain my bitterness. If only it was just Adam's sister. His mother had been in our business not so long ago.

"Yes, I misspoke. Forgive me. I should've said presently. Maggie and others don't understand why you, Adam, have been allowed to play around with this outsider. It may not seem like it, but we have been lucky to keep what Anna is a secret. And only a few know of the queen's involvement. Maggie is completely in the dark on this point," Mr. Seacrest said, looking at me, as if that should make me go easier on her.

"You know what, this is all very interesting, but I think I'm bleeding to death, so, can we talk about all the intrigue later and get to the saving?"

Crammed in the tiny bathroom, Adam on speaker, I watched my arm. No longer festering. It was as if the wound was healing itself.

"It's getting better," I said, surprised. "I feel like I'm watching a video in reverse. So weird."

"That's was I was getting to, if you had a bit more patience. I haven't separated you two, against my better judgement, because you're linked."

This was not the first time Mr. Seacrest had said this, and I hated that he, or any of them, thought they had power over me. That they could hold a council, or make a phone call, and control my love life. Screw them.

And yet, I didn't like the idea that I couldn't physically be parted from Adam without risking physical danger. Though I was a romantic at heart and loved Adam with all I had, I was still realistic. How were we realistically supposed to live our lives if we had to be in close physical proximity to one another?

"You think that just my voice is helping Anna? Isn't that outlandish? Have you come across this before? What? Wait just a sec-."

Adam's line went dead.

"What's going on?" I asked, knowing whatever it was, it was Mr. Seacrest's doing.

"I want to be certain of my theory. This was the best way," Mr. Seacrest said, not even trying to keep his actions a secret.

I was furious. "Don't you know you're not allowed to experiment on people without their consent?"

"Those are not our rules."

"You're evil."

"No, I'm practical. This is a piece of information we need to know. I seriously doubt any harm will come to either of you. It's worth the risk."

"Worth the risk of losing our trust?"

Mr. Seacrest's eyes cut through me. His anger felt like a slap, but it wasn't directed at me. It was anger at his own inability to control the world and the evil in it. I'd hurt his feelings.

Before he spoke, he took a moment to compose himself and hide his emotions. "The world is a much worse place for me and my people. You speak from a place of youth and passion and untried conviction. I act from centuries of senseless horror. I have devoted my life, my very being, to winning the war and bringing the end of all the Families."

Mr. Seacrest slumped against the curved bathroom wall. "I don't have room in my heart to care for you, Anna," he said, letting his guard down to show me what he really meant. Jaw-dropping sorrow and loss was behind those words, not malice. "You need to understand the Family way. Those in charge act, and those beneath comply. I am in charge. I am using my vast networks to keep you unnoticed and untouched. You may not understand my tactics, but I am working for you. You and my nephew. I know you don't trust me. I know you both hide information from me because you think we have different goals. We may have different methods, but the end of the Fourth and the peaceful natural deaths of the First and Second is our common mission."

"You want to bring about your own end? Most people will do what they can to hold on. Few would hand over immortality."

"Few have had to live with the deeds I've done and all I've lost. Fewer still see what I see every night."

Mr. Seacrest pulled upright, closing himself off again. "I'm going to bandage you, but you should stay in here for the duration of the flight, a little less than two hours, in case your wounds open again. I'll tell the others you're sick. And I'm taking this," he said, picking up my phone. "I will confirm the strength of your connection to Adam. I am sorry if it brings you any discomfort. It won't last long."

"Fine, but could you bring me my book?" I said, resigned. There wasn't much I could do to get out of being his little lab rat.

Corey came back a few minutes later with my book, along with a couple of blankets and a pillow.

"Want me to stay?"

"You barely fit! Thanks, but no. I'll be fine," I said, willing it to be true. But honestly, I wasn't feeling too hot. I really was starting to feel lousy.

I tried to get as comfortable as possible, wedging up against the wall, my feet up on the tiny sink.

I'm not sure how long I read before my head filled with cobwebs and sleep threatened to pull me under. It was late and I was frazzled and completely spent. Just as I was drifting off, something caught my eye in the bathroom mirror.

Emma with the krim in her stomach.

My hands flew up to muffle my cry. The sudden movement jerked my wounds open, blood gushing through the bandages. I looked at my arm and back to the mirror, fully awake. Mine was the only reflection.

Unraveling the bandage, I saw my forearm was in bad shape. The four scratches on my arm looked like they'd been made with razors, not phantom fingernails. And they were fresh. The blood was now freely flowing and I was feeling lightheaded.

Some time later I heard the seat-belt light ding overhead and the pilot announced we were about to land.

I felt Corey approach the door. "Anna, you need to take your seat. We're about to descend. Anna," he said, opening the door. "Oh shit!"

There was blood everywhere as I cradled my arm.

"I think I need help," I said listlessly.

I could tell Corey was about to lose it and bring the whole cabin to my assistance. But how could this be explained? They would surely think it looked like I was trying to commit suicide.

"No, Corey. Get Mr. Seacrest and hand me your phone."

Chapter Thirty-One

Corey closed the door and convincingly said to the cabin I'd made a mess in the bathroom and needed a change of clothes. I wasted no time dialing Adam's number.

"I'm at the airport. Is she okay?" Adam asked, thinking it was Corey.

A bolt of electricity ran through me as soon as I heard his voice.

"It's me. Please just talk to me."

"You sound pitiful. You would not believe what Uncle did. I'm beyond pissed. How's your arm?"

"I can't really talk," I said. I only had enough energy to listen to him and hold on to consciousness. I couldn't carry on a coherent conversation.

"Anna? Anna? What's going on?"

"Please, just tell me a story about Crimson Hall. A happy one."

I leaned my head back, listening to his voice.

Adam had just begun as Mr. Seacrest opened the door. The look of horror on his face barely registered with me.

"I just had to hear his voice one more time."

"This is not happening!" Mr. Seacrest cried, outraged and a little scared.

The rest was a blur. I remember Mr. Seacrest taking Corey's blood-soaked phone and putting Adam on speaker, commanding him to keep on talking and not to stop for any reason.

Mr. Seacrest left and Corey appeared seconds later. I could hear Mr. Seacrest announce I was seriously ill, that an ambulance would be taking me straight to the local hospital.

"Can I see her?" Meg asked, wanting to comfort me.

"She might be contagious. We want to minimize contact, if possible," he said, making it clear they were to steer clear of the back of the plane.

As I was listening to Mr. Seacrest, Corey was swearing up a storm, putting pressure on my wounds. Adam's voice was the hardest for me to find. He was always the closest to my heart and mind, but he felt far away. Too far.

Blood was oozing between Corey's fingers. "I thought she had crazy-ass healing abilities. Remember her broken leg that wasn't broken? She's still bleeding. I can't stop it and it's not like she has an infinite amount of blood."

Adam took a pause from his story about Crimson Hall. "I've been ordered to talk to her nonstop. I will continue my story but I'll be listening to you. Pease tell me what you see," he begged in the middle of telling me about one of the many times he'd gotten in trouble at school.

"You don't want to know. I don't want to know. She looks dead but she's breathing. She just grinned at me. The pilot said we should be landing in five minutes. Thank goodness we're flying into Paducah – no air traffic."

"Corey? Update?" Mr. Seacrest asked, appearing over his shoulder.

"She's still bleeding, but I think it's slowing down. Maybe, I don't really know."

"Anna, Anna," Mr. Seacrest called to me. "You need to stay awake."

This I knew I wanted to do. Whenever I closed my eyes, Emma was standing there. I had a feeling if I allowed myself to go to sleep I wouldn't be waking up.

"This is going to feel strange, but it will help you focus. You need to focus on pushing it out. Closing it off. You can say no. Something is intruding on you. You can say no. This will prick." He put something around my neck.

I had felt the power of the pulse of that necklace before, maybe? Everything was hard. It was hard to think and see, hard to will.

"Werden?" I whispered, looking up at Mr. Seacrest, naming the object he'd put around my neck. It was always on him, giving him protection.

"Find your way to her and direct it. Use your will."

"I can't. I just need to rest. Just leave me alone," I said, trying unsuccessfully to shoo Corey's hands away.

"How's her arm?" Mr. Seacrest asked Corey, as Adam continued to talk, hardly knowing what he said.

"The bleeding has stopped. See," Corey said, pulling back the bandage.

By their reactions I was glad I didn't have the energy to look down and see my hamburgered arm.

"What did this to her? She was just fine. Do you know?" Corey asked.

"Once Anna is well, we'll find those responsible," Mr. Seacrest replied. I liked his answer, for in his voice I felt the certainty that I would recover and we would make "them" pay. Emma and I deserved to be avenged.

"I'll be with you soon. Hold on," Adam said, his story forgotten.

"Don't stop talking to her. She needs to hear your voice. Anna, feel out for Adam. Use his strength and Werden to come back to us. We need you. I swear to you I will make this right. Come back," Mr. Seacrest coaxed.

I didn't want to disappoint them, all the voices pulling for me. But just as I turned toward them, a wide ocean opened to my right, offering a different kind of solace, diverting my attention.

The tires hit the tarmac and my heart took off. I could actually feel Adam, faintly, but enough to give me the jolt I needed to connect to Werden. Both were grounding me to the real. This world.

I found Adam's voice again. He stopped his story midsentence. "Yes. It's me. I'm here and so are you. You are going to be okay."

I came up through layers of consciousness, fighting the entire way. Fighting past images, so real, of Emma. Dead Emma. Alive Emma. Utterly astounded Emma as she realized what was happening - I was winning and she was losing. This thought had never crossed her mind, her mind that was opening to me.

Emma was the one attacking me!

"You weren't supposed to survive this! They promised. Not possible!" she screamed, now buried in the dirt beneath the dead tree, only her face exposed.

"What are you talking about?" I yelled, the wind picking up.

"What are you? How did you beat me? You are nothing. Just a girl. This is not the plan! They promised! Help me!"

I wanted to help, but I knew if I stayed, she'd try to best me. Kill me. I had to start running, pushing forward. It didn't matter what I saw, what was said, whispered, or screamed at me, I had to keep going until I broke through the top.

I came to, gasping for air as if someone had been holding my head underwater. Corey was kneeling in front of me, Mr. Seacrest at the bathroom door. All three of us, everything around us, covered in my blood.

"She's coming to," Corey alerted Mr. Seacrest, who looked up from his phone.

My flayed arm started healing.

"What in the world," Corey swore.

Right before our eyes my arm knitted itself back together, Adam arriving to see the final pieces of flesh melt together, leaving my arm whole again.

"I. Can't. Even," Corey exclaimed, rocking back, landing on his butt.

"Anna!" Adam called out, trying to get past Corey.

"Just a sec and I'll get out of the way."

"In fact, Mr. Edwards, I think you should change and go back with the others. This would be best all the way around."

"Anna?" Corey asked me. He wasn't about to leave if I didn't want him to.

"Mr. Seacrest is right," I said, feeling lightheaded. "Would you mind trying to make it right and normal for Jade and Meg?"

"I'll try. Are you going to be okay though?"

"I can't explain it. I feel... I feel fine, physically. A little woozy, but not much. I should feel like crap, I almost just died in some weird supernatural way. But...I feel basically normal."

"Yeah, well you're weird. We all know that," he joked, using my knees to help himself up. "If you need anything, call. Okay? Promise?"

"Yes, promise. Now, go be normal for all of us."

"Ha ha. Fool's errand. You're weird and I'm the fool."

"Always."

"Take care, A. See you soon," Corey said, Mr. Seacrest following him out.

"Stop right there," I said to Adam, who was about to swoop in and hug me. "No reason you need to be a gory mess too."

"I don't mind," he said, smiling at me, trying to pretend that seeing pints of my blood decorating the airplane bathroom wasn't upsetting.

"Just hold up. Let me change and clean up."

"No. You can change but someone else will get this."

"I actually don't think I could change in here without my fresh clothes getting gross."

"Strip down in there and come out. I'll pull the curtain and leave your bag for you. But you won't be alone. I'll be on the other side."

Even though I felt amazingly well considering what I'd been through, I was feeling emotionally vulnerable. Adam's thoughtfulness and trustworthiness had me in tears. I couldn't hold back as I took off my clothes and worked to scrub the blood off my body.

"You okay in there?" he called.

"Yes. I just… I just love you so much. You are such a good guy," I sobbed.

"Never been called that before," he laughed, which made me happy.

I loved that he'd never been this person with anyone else but me. His real self.

I quickly dressed, sticking my soggy hair up in a bun. I pulled the curtain back and he grabbed me, holding tightly.

"Don't ever scare me like that again. I can't take it," he said into my neck.

Our peace was disturbed by Mr. Seacrest, all nice and neat in a fresh clean suit. "I'm going back in the limo with the others. Echo will drive you two. Since you're mobile, I've told the others you're coming back to be checked out by the set medic. Corey's proving useful."

"Helpful," I corrected Mr. Seacrest's poor choice of words. "I'm sure he is."

"No stopping please. Straight back. Echo is ready for you. I'd like for the others to see you exit the plane in one piece and on your own. Follow me, please."

Adam gave me a smirk that said *That's my uncle. Whatcha gonna do?*

He retrieved my stuff from the plane, my suitcase already in the trunk. I let him help me to the waiting car, waving to the others as I walked.

"Good to see you, Anna," Echo greeted.

"You too. Any water in here? I think I'm dehydrated."

"Losing your body weight in blood will do that to a person," Adam joked.

"Guess so. My first time, so not sure what to expect," I said, lying down in the backseat, my head on his lap.

I felt a million times better physically. I was fairly certain it had to do with being in such close physical proximity to Adam. I was still exhausted, it was the middle of the night. I didn't have the mental strength to explain the last 20 hours to either of them. Adam played with my hair the entire ride back to Martin as we rode in relative silence, save the music.

Sylvia was on the front porch with *Ghost House's* on-call doctor, the rest of the manor silent.

Echo carried my things up to my room as I was examined.

"How are you feeling?" Dr. Glass asked.

"Fine now. Just really tired."

She had me take deep breaths, listening to my lungs with her stethoscope, tested my reflexes, and shone her penlight into my eyes while asking me questions.

"Everything seems normal. Almost too normal," she noted with a frown. "Your eyes are slightly dilated. Probably just need to change your contacts out. There's nothing else I can do right now without running tests. I'm going to draw some blood," she said, getting her rubber tourniquet.

"Are you sure that's necessary? I don't like needles." I couldn't imagine losing any more blood today, not even a little.

"Few do. But, yes. Let's be on the safe side. Which arm?" she asked.

I automatically stuck out my right arm, my dominant arm, without thinking.

"Unusual," Dr. Glass said, commenting on the very thin lines left on my arm from spectral Emma. The lines were very thin that no one would notice them unless they were looking really closely… or looking for them.

I didn't know how to respond, so I didn't. I turned my head to the side as she stuck the needle in. In that moment, I had a flash of intuition. I knew Emma Vitali, the real Emma in the real world, was dead.

Dismissed by Dr. Glass, I headed straight for bed. The grandfather clock struck 6 a.m. as I hit the second-floor landing. I thought about finding Adam, but the idea of doing anything more than putting one foot in front of the other until I bumped into my bed made me giggle. Yeah right. As if I could do anything else.

At the top of the third-floor landing stood Mr. Seacrest and Adam, Echo sitting quietly behind them by the widow.

"Sorry, gentleman. Store's closed. I got nothing to give. Not here or there. And you know where there is."

Mr. Seacrest began to protest, but I cut him off by raising my hand, startling him by laying it on his heart. "I am completely done tonight. I need sleep, real sleep. No supernatural dreams. No clandestine meetings. No training in caves. I. Am. Going. Now," I said definitively, turning on my heels.

With the little power I had left running in my veins, coupled with the powerful talisman around my neck, I wished for normal human sleep.

Sometimes wishes come true.

Chapter Thirty-Two

I woke up and reached for my cell. It was 11 a.m. I lay in bed, trying to think about the day before. I soon gave up and drew myself a bath. The house was strangely quiet. I usually had people hovering around me 24/7. I was betting the floor had been evacuated for my benefit. I could feel them, my crew, circling beneath me, going about their business, living their lives.

I sat in a bubble bath until my poor toes resembled prunes. I dried off and dressed in my favorite sundress, and left my solitude for food.

Adam found me in the kitchen and gave me a kiss. "Have a good night's sleep?"

"The best," I answered brightly, the warm sun streaming through the windows, the summer not wanting to let go. "And you? How long have you been up?"

"Not long. Yesterday was exhausting for me too."

"I'm sure," I said, almost dropping my sandwich on the floor. "Did... did you get hurt yesterday?"

"We are not alone," he said casually.

I looked around the kitchen, but I knew what he meant. We couldn't talk here. Not now.

The rest of the day was uneventful. Sylvia came to check on me midday, telling me she'd banned nonessentials from the manor until tomorrow morning. Even though I protested, assuring her I was fine, she basically ordered me to do nothing for the rest of the day.

"If you're ready, go ahead and resume your schedule tomorrow. If not, we can shoot around you for a few days.

Anna, I've been in this business a long time. Take care of yourself now or pay later. And the whole production will suffer. I need all my people well. Time is money. Better a little now than a lot later."

"Can I ask you a question?"

"Yes?"

"Why did Emma get written off the show?"

This question slightly upset her, her motherly concern slipping. "The writers wanted to go in a new direction and I agreed. It's a hard business. In one day and out the next."

While I could see that what she was saying was true, there was more to it. Sylvia was hiding something, and it felt weird. Super weird. I'd never picked up that kind of vibe from her before.

"Why do you ask?"

"Curiosity. I guess, honestly, I'm worried I'll be out because of not feeling well. I mean, this is the second time. I hate being a burden. I feel very unprofessional."

"Quite the contrary. While I will never guarantee anyone's position on *Ghost House*, production doesn't work that way. At least not mine. Exhaustion is common, especially given what you're dealing with."

She read the surprise on my face and clarified. "I must say you are dealing remarkably, and professionally, with the passing of your mother. I know how much you loved her. I read a few of her books."

"You did?" I asked, shocked to hear Sylvia Diaz read paperback romance novels.

"I'm not all business," she laughed, turning pensive. "My mother and father were taken from me. I understand what you're going through, as much as one person can understand another. Each person has their own particulars. I don't typically do this, Anna, but if you need to talk, you can come to me."

"Thank you. I'm sorry to hear about your parents. Thank you for sharing."

Sylvia was done being open. She was good at closing herself off. I had never guessed that level of horror was in her past.

Standing up she said, "What I need is for you to take your mental and physical health seriously. Got it?"

"Yes, ma'am."

Sylvia left and Adam wandered into the second-story sitting room soon after.

"Were you listening to that?" I asked as I moved my legs to make room for him.

"Definitely," he said, kissing my head. "Tell me, are you really worried about being cut?"

"I think so. I don't like to come across as weak and I've been nothing but a mess since we got here. People will give you a little latitude, but just a little. We tire of other people's crosses easily."

"Who cares what other people think?"

"Apparently I do. I wish I didn't, but, I at least want people to see me as competent, and certainly not weak or the weak link."

Adam nodded. He really didn't care what others thought of him. Regular people at least. He had begun to care about his reputation among people in his world. The tougher you were, the more power you had, the longer you survived. The Families were poster children for survival of the fittest.

Adam and I hung out the rest of the day, reading. It gave me great joy to look across the couch and see him completely absorbed in a book. Several times I looked up from my book, sighing, knowing a full-blown explanation of hell-day would be expected.

"Do you mind? I can't read when you're staring at me," Adam said, not looking up.

"Is it time?"

"Not today, love. Today is free. A day to recover."

"Tonight? Is that any better? I'd rather just get it over with and sleep hard tonight."

"No, not tonight. I've already squared it with Uncle. I've scheduled us a private meeting with the great Mr. Seacrest for tomorrow, lunch time. Now, can I please go back to my book?"

"Love you," I said, my heart in total meltdown at his thoughtfulness.

"I know, I'm too much. Here, give me your legs," he said, patting his.

And for the next hour, he massaged my feet with one hand as we continued to read.

Chapter Thirty-Three

Fall was trying to get a hold in Martin. But it was hard. Summer was a fighter and loved to linger longer than socially acceptable, at least from my point of view.

I woke at my normal time, and even though the morning was calling me, I didn't feel like running. Echo tapped on my bedroom door.

"You ready?" my running partner asked.

"I want to do something different. You up for Pilates?"

Echo made a face but shrugged his shoulders. He was in.

"You don't like Pilates?" I asked.

"I don't have an opinion. Only done it a few times. Suzanne loves Pilates. Shall we ask her along?"

"Sure. Might as well ask Corey, too. He's way better than I am. He'll probably end up leading our little class."

"If Suzanne will let him," he said as he went down the hallway to invite her.

Half an hour later we were on the floor of the library. Corey had found mats for us in the prop room. It felt great to stretch and feel my body growing stronger.

I was rested, physically and mentally, and ready to face the day. Adam was shooting a scene on the football field and I had tennis practice, so we walked to the school set together.

I was preparing for what to say to Meg when I saw her on the court. We hadn't talked since the L.A. trip. She was unusually quiet as we volleyed, while Maggie was characteristically mean to me, correcting my form and technique, praising everyone else.

There was an extra level of hostility coming from Maggie today, and an odd vibe from everyone else.

Practice over, Maggie gathered us to give us notes and tell us what she had planned for the rest of our time together. Everyone was weird. Katie wouldn't make eye contact with me, Meg kept shifting her weight from foot to foot, Suzanne seemed super pissed, and Maggie's rage was barely contained. I had to ask.

"I'm sorry, I'm clearly missing something here," I said to the group.

"Like your last period," Lucy snickered.

Katie's eyes widened like saucers and Meg whacked Lucy's arm.

"What? Just saying what's on everyone's mind," Lucy said, feigning offense.

"I don't understand," I said, looking around the circle.

"There's a rumor going around that you're pregnant," Suzanne said.

"What?" I choked.

"And not just on set. It's in the tabloids. Happy Monday morning," Suzanne said sarcastically.

"When did you know this?" I demanded. I'd just been with Suzanne at the Manor. How could she not tell me? Allow me to be blindsided and humiliated this way?

"On the court. I didn't know earlier. Swear."

I closed my eyes. I felt out to hear what was going on with the tennis team, each one an open book to me.

There was genuine shock and pity from Suzanne, Meg, and Katie.

Merriment mixed with a very small amount of pity from Lucy.

Downright seething hatred from Maggie.

"You all should know better. Just because you read something online doesn't make it true. I can't believe you!" I felt completely betrayed. If the people who knew me didn't give me the benefit of the doubt, I had no chance with others.

I couldn't stay, couldn't look at them. I felt incredibly violated. People talking about my very private life. People who should know better, who would expect me not to believe rumors about them. How quickly people turn on you.

"It's not just about you, Anna," Lucy barked out self-righteously to my back. "What happens when you get big and bloated? How's that gonna play out? That affects us all."

I walked back and said softly but firmly, "Not that it is any of your business, but I am not pregnant."

"You *have* been sick lately. And let's be honest. You've gained weight."

I went from hurt to royally offended. About to read her the riot act, I remembered my dad's advice. I get to decide how to react when people attack me, assume things about me. I get to decide to be mean and nasty back, or take the high road. Someone had started a nasty rumor about me, but whoever it was didn't own me. No one could push me around without my consent.

Not today, sister. Not today.

I could feel Suzanne following me back to our trailer. I was too mad to want to hear whatever she had to say.

"Hey, wait up."

I didn't stop, making her jog to catch me.

"You must be doing something right," she said, catching me off guard with her compliment.

"What do you mean?"

"People only start rumors about those they deem a threat or are jealous of. It means you've arrived."

"Thanks, but no thanks."

"You know it's all part of the fame game."

"Yeah, well, I hate it."

"And I can't believe you didn't deck that little bitch. I almost hit her for you."

"She's not worth it. It would only give her power over me."

"I envy your self-control. I only dream of being able to hold back like that."

"I don't want you to get you the wrong idea. I didn't have all those rational thoughts in the moment. By nature I have delayed reactions. Only works in my favor some of the time."

"Yeah," she agreed. Suzanne was a fighter. Her hot temper could get her in trouble in everyday life, though it rarely did. But those instincts, her quick reactions, were the reason she was still alive. One of the reasons I was glad she was around to protect me.

She was the optimal warrior: in tune with her body, emotions, and environment. And me? Most of the time I stumbled around, stunned when confronted with Family or supernatural issues.

These thoughts led me to change the subject. "You ready for the table read today?"

"You know I'm no coward, Anna. But I'm terrified to be in a room with him. I've been able to, thankfully, avoid him so far. Guess today my luck runs out."

"What are you nervous about?" I asked, hoping I wasn't prying.

She was about to tell me when she saw Corey, and her mood shifted. She became her regularly closed-off self.

Corey stopped and talked to me as Suzanne went in the trailer to shower and get dressed without saying a word to him.

"What's that about?" he asked when the door closed.

"You'll have to ask her. How'd it go this morning?"

"Fine. You?" he asked, though I could tell he'd heard the rumor.

"Yeah, I heard it. Yes, I'm pissed. But your girlfriend gave me some sage advice and I'm just trying to ignore it all. You know, it's really the least of our problems."

"I know that. We all know that. But you're a bigger person than I am, A, I'm telling you. See you at the table read," he said, going off to get ready too.

I was finally about to get in my trailer and decompress when I felt Maggie walk up. I wanted to pretend I didn't know she was there, but she called my name.

"Is it true?" she asked, her hatred no longer shielded. There was no one around to put on an act for.

"You know it's not. You're the one who told me about the stupid rules."

"How can I know you're not lying? Didn't find some way around?"

"I really don't care what you think."

She grabbed my arm lightning fast. My heart rate tripled and I wondered, in that second, if she had snapped like her mom. Maybe she was going to kill me and there was no one to stop her.

"You listen to me. You may not care what happens to Adam, but I do. He's my responsibility now. If word of this gets back to the Family… if they believe it, my mother may come to investigate, and trust me, you don't want that. That visit you won't live through."

"Let go of me," I said, yanking my arm back.

"I don't care if you hate me. Just to be clear, the feeling's mutual. You are nothing but bad news for my brother and I won't have you destroy him. I'm not above taking action on my own."

"Are you threatening me?" I asked rhetorically, because it was clear she was. I was really just trying to draw this out, hoping to calm her down, because she was trying to decide whether or not to kill me right here and be done with it. The only thing holding her back was Adam's inevitable anger and hatred if she did.

I was working out my own way to subdue her. The longer we talked, the clearer my plan became.

"You are on thin ice with me," she said.

"I don't understand why you hate me so much. I love your brother, and I loved your sister, my aunt, with all my heart."

"And how did that end up for her? She's dead because of you."

"That is not fair."

"But it's the truth. If she hadn't been so interested in you, she'd be here today. You have no idea what it's like to lose a twin. To lose."

"You are wrong," I said, feeling the rawness of the death of the women I'd loved most fiercely. Gone. Both. And violently.

Suzanne swung our trailer door open. "The shower's all yours, Anna. Oh, Maggie. Want to come in?"

"Her I like," Maggie said, pointing at Suzanne but looking at me. "I'm not done with you." Then she turned to Suzanne and said brightly, "Some other time. You're doing smashingly at practice. I'll see you tomorrow on the court. I've got some business to attend to."

"What was that about?" Suzanne asked as I slumped onto the couch.

"That? Oh, same old same old. You know, someone threatening to kill me."

"What?"

"Yeah. She hates me. Really hates me. Like, almost actually took my head off in full daylight kind of hate."

"Huh. For such a nice person, Anna, you really know how to make enemies."

"That's all you got for me? Some bodyguard!"

"I'll talk to her," Suzanne said, feeling chastised but confident she could make things better between me and Maggie. "Was it the rumor?"

"I think that was the final straw. She said if her mom finds out, she'll come. The queen can't come. She's … "

"Yeah, I know. I bet she won't. The rumor isn't credible."

251

"How come you're so sure? You seem to be the only one."

"Because no matter how foolish Adam can be, there is no way he'd be that dumb. He knows the consequences. Just no way."

I was still livid when I sat down for the table read. I hadn't had a chance to talk to Adam about the rumor or my encounter with his sister.

I sat down in a huff, though my self-pity wasn't meant to be long lasting. Pricks ran down my spine. Finn and company. Back in town.

Suzanne was already at the table. I watched her, waiting to see when she'd become aware of his presence. She caught me staring at her.

"What?" she asked.

"Nothing," I said, eyebrows raised as he was oppressively close. I couldn't believe she didn't notice.

"Oh," she said, trying to look unconcerned. Trying and failing. I was burning with curiosity to see Suzanne and Finn together, interacting. I did have enough of a conscience to feel ashamed of myself, knowing this was hard for the both of them, and possibly devastating for my best friend.

Suzanne took the high road and nodded at him when he walked in. I would've pulled out my phone, for sure, or done something to not have to acknowledge Finn, if I were her.

Finn came right over to me. "This seat taken?"

"All yours."

Suzanne was sitting on the other side of me. I was in an awkward sandwich.

"Hey, Finn. How are you?" Suzanne asked.

Her greeting was straightforward enough, but her delivery almost broke my heart. In that instant her soul was clear to me. I saw her deep pain and sorrow. Her regret. Her fear and uncertainty of what it meant to see him.

"Nice to see you again. Thought I never would," he answered.

No need to be someone like me to hear, clear and as fragile as glass, where Finn stood in relation to Suzanne.

His openness and sincerity closed her down immediately. She'd expected a lashing. She wouldn't have been surprised if he'd ordered a hit on her. She had not expected his warm and earnest reception. Slightly dazed, she turned towards the door where Corey and Adam stood.

The read-throughs were never boring, though they were incredibly hard. It was hard because I had to wait week-to-week to find out what was going on at *Ghost House*! No one told us where the story was heading, and I had no practice watching shows week to week. I was a binge watcher or reader. Never an episode or chapter at a time, I wanted it all - the entire story - in one sitting if possible.

In this episode the formation of the Westview ladies' tennis team and coach – played by the fabulous Maria Sousa - were introduced, and the friction for scarce school resources between us and the darling football team, Title IX be damned. I had to swallow my bile when we came to an over-the-top sexed up scene involving Adam and Lucy, a rope pull contest, and copious amounts of mud.

Yuck.

And then there was the twist I wasn't expecting. Finn, a.k.a. my older brother, finding Suzanne's character attractive. He asks me about her and I razz him back. It was clear to me where this storyline was heading.

It was hard to stay present, still fuming over the rumor mill. I made eye contact with Adam several times, but he gave me nothing back. He wasn't thinking about the gossip. He seemed more focused on Finn Varga and the minions he traveled with.

Yeah. Sure. Total double standard. I didn't know for certain, but I would've bet Adam was rumored to be the baby-daddy, and no one gave him a second thought – not even Adam! No one cared what he did in that department. But me? A girl? We were held to totally different standards with very different, and worse, consequences. It wasn't fair.

Fair? I laughed out loud. Unfortunately it was in the middle of Meg's and Corey's reading of a spooky scene set out behind the manor barn.

I grimaced my apologies and they continued.

Fair? Since when was my life fair? No one's life was fair.

I didn't deserve to witness the murder of my aunt and mother. I didn't deserve to be almost driven crazy with my prophetic dreams. I'd been almost killed, twice now. Caught up in the supernatural. None of this was fair.

I felt Adam's eyes on me, almost yelling at me to calm down. I automatically felt for my hair, smoothing the stray hairs that I hoped just looked like static electricity. Adam went back to the script, but my eyes stayed on him and he knew it. He smiled.

My brain responded. *Fair? Anna, you want to talk about fair? You think you deserve to be on Ghost House? You think you deserve to have a BFF like Corey? You think you deserve Adam? A father who loves you so completely? Even your abilities. They are gifts. Gifts, Anna. You don't deserve them. They were given to you. You are not owed anything, not even your existence. So SUCK IT UP!*

I was right! Yeah, it did suck to be misunderstood and gossiped about, but I had much more going on in my life. Yes, I was nearly killed by a phantom, nearly bled to death thousands of feet in the air. But I hadn't!

I looked at my arm, at the microscopic silver thread marks. I wondered what they meant. How could they be there, what did they mean?

I was checked out from the read that I almost missed my line. But Finn nudged me under the table, causing Adam to cringe and me to slightly overact.

It was midday before I was finally alone with Adam. First thing out of his mouth?

"So, you're having my baby? Why didn't you tell me?"

"Why do you think this is funny?"

"'Cause it is. Small minds, love. Small minds grasping at bigger ones. Have you figured out who did it?"

"You'd think Lucy. She called me fat! But it wasn't her. Who told you?"

"Dom."

I stopped dead. I knew, just knew, it was Dom. Dom had always been nice to me, but it had felt fake. Everything he did was fake.

Ever since I'd gotten off that plane and inadvertently killed his sister, I couldn't look at him. I was certain she was dead in the real world, yet Dom hadn't said a thing. Did he know? Was he blaming me? Was this payback?

"I know what you're thinking. It wasn't him. I didn't catch that vibe. You're not the only reader. Though I know it's hard for you to believe, I'm incredibly perceptive. More than you, if truth be told. So please, if you want to avoid me killing someone at the next table read, don't let him causally touch you like that."

Adam was back to Finn. How strange that he saw nothing wrong with Dom, yet he saw the devil in Finn. "Empty threats. And I'm not responsible for other people's hands."

Adam did not like that characterization.

"You know I didn't mean it like that. You saw him. He almost kicked me, nothing sexy about it."

"Assault is better?"

"You're impossible!"

"Yes. Remember that. I am utterly unreasonable when it comes to him and his kind."

"False and false. You've demonstrated remarkable restraint and compassion towards Finn Varga," I said, kissing his cheek.

"And the second false?"

"Suzanne. She's 'his kind.' And so is Corey, which I keep forgetting."

"I don't have to worry about them."

"It's a record. Three falses in a row!"

"What?"

"You definitely need to worry about Suzanne. Finn Varga is madly in love with Suzanne and she is deeply conflicted. She's still attracted to him. I mean, she didn't take him with her because she loved him. I'm pretty sure she still loves him, but she's not ready to admit it. Which pisses me off."

"'Cause of Corey?" Adam guessed.

"Yeah. Because I'm selfish. I should, of course, be worried that if the two of them get back together all hell will break loose and we'll all die."

"Yes, you should. But you're not. You're worried about Corey. You're always worried about him."

"Mr. Jealous."

"No. Well, yes I am. Absolutely I am. I don't want to be, but I'm selfish too, Anna. Thoroughly selfish."

"Man. Fourth false in a row. That's gotta be some kind of record. You give off the vibe of really not caring – and you don't, about unimportant stuff. But when it comes to real stuff – good vs. evil kind of stuff – you are incredibly giving."

"I'd like to give you something, Ms. Ellingwood," he said, putting his arms around me.

"I'm sure you would," I teased.

"Come here," he said, kissing me.

We walked back silently, hand in hand, the rest of the way to the manor.

After dinner we began the first of a four night shoot in the woods behind the manor. A small path had been cleared by the crew to get all their equipment to the barn.

When I'd read we were at the barn, I was shocked Sylvia had found it. I had the feeling the Gold Ghosts had been hiding the barn, protecting it. I wanted to be optimistic. Echo said the set crew had been in and out of the barn all summer and there'd been no incidents.

But we knew that no mayhem in the past didn't mean there wouldn't be any in the future. And the only reason the barn had been found was because the ghosts wanted it to be. Not a happy thought.

The first night was rehearsal. Most of the principal players were involved in a Gold Manor treasure hunt. In the first episode of season two, Meg is in the old beautiful library when she finds a map of the estate, and notices an out building, setting up one of the season-long story arcs.

Since my character is possessed by the Gold Manor ghost, I lead her, Lucy, and Corey on a wild goose chase in the forest, intentionally misdirecting them. The last scene in the episode is of Meg alone, separated from our group, and standing on the threshold of the barn.

The barn was going to be a location this season for parties, intrigue, and lots of general mayhem. When I emerged from the trail cut into the forest, I rocked back in my boots. The barn barely looked like the one we'd encountered last year. It had been transformed from a structure on the edge of collapse, a sure deathtrap for anyone who ventured in, to a barn ready to hold weddings on the weekend.

"What happened to it?"

"You don't approve of the face lift?" Sylvia asked behind me, walking at a clip.

"Uh…no…It's great…" I stammered.

What'd caught me completely off guard was not so much the total cosmetic transformation, but the feeling that it had been cleansed. The atmosphere was like Clorox, like using heavy duty products to get rid of a little dirt. The place reeked, in my mind at least.

"Adam?" I said, cocking my head to the side, trying to gauge what he felt.

"Uncle said the place was safe. This must be him. You know what he hates."

What did Mr. Seacrest hate, apart from the Fourth? Supernatural creatures such as the Gold Manor ghosts.

"I can't imagine this would make them, you know, happy. They are vindictive."

"But only if they know. This is not the first time Uncle has dealt with that kind. Let's hope whatever he did holds, and there isn't a backlash."

"That's a pretty big hope."

Corey was coming up behind us. "I probably don't want to know what's going on, do I?" he asked.

I shook my head.

"Well, you better put your game face on, you possessed actor, you. Give'm hell," he said, walking past us and over to Suzanne.

"You see that?" I asked Adam, watching Suzanne and Corey, his arm slung over her shoulder.

"What am I looking at?"

"My best friend, who is happy right now because ignorance is bliss."

"You are going to pop his balloon?"

"Do you think I should?" I asked, wanting advice.

"Absolutely not. That's their business."

"But it's not fair to him. He has a right to know his girlfriend is not over her first love."

"I disagree. But either way, it shouldn't come from you. And you don't know the future. You get in there, in between them, and you could screw up their relationship or, worse, your friendship."

"But if I say nothing, isn't that worse? Not looking after him?"

"Anna, Corey's a big boy. Let him work out his own love life. Trust me on this."

I nodded, but a nasty thought ran through my mind. *If I had trusted my own instincts instead of Adam's, maybe my mom would still be alive.*

Adam felt the jolt of anger run through me, though he didn't know what it meant. At least I hoped he didn't. Because I didn't really blame him. Or at least I knew I shouldn't.

Chapter Thirty-Four

Adam stayed with me while my hair and make-up were freshened-up. I could feel Finn's approach, involuntarily shuddering before he reached us. Luckily, he wasn't paying attention to us because he was on his phone.

I watched Finn out of curiosity as Adam told me that Andrew was coming up for a visit in a few days. I happened to see the exact moment when Finn smelled "the cleanse" too. He let out a string of expletives and snapped to attention, his spine straightening, ready for a fight.

All eyes were on him, wondering what'd happened.

"Sorry, all. Just got some bad news," he waved his phone. "Go back to whatever it was you were doing," he said to the cast and crew, regaining his cool. For the most part.

Finn looked around and spied Suzanne, locking eyes on her.

I knew what he was about to do, but felt frozen. Should I...do something?

He marched over to Suzanne and went to grab her by the arm. He was about to yank her away – surely for an explanation – but thought better of it and dropped his hand.

"Excuse me. Suzanne, may I talk to you in private?"

Poor Suzanne. This was the first time Finn had talked to her outside of table reads and I knew she felt incredibly awkward. From her body language I was fairly certain she didn't know about the exorcism of the ghosts from the barn. She had no idea what he wanted.

Corey looked mad as hell. As they walked away to talk in private, his eyes met mine. I gave him the *get over here right now* stare.

Corey tried his best to casually walk over to me. "You know what that's about? What does he want?"

"I'm pretty sure he's now aware of the ghosts and he wants her to tell him what she knows."

"What is he saying to her?"

"I don't know exactly. I don't have supersonic hearing, you know."

"Why the hell not? Now that would be useful. Why can't you have something that would actually help?" Corey snapped.

"Watch it," Adam cut in.

"A can lookout for herself. She doesn't need you to do that. Besides, she knows I didn't mean anything by it."

"All the same," Adam replied, not backing down.

"Hey, guys. Let's take one crisis at a time. We don't know what Finn can really do or sense, right? I can feel from both that Suzanne is very safe. Let's move along. No reason to tip Finn off."

"What do you mean by very?" Corey said, turning to me.

"Stop it. Come on," I said, deciding at that moment that Adam was right. Suzanne and Corey had to figure out their own relationship.

Truth be told, I was glad for the diversion. I was not looking forward to this shoot. We were pulling an all-nighter in a cold, damp, scary forest – now with angry ghosts lurking nearby. Tonight I had a fight scene with Lucy and Meg while possessed, and a make-out session with Jade.

I didn't know which made me more nervous. I didn't want to kiss Jade, but we were comfortable with each other. From the first time I'd met Jade, something about him seemed right to me. I'd had a similar feeling when I met Corey in 7th grade.

When I met Corey, I had a gaping hole right in the center of my chest. He was my lifeline to the world. When Jade came along last year, I was in a very different place. Jade offered me unconditional friendship. He didn't need anything from me, saw that I was surrounded by craziness, and decided to be kind to me anyway. Being around Jade was the easiest thing. Natural.

That is, until the TV romance. It made us both uncomfortable. Jade didn't know about the world I was caught up in. He only knew the normal facts about me, one being that I had a rock-star, entitled, jealous boyfriend.

Jade didn't know I could read him. It was unfair of me, and I felt bad to have all this extra information about him, but it wasn't intentional. I wasn't trying to violate his privacy. My reading others was almost like another sense. Very similar to seeing.

So, while I didn't relish the idea of kissing him, it made it a lot easier knowing he didn't want to kiss me either. Not because he wasn't attracted to me, but because he was a gentleman. He wasn't interested in taking without asking.

And yet, it was still awkward.

The night began normally, professionally. All the principal players were in the barn, decorating it for the dance. Meg's character tells the other girls she's found another entrance to the tunnels that run out from the house, setting up a story arc in the tunnels. Suzanne asks if my brother's coming tonight and Lucy gets jealous, while Adam and Dom razz Corey about Katie, the new girl.

Most of us took a break while Meg and Lucy shot in the forest. I knew what was coming up, my kissing scene, so I tried to relax. I'd napped most of the day and had a lot of energy surging through me. Adam sat next to me, holding my hand, saying nothing but lending me his solidity. I was glad I didn't have to worry about his emotional state right now.

Meg and Lucy finished and the extras began getting in place for the party shoot. I was getting up to get my hair and make-up touch ups when Meg approached us. She was freaked.

"Anna, you have a sec?"

"Sure. Just on my way to hair and make-up," I said, kissing Adam goodbye. Adam felt the waves of panic coming from Meg too. He nodded at me.

"You okay?" I asked as we walked away from Adam.

Meg pulled me to the edge of the clearing, looking around. "I am done with this place! If I could, I'd quit today and never come back. I am just done!"

"You saw one?" I whispered to her, putting my hand on her arm, trying to calm her down.

"How did you know? Have you seen one too?" she asked, eyes as wide as I'd ever seen them.

"No, not yet. But I have seen them here, at the barn, before."

I tried to sound causal and serious at the same time.

"How do you do it? I feel like my skin's about to come off! That's it. I've just decided. I'm quitting. My life and sanity are worth more than my career."

I looked Meg in the eye and said as kindly as possible, "It's not that easy. If they want something, they'll find you. There is no walking away."

"What do you mean?" she asked, horrified.

"Last year, on holiday break? I was with Corey at his house and…."

"No!" she shrieked, holding her heart. "No! This can't be happening! Not again."

The hair all over my body stood on end. She'd caught me completely off guard. "What do you mean *not again*? Have you seen one before?"

"Anna, I can't."

"No, Meg. I'm in this too. We've got to work together."

"You're going to tell me all your secrets? This set's the worst! It's usually petty stuff, but not here. It's much more. You know I see a lot."

"I thought you didn't want to know."

"And I don't. Forget it. Let's forget the whole thing," she said, brushing past me and back into the bustle of the set, completely shutting me out.

Adam, who'd been watching us, came up to me once she was gone.

"What happened?"

"I can't believe it. Gold Manor is not the first time Meg has encountered a ghost! What does that mean?"

"I don't know. Huh."

"I'll find out more as soon as I can. I think Meg will talk to me."

"And sooner rather than later. Now that Finn knows about them too, well, the Fourth and ghosts really don't mix."

"What do you mean?"

"Let's hope you don't have to find out."

"Thanks a lot. You know, I did tell Finn I saw a ghost. Should he be this surprised?"

"Hearsay and feeling it is very different."

"True. Hey, you tell Corey to pretend he doesn't see any ghosts if they show up. I don't want him outing himself in front of Finn."

"Sure, love," he said, as I kissed him on the cheek. He grabbed me around the waist and kissed me until my head spun.

"You remember that when you're kissing Jade tonight."

No words came to me as I righted myself and walked off. That was my secret to "great acting" with Jade. I just pretended he was Adam. That's all I needed to get carried away into the passion of the moment.

Our scene went fine. Jade made it easy, laughing with me, putting me at ease. I was glad Adam wasn't watching. He was getting ready for a scene with Dom and Corey.

When we finished, Jade and I headed over to his next scene with the other guys. It took forever. I should've gone to bed, but was too tired to think clearly.

The only people left in the woods were those in the scene, Sylvia with her usual minimal crew, and Finn.

I was sitting in Corey's chair when Finn took a seat next to me.

"Surprised you're still here. It's nearly three a.m."

"I'm too tired to move. You?"

"I'm amped. Got some disturbing news today."

"I'm sorry. Do you want to talk about it?" I asked him, eliciting a laugh.

"Thanks, but no thanks," he said, surprised I'd asked what was going on with him. "I don't mean to be a jerk, it's just, when you're someone like me or Meg – she gets it – people usually don't know what to do with us. I mean, they know what they want from us, but not how to genuinely interact with us. Make sense? You'll see soon enough."

"I think I understand."

"Take your boyfriend, Mr. Famous Rock Star, who at this very moment is trying to intimidate me by staring me down. I know. I get it. He doesn't like me. Or he likes you a lot. Or he doesn't trust you. Or anyone. He knows the game. He's been in it a while, but I've been in it a lot longer."

"Is that why you took time off?"

"Not really. Family reasons, mostly. How well do you know Suzanne Browne?"

He said her name like it was a question too. I'd bet that wasn't the name he'd known her by.

"Honestly, not well. I mean, we've been friends for over a year, but she's hard to get to know. Why?"

"I used to know her. In fact, we used to date. I loved her," he said, eyes glazed over.

It was quiet for a few beats, feeling too intimate for me.

"Well, I should tell you that while I don't know her very well, she is currently dating my best friend, Corey," I said, not unkindly. I just wanted him to know where I stood. There was no way I was going to help him out with Suzanne.

"I gathered you were friends with him. Best friends though?"

"Corey and I have been friends since the 7th grade. I love him."

"Adam knows this?"

"Not that it's your business, but I'm a package deal."

"Not to be insulting, but you're an idiot. You don't know guys, and certainly not ones like your rock star. Now I know why he acts the way he does when it comes to you."

"I think you're taking this big brother thing too far."

I wanted to defend Adam, but it probably was better if he thought Adam was just crazy jealous.

"Fine. But, hey, I've got a different question for you. Ever see anything strange around the set?"

I instantly decided how I should handle this, with a slice of the truth. "Do you know *anything* about last season?" I asked sarcastically.

"My agent's really going to hear it. Go ahead. Lay it on me."

"I already told you about most of the stuff."

"Most?" he bit out.

"Yeah. The ghost I saw was on set. In the woods"

"I assumed that's what you meant. If you see one and you're with Suzanne, get out of there and take anyone else who's there with you. Remember what I told you. I mean it, leave them alone."

"Am I supposed to think you're crazy now?" I asked, trying to lighten the mood.

He turned toward me, put his hand on the edge of my chair and said, "You know I'm not. You've seen things you can't explain. Please trust me on this, but don't tell anyone else. People do tend to think you're off your rocker when you talk about the supernatural. Lucky for them."

"What do you mean?"

"Ignorance is bliss," he said with great sorrow in his voice.

Chapter Thirty-Five

It was almost dawn when I got to my room. With no place I had to be until five p.m. tomorrow, I thankfully put my phone on silent, intentionally not setting an alarm.

Instead of an early morning run, I rolled out of bed at a glorious 1:14 p.m. I went outside for fresh air and found Echo reading on a bench.

"Ready for a run?" he asked.

I declined, opting to putz around until call time.

Time flew by, leaving me feeling like I'd lost a day when I sat in the hair and make-up chair in Gold Manor's basement.

I hated the wardrobe Drake had for me tonight. Really trashy: tight, semi see-through, and fishnets? A little too obvious for my taste. I had thought long and hard how to combat the sexism in the industry, and my current plan of making small changes whenever I could felt pathetic.

"Can't we do something about this one? I certainly don't look like a teenage girl. I look easy. How will anyone hear what I'm saying when they can see so much of me?" I whined to Drake.

"Believe it or not, I added an inch to the skirt. And pockets. I know you love pockets. Sorry, Anna, but this is it. If you want a change, you're going to have to take it up with Sylvia."

In my hideous getup, I walked out to the barn for the shoot with Jade. Sylvia muttered something about the footage from yesterday being damaged. She was put out and not to be messed with, so I decided not to push the awful outfit issue.

The barn felt different today. Alive. I could feel the souls of those who'd gone before me as I passed through its doors.

Sitting on a bale of hay as the crew set the lights behind me, I couldn't help but beam. This barn felt like it used to be a happy place. A useful place. A place of refuge. The rafters had stories they were dying to tell.

"What is it?" Jade asked, referring to my goofy smile.

"I don't know. It's this barn. I can't help but imagine what it was like when it was lived in."

"And that makes you smile? Let me tell you. I grew up on a farm, and if our barn could talk, it would tell you how hard life on a farm is."

"But I don't think this place was a farm like yours. Soybeans, right?"

"Livestock too."

"This place was for animals and parties," I said, trying to explain the visions coming to me. Trying and failing.

"You *are* from the city," he teased.

"All right. We're ready," Sylvia called.

We filmed our kissing scene. When it was over, Sylvia yelled cut. I started to drop my arms from his waist.

"Wait," Jade said, holding my hands right where they were, filling me with fear. "You feel that?"

I did. His sides were warming, unnaturally hot.

Jade looked at me, lifting his shirt. His sides were glowing, and getting brighter.

"Anna, what's going on?" he asked, alarmed.

I looked around, but no one was paying attention to us. The crew had followed Sylvia out of the barn, on to their next shoot.

"Help me!" he said, dropping to his knees, clutching his sides.

His cry caught Echo's attention and some of the others. Echo, at the mouth of the barn, turned to us, but the barn doors slammed shut, closing us in, keeping them out.

Jade was now on the dirt floor, writhing. I looked around for help.

There was no help, just the opposite – the gold ghost was staring us down through the window. She hovered just outside the area Mr. Seacrest had cleansed.

I looked back to Jade, determined to use whatever power I had to heal him – if possible. But he was levitating in the air, out of reach, and heading for the window. The ghost pulled him from the barn, through the window, the glass ripping his flesh apart.

"No!" I screamed. "No!"

Within seconds I was surrounded by the inhabitants of the third floor, Adam at my side, soothing me. "It was just a dream, love. Just a dream."

But everyone there knew I didn't "just" have dreams. Adam was the only one I'd shared my precognition with. That's all *my* normal dreams had been of late.

Adam sent Echo and Suzanne away and I checked my phone. 1:14 p.m.

"It's Jade," I said, gripping Adam's arms, sobbing. "The gold ghost took him right from me, right out of the barn."

"That's not possible. Uncle –"

"I know what I saw. It was real. Adam, not him. Not Jade!" I said, my sobs subsiding as my thoughts turned to action. "Call your uncle. I want to speak to him right now."

"I will call him, but you've got to calm down. Jade is nothing to my uncle. If he's going to help us, you've got to get control," he said, pushing call on his cell.

"Uncle? Anna dreamt. Yes. Yes. One of those dreams. No. The barn. Yes. Fine, ten."

"I don't want to go there," I said, the horror of the night fresh in my mind.

"But we still need to go," Adam cooed.

On the way out to the barn I grabbed a banana. To the crew in the house and any other onlookers, Adam and I looked like two young lovebirds out for a romantic walk.

If only.

Echo was reading on a bench in the backyard. "You want me to come with you?"

"No. We'll be fine. But stay close, okay?" Adam replied.

"Sure thing. Anna, up for a run when you return?"

"Still freaky," I mumbled. Both guys nodded, Adam knowing this was familiar to me.

Almost to the clearing, I felt Maggie.

"Did you know she was coming?" I asked Adam, miffed.

He looked at me puzzled until he felt her too. "Uh, no. Impressive range."

"I don't want to talk about anything if she's going to be there."

"Try to play nice."

273

"Oh, you have no idea how I've tried. I really have. Your family just doesn't like me."

"It's hard, but you're right. I wish it weren't so. If your father knew, I can't imagine he'd approve of me either."

Before I could respond, we saw them standing just outside of the barn.

"Be nice," he breathed, squeezing my hand. "Uncle. Sis, surprised to see you."

"Really? I was having lunch with Uncle when I heard of your girlfriend's vision. Though I doubt it has much merit. I'm the one who installed the wards around the barn. It's as safe as safe can be."

I knew what I'd seen. What I'd felt. I was getting better at figuring out which part of my dreams were normal, which were foreshadowing, and which were downright predictions.

"Mr. Seacrest, with all due respect to Maggie, I know what I saw in the dream. I'm not claiming it's going to happen just like that, but if we do nothing, Jade's going to die."

"Tell me what happened," Mr. Seacrest said as we walked into the barn. He had me show him where Jade and I had been in the dream, and every other detail I could recall.

"Any additional information?"

"I woke up at 1:14, just like in the dream. And Echo was outside on a bench asking if I wanted to run," I said, trying to think of other parallels.

"Really? Where did you find this girl?" Maggie scoffed.

"Margret," Mr. Seacrest warned.

"No. I've had it. I don't know what power she holds over you. Adam's young and stupid, but you really should know better. Don't you see how she's got her hooks in him? I can't believe this has been allowed to go on for so long! I know the queen is unhappy," she said, turning from Mr. Seacrest and pointing at me. "Believe me, little girl, if the queen doesn't get her way, there will be hell to pay. And you're going to pay it!"

Maggie was being awful, and I knew it was partly due to ignorance. But my heart was torn up. I wanted to defend myself. I expected Adam or maybe even Mr. Seacrest to come to my rescue, but they were silent.

"Nothing? Really? This is golden. You twits!" Maggie stormed off.

"Let her go. It's better this way," Mr. Seacrest said.

But Maggie wasn't done.

"Don't you do that," she screamed, coming back for more. "Ever since I arrived, there's been nothing but lies and subterfuge. You think I don't know? I sniffed out those Fourth before I set foot on set. Either you tell me what the hell is going on or I'll take care of the problem myself."

"You will not threaten me," Mr. Seacrest said calmly, though his voice held the real threat.

His warning sobered up Maggie's rage. "I do deserve the truth. Adam, what has she done to you? First our sister and now you? Talk to me."

Adam was caught. He wanted to tell his sister, but knew it wasn't wise.

The vision of Jade being ripped through the window popped into my mind. I was here to help Jade. Couldn't Maggie wait? She wasn't slated for death just after sunset!

Adam felt my agitation.

"Can we just get this over with? I want to find a way to save Jade," I said truthfully, if somewhat imprudently.

Maggie, who had finally settled down, flared right back up.

"I can't believe you fell in with a witch like that!"

"Stop it. You don't understand. I love Anna. She -"

Adam was cut off by Maggie gearing up to tear him a new one. "No you don't! You better hope Mother never meets her. On second thought, maybe I should ring the queen right now. I know she loves updates on her favorite child."

"They have met," Adam said, staring his sister down.

"What? Why haven't I heard about this? There's no way Mother would allow this abomination!"

"Maggs, I don't know what you think is going on here. What gives?" Adam asked, trying to find out what was really bothering his sister. With his question, a crack appeared in Maggie's armor. Fear.

"No, Maggie. You're my sister. I'm never leaving you. Never," Adam said, laying a hand on her shoulder. Maggie wasn't ready for comfort. She wanted answers.

"Tell me. Tell me everything. I mean it. I see the looks you're exchanging."

"No," Mr. Seacrest said authoritatively. "No lies, but not everything you seek. Not yet."

"Who do you think you are?" Maggie said, put out but calming down.

"The last of us. The end of us. The protector and holder of knowledge. You know who I am. Do not test me. But we will tell you more than you need to know. More than you want to know, dear one. I am sorry for you," he added, growing tender.

I guessed at what Maggie was allowed to know, but I wasn't going to say it.

"Mom has known about Anna for some time. Anna and I tried to hide ourselves from her gaze, fruitlessly. At the end of the shoot in March, Mother came to town. I was helping Anna pack and the queen was furious, out of her mind – as she often is of late. In the middle of her speech forbidding Anna and I to be together, Anna's own mother walked in on the scene. Without word or look, the queen reached behind her and … snapped Anna's mother's neck.

"So yes, Anna has paid. Her family has paid the ultimate price for being entangled with me. The queen's one restitution, when she was brought to her senses, was to leave Anna alone forever."

"The woman must have been armed. She attacked," Maggie countered, shaking her head.

"No, sister. It is the end, as Uncle said. Mother is gone. Only madness remains. We are leaderless and the Fourth are moving throughout the world. You know of the report of the dreamers? Anna is the only female dreamer left."

"Why her? I know she is powerful, but she took Diane from us," Maggie said, still indignant.

Mr. Seacrest answered. "Anna is tied to our Families, it is true. I am personally training her. Adam and Anna have become intertwined in a way I haven't seen before. I have yet to unravel them, so we need you to stop interfering. We are better if they are united and we work as a team."

"I hate that," Maggie conceded.

"And yet it is. You must trust me. We have told no one of the queen's instability. Those at court, close to her, will say nothing as well. We all know the chaos and war courted if it becomes known the queen is incapacitated and we are leaderless."

"Why do you dislike me?" I asked her.

"You know, everyone thinks I've been this out-of-touch drunk. I was, but not for the past years. I've been watching, listening, and I was about to get back into the fray, my brother at my side. Then you came along. And you weren't just some girl. You were powerful, yet you allowed my sister to be killed. All I see is death if he stays with you."

"You blame a child for Diane's death?" Mr. Seacrest chided. "You insult the memory of a great woman with that profanity."

"You are jealous and angry," Adam said pointblank to his sister.

"Yes," Maggie conceded, still full of hate.

"This has nothing to do with Anna and everything to do with your own weakness." Adam said, pushing too hard.

"How dare you! You don't know the life I've lived."

"Your story is yours to tell," Mr. Seacrest said, bringing the heart-to-heart to an end. "What do you plan to do now?"

"I will leave Anna alone. But you've said nothing of the Fourth scum you've allowed to live."

"Finn Varga is the son of Dane and Lillian. Kill him and the Fourth will descend. We cannot have that," Mr. Seacrest explained.

"Surely not to protect your entertainment venture," Maggie said incredulously.

Mr. Seacrest gave her a look that said he would not dignify her accusation with a serious reply.

"This place, the ghosts, Adam and Anna, and more that is to come, must be protected from outside interference. You know of my work."

Maggie looked down and then back up at us all, a new resolve on her face. "And you know of my work and my duties. If the queen is unable to rule, I will take her place. You have narrow interests, whereas mine span all the Families. For the time being I will extend this courtesy you request, because of your long service, Alastair. I will return to Crimson Hall to see if what you said of our queen is true."

Maggie had pulled her emotions close, and closed off any further route of being understood.

I stood silently, wondering at the warning in her words.

"Anna, I am sorry for my mother's actions."

"She deserves more than that. You've done nothing but torture her ever since you arrived," Adam said, exasperated.

"And I wish she didn't exist. Sorry, but it's the truth. There is something about her... deadly, dangerous."

"I love her, sis. She makes me happy. Why can't that be enough for you?" Adam sighed.

"You are still so young, so blind. Love and happiness are not for us. I knew you weren't listening in school. Your purpose is to defend the Families. Pure and simple. She is your undoing. I will not let her be mine."

Chapter Thirty-Six

Maggie was going to be a greater problem than I'd anticipated. I thought she was simply the big sister that hated her little brother's girlfriend. If only. Maggie as queen... that didn't sound like the best solution to the leadership problems in the Families. But what did I know?

What I cared about presently was making it through the night with Jade in one piece.

We gathered our bunch in the Gold Manor library where I told them about my dream, and Mr. Seacrest gave us the plan.

"Not only do we want to save Jade, we need to keep people in the dark about the ghosts," Mr. Seacrest reiterated. "A hint of the paranormal and we'll draw unwanted attention. My plan is simple. I'm going to call a meeting tonight in the clearing at the barn. I will notify Sylvia at the last moment, making her unable to shoot tonight."

"Won't that just push things off? How is that really going to help?" Corey asked.

"I have many resources," Mr. Seacrest answered sternly, making it clear this wasn't a brainstorming meeting. He didn't want our help or "insight."

While I thought Mr. Seacrest's plan was good, I knew Sylvia. She might not bite. What would I do if Sylvia ignored the meeting?

Mr. Seacrest was unaware of a side experiment I'd been running. I had wondered about how set the future was. If I really dreamed about the future, could it be changed? Maybe my dreams were simply projections of what might logically occur in the future, given the state of the world in the present.

I wondered if I had an unconscious ability to pick up on information and details that my conscious mind could never process. The dreams were a result of putting the pieces together.

I'd started keeping a record of my dreams in my journal. I wrote what I saw, what I felt, what I was able and unable to do. Side by side, I'd write about my day and connections I saw between the waking and dreaming states. I wasn't consistent in my note taking, but I was beginning to make correlations.

On a couple of occasions, when I awoke from a dream I'd felt was telling me about what was going to happen, I'd tried to change what seemed a significant detail, and therefore the outcome. Both times I had failed. The outcome I'd tried to change happened anyway.

Unfortunately the dream I'd had last night probably fell into this category. It was still hard to tell. What if the outcome was a foregone conclusion and there was nothing I or anyone else could do to save Jade?

I was nervous as all get-out sitting in hair and make-up. Drake came in with my outfit. Just like in the dream.

I ran through my protest of the outfit, that it was undignified, that I felt objectified, but my heart wasn't in it.

Echo walked with me out to the barn, the crew already there. When my cell buzzed with the news of a mandatory meeting in 15 minutes, I started to calm down. The pieces were falling into place.

"Hey, wait up," Jade called from behind us.

I was relieved to see him alive, I almost threw my arms around him. But that would've been weird.

"Glad to see you!" I said, grinning so big I think a tear leaked out.

"You too," he laughed. "You ready for this?"

"Oh, didn't you get the text? Don't think we're going to shoot tonight after all. There's some important cast and crew meeting in about 10 minutes."

"My phone's off. Guess I'll check it," he said, shrugging as we cleared the woods.

"All right you two, let's get this done," Sylvia barked when she saw us.

"But the meeting?" I asked, confused.

"They can wait. Come on. Let's get a few takes in."

My mind ticked off another correlation – Sylvia's mood. In my dream she was mad, just like now.

I thought about refusing. I could fall and pretend to hurt my ankle. Heck, I could easily throw up right now.

"Just trust it's going to be okay. Mr. Seacrest knows what he's doing. I'll be right here," Echo counseled.

I grabbed Echo's arm. "Whatever you do, don't leave the barn. Okay?"

He nodded, looking at my fingernails digging into his skin. "I'll be right there. You'll see me the whole time," he assured me.

I went to my mark. I couldn't hide my anxiety when Jade sat next to me on the hay bale.

"You look sick," he observed.

"I am," I said, starting to panic.

"Okay. Everyone ready?" Sylvia asked, pushing to get her shots in.

It's not like we were filming any old scene. I was about to have an intense make-out session with Jade, but all I could see was his mangled body in my mind's eye.

"Give me a moment, please," I said, trying to center myself. The sooner I could get into character and through the shoot, the safer Jade would be.

It's hard to calm down when you're pressed for time and it's a life or death situation.

Jade knew I was struggling.

"Not that you need advice, Anna, but maybe just let go of whatever's throwing you off. This is awkward for both of us."

"It's not that. It's just… I had an awful dream last night and I can't shake it. That ever happen to you?" I asked, trying to distract myself.

"Can't say it has, not really."

"And I hate this outfit," I said, pulling the dress down, which just showed more cleavage. I compensated and pulled at the top, making it shorter again. There just wasn't enough of the dress.

Jade, like the smart guy he was, made no comment on my outfit.

The banter helped me calm down enough to shoot the scenes. Jade and I had just climbed into the hay loft for the last take when Sylvia's assistant came running in. "They need you, right now, at the manor. It's Meg!"

Sylvia grabbed her phone and ran out of the barn, the small crew following in her wake.

"Let's go. Maybe we can help," I said to Jade.

Before I was down the stairs, I felt the ghost. I knew we couldn't make it out of the barn in time. And wouldn't it be worse to be an open target in their forest?

"Jade, listen," I said in a rush. "Last night my nightmare was about you. You died. I know this sounds crazy, but please trust me."

"Do you see that?" Jade asked, pointing at the widow.

I didn't need to look to know he was talking about the gold ghost.

I'd brought a back-up plan. I knew this was about to ruin our friendship forever, but at least he'd survive.

"We're getting out of here," I said as the barn doors slammed on their own. I grabbed Jade's wrist, taking a crystal from my pocket with my other hand. He was almost out of time.

My plan was to use my crystallized energy to get us out of here, but the crystal wouldn't budge. It wasn't reacting to my touch. I couldn't get it to release the energy stored inside.

I let go of Jade to rub it between my palms. Nothing.

"Anna!" Jade yelled, already ten feet off the ground, being pulled toward the incensed ghost.

I was out of time. I popped the entire crystal into my mouth and made my mind as blank as the night sky. I said clearly what I wanted, for Jade and me to be far away from here.

I should have been more specific.

Chapter Thirty-Seven

"I... I've never been to the ocean. Am I having a psychotic episode?" Jade asked me as we stood side by side in the sand at Huntington Beach.

"Oh crap! I think I overshot," I said, looking around, head spinning.

He sat down in the sand. "I think I'm hallucinating."

"No, no, no! Not this far. How are we going to get back? How could this ever be explained?" I said more to myself than him.

"It's amazing here. Are we staying?" Jade was in shock.

"Definitely not," I said, feeling the hum of the energy radiating through me. "Come on," I said, dragging him to his feet. We walked to the parking lot and I crouched behind a car, pulling him down with me, making sure no one was watching us.

"Gold Manor, my room, both of us," I said clearly, seeing my room in my mind. And then we were there.

"I've never been here before either," Jade said, eyes bugging out. He was a man who could not make sense of what he'd seen because it really was nonsensical!

"Jade, I'll try to explain, but we need to make an appearance in the backyard. Can you do that? I'll tell you everything I can, but I need you to not tell anyone what just happened, okay?"

"What did just happen?"

"I honestly don't know. I'm just odd?" I offered.

"Maybe I'm dreaming?" he countered in a daze.

"Maybe you are. Come on," I said, checking to make sure the hallway was clear. "And remember, quiet, okay? Can you do that?"

"I don't have anything to say," he answered from behind me.

Right now he didn't. But he would, which I couldn't think about at present. At the moment we needed to get in place without raising suspicion.

As soon as we neared the first floor, we heard voices. We retreated and ran through the second floor, taking the back staircase down to the basement.

"What are we going to do down here?" Jade asked, looking around.

I hated what I was about to suggest but it seemed our best option. "You know the tunnel they recently found? We can take it all the way to the east side of the grave yard."

Jade didn't put up a fight until he saw the entrance. "I don't know, Anna. I don't like small spaces. I don't even know if I'll fit."

He was exaggerating. The tunnel to the cave wasn't very long and definitely big enough for a large man to crawl through.

"You'll be fine. I'll be with you," I said, reaching for his hand. We didn't have time for this. If we didn't make it to the clearing soon, people would start to notice.

"Stay behind me. I won't let anything happen to you," I said, feeling the promise I'd just made. Could I keep it?

This was twice now. Twice a Gold ghost had tried to kill him. One time may have signified nothing, but two times? How was Jade linked in this mess?

Out of the tunnel and into the cave, Jade's phone buzzed.

"Hello? Yes. Sure. Anna – it's for you," Jade said, handing me his phone.

"We're okay. Barely though, and I screwed up. I mean, it was my only option," I told Adam, who understood the gist of what I was getting at.

"I want to hear all about it. Where are you?" he asked.

"In the cave right outside of the basement. On our way to the meeting."

"Anna, get out of that cave! Go back the way you came. Now!"

"How can we explain being in the house?"

"The meeting was moved to the first floor. We're above you. If anyone asks, say you took the cave here, I don't know. Just get the hell out of there!"

I handed Jade his cell back and said, "They're all in the house. We're going back."

Jade sucked up his fear and followed me. I could feel how hard this was for him and I admired his courage. Courage wasn't the absence of fear but pushing past it and acting anyway.

Right before we began to ascend the stairs to the first floor, Jade stopped me.

"I'm not crazy, right? You saw what I saw?"

I nodded slowly, wondering what he wanted from me.

"And everything that happened tonight, you weren't surprised."

"I was," I said, sidestepping the truth.

"But not like me. Right?"

I nodded again.

"Maybe, sometime, you'll explain?"

"Let's get upstairs, okay?" I said, not wanting to make empty promises. I knew what he deserved, but I didn't know what I could deliver.

The first floor was full. The cast and crew were assembled and Mr. Seacrest was already delivering his news.

"That was the good news. Very good indeed. Good work. The show's success is because of you. Sylvia, I congratulate you and want to let you personally know the studio has agreed to your personnel request. What I can publicly tell all assembled here is that Finn Varga has signed a contract for the remainder of the season. We've gotten a full order of 22 episodes.

"As for the bad news, the show is being sued. The death of Kayla and John were fully investigated and deemed an accident. One of the families filed a wrongful death lawsuit. This will take time and money to fight, but we will win. You are all to say nothing to anyone, post nothing to any social media site about the case. Absolute silence about this matter is what I expect from the *Ghost House* family. Clear?

"Tomorrow the lawyers will come. I expect everyone to take this seriously and fully cooperate."

I barely heard what Mr. Seacrest said. While he spoke, anger had gradually become my dominant emotion. Thinking through what had happened with Jade in the barn, it felt like a set up. I'd been set up.

Mr. Seacrest was the only one who could've done it.

Chapter Thirty-Eight

I had enough self-awareness to know if I stayed one more minute in that man's presence I was going to lose it.

"Everything's fine. Okay? I'll be back," I said to Jade, who was pretty much tuned out.

I scooted along the back of the crowd until I let myself out the front door and into the fresh, late September night air. I wanted peace to work through what had happened. No such luck. Maggie was sitting on one of the porch swings.

"You know, I'm not as bad as you think. I need to protect my family and the Families," she said to me from the dark.

"I've learned enough to know when anyone wants to protect the Families, that's probably going to be at my expense."

"Anna, ever since you showed up in my bar, I've been paying attention. Of course I knew about the death of the other dreamers. But not you? There are other things I know, things that should've taken you down and haven't. I came here to see for myself."

And then I saw the truth. "You're the one who set me up tonight," I accused, appalled. "Why?"

"To test you," she said, unapologetically.

"You almost killed my friend! I..." I stopped. Every name I wanted to call her, everything I wanted to do to her, wouldn't change a thing. She would have more ammunition against me and the damage was already done. The only positive I could see was that now I definitely knew she couldn't be trusted.

"No one was injured," she said with disdain, as if I was making a big deal out of nothing.

"You are wrong," I said in exasperation, done with her.

As I turned to walk away, she said to my back, "Don't you want to know if you passed?"

I was proud of myself that I didn't give her the satisfaction of a response. She was her mother's daughter. She thought she could toy with me and Jade, risking his life and sanity with no consequences. She was mistaken.

If Maggie was going to say anything else, she was cut off by the mass exodus of cast and crew from the manor. I pushed past the flow, finding Jade where I'd left him.

"We're due back on set in 30 minutes," he told me somewhat numbly. "Supposed to go to hair and make-up first."

"Hey, you okay?" Adam came up to us.

"I can't even begin to answer that," I said to him.

"I look forward to hearing all about it," he said too brightly, putting his arm around me. He added under his breath, "You're almost glowing. You need to get out of sight."

"He's in on this too?" Jade asked, trying to keep his voice even and cool.

"Let's go downstairs," I suggested.

We deposited Jade at hair and make-up and I pulled Adam down the hall, explaining what the last 30 minutes were like. I was glad he took my side, cursing his sister.

"Uncle is going to be royally pissed. He does not want you messed with. What gives her the right?"

I'd thought he was going to try to calm me down, but I was the one who had to breathe reason into him, and I had short supply.

"Now I'm really screwed with Jade. I've got to explain this to him somehow, but I don't know what, or how much of the truth, to tell. Too bad I can't erase his memories."

"Unfortunate, but we'll figure it out," Adam said, trying to shake off his anger.

"And tonight, after the shoot, I'm not hanging him out to dry."

"You can't go back to the barn. It's not safe."

"It is. I saw it in Maggie. She'll put the protection back up now her experiment is over. I'm sorry, Adam, but I don't like your family. They're awful."

"Yeah, I know. But it wasn't always this way."

"And you think it doesn't have to be. I don't know. Maggie seems pretty sick to me. And tricky. Did you know that about her?"

"Not really. Sometimes it's hard to see the ones you love clearly."

Chapter Thirty-Nine

Shooting finally over, I asked Jade to come back when the manor would be quiet. I met him in the entry way, just as Sylvia was leaving.

Sylvia nodded at us with a puzzled expression, but she didn't ask.

"Since they added a 24/7 security detail, and with people coming and going, this place is rarely private. Let's try the library."

"May I ask you something?" he asked, following me.

"Shoot."

"Why do you stay here? Why not move out, or stay with Meg or Lucy? You could get your own place, or even stay with me. Something's not right here," he said as we entered the library.

Adam walked in behind us. He'd gone to the kitchen to get me a glass of water.

"Thanks. I'll see you in a bit," I said as he walked right back out.

I sat down next to Jade. "Let me start by saying I'm sorry."

"For what? As far as I can see, if it weren't for you, I would've been in a lot of trouble," he countered.

Silence fell over both of us as I tried to work out what to say to him. I wanted to give him just enough so he'd know he wasn't insane, but not too much. More than what was necessary would be bad. And I didn't want bad things for him.

"Anna, I don't know what kind of responsibility you feel towards me, but I'm not as torn up as you imagine, I think."

"Why?" I asked honestly. If the situation were reversed, I'd be a puddle on the ground. I *had* been a puddle on the ground.

"You know I'm from here, right?"

"West Tennessee?"

"No," he smiled. "I'm from Martin. Born and raised. My family goes back generations."

I smiled back. But his smile faded as he said, "And we have stories. Family stories."

I tensed. The word "Family" now held a very different meaning for me.

"The woods around this house are pretty familiar to the local kids. Oh man, there was quite a reaction when we heard what the show was about. The woods are legendary for stuff like that."

"Like what exactly?"

"Being haunted. Being dangerous. Everyone knows about the woods. Most who go in come out injured. Or worse."

"What happened to you?" I asked, mesmerized. Why had it never occurred to me to look into local legends beyond the history of the Manor itself?

"Listen. I'm a country boy. It's all talk."

"You don't believe that. Will you tell me what you know?"

"I thought you were supposed to be explaining things to me."

"Please?" I asked, not letting him divert me.

"Did you know my family is connected with the Golds?"

"No. In what way?"

"Way back when, two of my ancestors married into the Gold family."

"Two? Were they twins?" As soon as I asked, I was sorry. That I guessed this served to unsettle him even more.

"That's incredible. Do you know the story, then? But, how could you?" he asked.

"I'm sorry, really. I don't know. Please continue."

"Yeah, well, they were twins and cousins to my second or third great-grandmother, Iris. The three of them were best friends. Well, the story goes they had only been married into that family for a short while and were living at the mansion."

"That's incredible. You are related by blood to the ghosts. The ghost tonight has a twin. They are the twins killed in the massacre."

Jade took a beat, trying to absorb that bombshell. Maybe I'd been too blunt.

"Soon after the Gold family was killed, my great-great-great-grandmother died. Of exposure."

"Exposure? Around here?"

"Every once in a while we get big snows."

"What was she was doing out in the snow?"

"I don't know details. The story is that she was really upset and went over to the house after the massacre. She apparently went into their old bedrooms, looking for something. That part is sketchy."

I interrupted. "Which rooms? Do you know?"

"I think one of the rooms was the one Meg stayed in when she first got here. I can't be sure."

"Sorry. Go on."

"There's not much more. About a half hour later she ran out of the house, through the back, toward the family cemetery and was found dead six days later."

"What else?"

"They said her hands were torn and bloody, as if she'd been digging in the dirt. What was she doing? Was she burying something? Or unearthing something? We'll never know."

"Is there anything else?"

"We don't usually talk about this, but you're obviously a basket case, so I'll let you in on the biggest family secret."

"What is it?" I asked, completely enthralled. He was a man of few words. But when he spoke, wow.

"She was found by an oak tree, and her parents thought it fitting to bury her there. The thing is, no one knows where the grave is anymore. It's like it vanished, tombstone and all."

"What about her husband?"

"She was never married. No one knows who the father of her baby was. You know the South, skeletons in every closet."

"I don't think that's just the South."

"Well, that's our family's deep dark secret," he said, ready to hear mine.

"Let me ask you this. Do you believe in ghosts?" I began.

"No, not really."

"Then what do you think people have seen in the woods? What about people who claim they've seen one? Are they all liars or crazy?"

"I'm not judging anyone else. I believe when you die you either go up or down. There's no hanging around."

"I used to believe that too. But now I know there are things that don't make sense," I said.

"There's no denying that. I think people see stuff, like you and I did tonight, but it's not always what we think. That's all."

"What do you think happened tonight?" I asked, hoping he'd worked out a scenario I could endorse.

"I really couldn't venture a guess, beyond the fact that you can do some unexplainable things."

"And honestly, Jade, I can't explain them. Not even to myself."

"Given what I saw, you have prophetic dreams. You told me I was in danger and then I was. You knew because of a dream. Are you psychic?"

"I don't really know. Maybe? Sometimes?"

"I've at least heard of psychics. Are you a witch?"

"I sure hope not! I really don't like magic," I shivered.

"Then how do you explain what happened?"

"I was thinking about telling you I drugged you and it was all a hallucination."

"Sounds good to me."

"You mind if we go with that for right now? I think we should probably focus on why a Gold Ghost wants you dead."

"You've named it?"

"There are two of them, the twins. The green one and the gold one. Well, sometimes they change color."

"You can call them anything you'd like, but I still don't think they're ghosts."

"Dude, they are what they are," Corey said, walking in with a bag of popcorn. "Want some?" he offered.

"Naw," Jade turned him down, slightly startled. "You know about the … ghosts?"

"Yep," Corey said, taking a chair across from us. I'd thought it might help to bring someone else in to normalize the craziness.

"How many people know?" he asked Corey, but I answered.

"We don't really know. But Adam, Suzanne, Echo, and the two of us, at least," I said. He didn't need a comprehensive list.

"And Meg," Corey added.

"No, not really. She's seen them, but she denies it. She doesn't want to be in the know. She definitely wants to be left out of it," I told Jade. I didn't want him to make the mistake of talking to Meg or hinting about ghosts around her. Not that I thought he would, but it was best to err on the side of caution.

"Oh. Uh, can I opt out? I don't want to know any more."

"You're in luck, then, because there's not much to tell. I've been told to stay away from them because they're unpredictable and highly dangerous, of which we've had firsthand experience," I said.

"I think I'll take Meg's route. You won't need to worry about me. I won't say anything to anyone about any of it."

"Great, man. I think I'm going to bed," Corey said, polishing off his late-night snack.

"Just a sec. Jade, we can't let you go so easily," I said regretfully.

"We can't?" Corey asked, confused.

"No. The ghosts want something from him. They've tried to kill him twice. We let him go, let him ignore it, and they might eventually succeed."

"Sheeze. Sorry, man. Guess you're a member of the team now."

"I think I'd rather go rogue like Meg, though," Jade tested.

And then it hit me. Meg. Team. We weren't making any progress on the ghost problem because we'd been on the defensive. Coming at this from the wrong direction.

At least one of the ghosts was out for Jade. At least one of the ghosts had tried to talk to Meg on several occasions. And we had no team because nobody wanted to deal with the ghosts.

The time for avoidance was over. That was yesterday. I made myself the head of the new task force: we would solve their riddle and win.

"This is the problem. We've been ignoring what they've been saying." I was trying to put into words what I'd just worked out.

"You've talked to them?" Jade asked, shocked.

"Not really. They've talked at us. In riddles. We thought maybe we had some of it figured out, but we may be wrong," I said, thinking of what the green ghost had said about the tomb beneath the ground, about "storm and sea," about me.

"Maybe the riddle means a lot of things," Corey offered.

"Yes," I said, bells going off in my head. "I've got to go. Gotta think. Jade, just please don't say anything about this stuff. Okay?"

"Wasn't planning to," he said, and there was something in his voice and posture that hurt. It was what I'd feared. Our delicate but real friendship had been sacrificed on the altar of the supernatural. I was no longer someone he simply connected with. I was a stranger and unknown. He would trust me because I'd saved his life and he had no options. But I was now at arm's length.

"I'm really sorry about this, Jade. Sorry this happened to you. Is happening."

"It is what it is, whatever it is. Your hair," he said, slightly alarmed.

I still had surplus energy running though me, and I'd let my guard down.

"Oh, yeah. Just add it to the pile of things we can't talk about."

"Sure," he said, getting up to go.

I watched as he left, and sat in silence next to Corey.

"Well, that went well," Corey scoffed, chiding me.

"Shut up," Adam snapped. He'd been there the entire time, hidden.

Corey jumped. "Give me a heart attack, why don't you!"

"Calm down. He was helping me figure Jade out," I said, defending Adam.

"Yeah, well, it's not right the way you two gang up on us. Pretty soon you're gonna find yourselves alone. Just the way you like it," he snapped.

"That was really mean," I said, hurt. "Is that how you feel?"

"I don't like being tricked," he said, not answering the question.

I asked again. "But is that how you feel?"

"Sometimes. Like a lab experiment. I wish you'd just chill out. Be you again, instead of a human lie detector. I mean, really."

"Yeah, me too," I said sincerely. I wished I were normal.

"And on the other hand, she should be pretty proud of herself for saving Jade. How do you think Anna accomplished that? By sitting back and being normal? Should she just say 'to hell with it all' and go back to regular life? You know what would happen to her? How long do you think she'd last? How long do you think you would've lasted if she'd given up?" Adam rebuked.

"That's enough," I said to Adam. "Now we all feel awful. And I didn't use my superpowers to ferret that out."

Corey set his empty bag of popcorn down and gave me one of his great big hugs. "I'm sorry, A. Really am."

"It's okay," I said into his chest.

He let go and walked off in the direction of the kitchen.

"Could he be Fourth or from one of the other families?" I asked Adam, incredulous, my thoughts back to Jade.

"I don't think so. I get nothing off him."

"Good," I said, slightly relaxing. "You think Jade's just plain old human?"

"Probably. But I think you're right. We haven't given thought to the ghosts themselves."

"Why is that? Especially with Mr. Seacrest and all his years and wisdom."

"I've always been told you leave them alone or run from those buggers. No use to stay and fight or try to reason with them."

"Then why are we still here? Living in a haunted house?"

"They are like sirens. In other words, if you know how to stay clear, you can go about your business. We have reasons to stay."

"Why are you here? Why did you want to be on this show?"

I had wondered this before. Why would he choose a life in the spotlight?

"I don't know."

"I mean, aren't you putting a target on your back?"

"It's a sort of reverse psychology. Anyway, there are billions of people in the world, and proportionately, just a few of us."

"Okay, so why?"

"What about you?" he asked, turning the tables, not wanting to answer. "Not vanity," he answered for me.

"I love it. I love acting. I love telling stories. It's the best job on earth. I get to lose myself and find myself at the same moment. I get to be surprised by myself and others. Constantly."

"Ditto," he said, smiling at me. "I believe Echo told you why *F&L* was formed? As a kind of 'timeout' for me? I'd been out of the fight for a year when I met Meg. She told me about her new show and I was drawn to the project. Guess I know why now."

"But with all the real drama, you think it's worth staying?" I asked, my stomach fluttering. He was looking at me the way he sometimes did. Piercing and intimate.

"Anna, there is much more going on here than shooting this show. The stars are lining up in a big fat row. For better or for worse, we are here."

"I guess, today at least, it was for the better. Without us here, Jade might have been another casualty of the ghosts. But then there's the Butterfly effect. Who knows what would've been if we'd never met, dragging mounds of baggage to this very small town?"

Corey walked back in with a plate of cold spaghetti, Suzanne with him. "So what's the plan? Do we focus on the ghosts? Or Emma and why she'd want to kill Anna? Or Finn and if he has some ulterior motive for being here? Or, heaven forbid, the production schedule. You look at that bad boy? Something's up with Sylvia. I mean more than usual."

"Now we've got to worry about your sister too," I said, looking at Adam.

Corey spoke with his mouth full. "What did she do?"

"Oh, you know. Same old story. Nearly caused my death."

"She wasn't trying to kill you," Adam said, defending her.

"She could've. She didn't know what was going to happen."

"Doesn't sound like Maggie's style," Suzanne chimed in on Adam's side.

"No, Anna. We are not ganging up on you about my sister. We just know her," Adam reasoned.

"And I don't mean to be insensitive, but maybe she's changed. It's possible. Does it sound like her to sacrifice an innocent bystander – Jade in this scenario – for information? Just to see what I could do?"

"She did what?" Suzanne shrieked.

"Yep, Maggie was the one who intentionally let the ghost into the barn."

"But how did she know the ghost would attack?" Corey asked.

"Mr. Seacrest told her what she'd planned was successful, if my dream predicted the future. I really hate time paradoxes."

"So what did happen tonight?" Corey asked.

"Maggie took down the barn wards and the gold ghost almost got Jade. And it's not that I didn't trust Mr. Seacrest's plan, I just wanted a plan B. Just in case. I got Jade out, but not before he saw the ghost and that I can do things I shouldn't be able to do."

"What did you do?" Corey asked, Suzanne swatting his leg. "What?"

"She'll tell us if she wants to," Suzanne chided.

"It's not that I don't want to, it's that I don't understand, myself," I said, looking for understanding but meeting a disappointed Corey.

"Yeah, sure, I get it," Corey said, standing up. "Off to bed. I've got a six a.m. call. And I know it's not just me."

Chapter Forty

We all had early calls, despite more uncertainty and drama.

Corey veered off to his bedroom on the second floor and I followed.

"Hey, I'm not ready for the others to know yet, but I got Jade out of the barn the same way I took you out of the restaurant."

"No way!"

"Yeah. But because I was under pressure, I overshot and consumed a big ball of it. We ended up at Huntington Beach," I said, pulling a few grains of sand from my pocket as evidence.

"That's completely insane," Corey whispered, feeling the weight of the secret I was sharing. "How is that possible?"

"How is any of it? Curses, centuries-old people with powers? All of it's nuts. I feel like, maybe, after today... after saving Jade, I might be ready to accept it."

"I thought you had. You seem so at home with it all, with him," Corey said, running his hand along the door frame.

"Partly, I guess. I've just wanted someone to make sense of the world for me. Tell me exactly what's going on and the reason for it. Like, the scientific reason. But no one can answer or is interested in those questions. At first it was maddening, all the uncertainty. But now I think no one knows the answers. The reason Mr. Seacrest hasn't explained what's going on with me is because he doesn't have a clue. It's not because he's keeping secrets."

"Sure he is."

"I know that, but not about this. Not about me. I think he can help me, but he can't lay it all out because he's never encountered someone like me."

"I always knew you were special," he said.

I laughed, but he didn't. Some of the feelings he'd had for me in the past were on the surface, breaking through.

"I want to be unique, but in a normal human way. Not this freak of nature way. But I am what I am."

"At least you're not part-killer like my Fourth ancestors."

"And you didn't need any of them to figure out how to be you and be in control. You're such a natural. I envy your ease. You are so consistent."

"Is that a compliment? Because I thought girls like mystery and adventure, not consistency. I gotta work on that," he laughed.

"Stop that. I like you just the way you are."

"Not enough," he said, peeling his eyes off the woodwork, straightening up and looking me dead on.

"I thought we were past this. You're with Suzanne now."

"Because you're with Adam," he answered honestly.

"That's not nice, treating her like a place holder."

"And what about her? You see how she looks at Finn?"

"She doesn't."

"Exactly. She can't even look at him. She's still in love with the bastard. What's wrong with me, Anna? Why do girls look at me and decide I'm not enough? Why am I not enough for anyone?"

"You are so wrong!" I shouted at him. "You are one of the best people I know. You're on the very short list of people I love and care about. You are more than enough. Anyone who doesn't see that is an idiot."

"Yourself included?"

"Nope. I see you, Corey. I see how great you are and I love you fiercely. I just don't love you in the way you want, or wanted. I don't know if you want to hear it, but it's the truth. As far as I'm concerned, you're my family. My forever brother, and I will love you until I die. Someday the right person will see you, and she will be lucky, and I will be jealous, and I hope to heaven I like her. The real problem will be finding someone who's good enough for you."

I went to bed thinking about how much I loved Corey and how sad I was to disappoint him. I wanted all good things for him, but I couldn't love him like he desired.

I drifted off thinking of the men I loved, happy. Despite all the craziness in the world, I was lucky to have so much love in my life.

Chapter Forty-One

My good mood was ruined when I opened my eyes in my dreamscape, finding myself in the throne room at Crimson Hall. Mr. Seacrest was seated on the highest throne, which struck me as both odd and important, though I wasn't sure why.

"Come, have a seat. We need to talk."

I took a seat at his right. "Is it just the two of us tonight? Is Adam coming?"

"I think you and I have a few issues to work through. It's time to tell me what you've been holding back."

I felt out to test what was really going on. Was I about to be ambushed? Was he setting me up, or did he want a genuine heart-to-heart?

Whenever I was with Mr. Seacrest, there were always questions of sincerity and authenticity swirling about him. I trusted him – to an extent.

"I'm not sure what you're referring to," I replied doubtfully.

"Ah, you mean which one of your many secrets am I asking for?"

"Don't you deal in knowledge and secrets? Let's not pretend with each other."

"Yes, my dear, but I'm not here to fight or best you. Let's start another way. Let me show you why I've brought you here. Will you come with me?"

He got up from the throne and crossed to the other side of the room. "Come, follow me."

I walked behind him as we made a full perimeter sweep of the room. I wondered if he was looking for something, but he wasn't. We made two more loops. On the fourth, I began to feel anxious. Halfway through the loop, we were directly behind the queen's throne. Mr. Seacrest bent down and pressed a stone in the floor, exposing a hidden door in the wall.

"This way."

I followed him into the dark, my curiosity piqued. I bumped into him occasionally as the path twisted and sloped.

Eventually he came to a stop. "This is a secret, Anna. Few know this exists, and only a handful know of its location. I'm trusting you to keep this secret and to do as you're told."

"Okay."

"This place will hold you to your word," he warned.

I heard him fumbling in his pocket, a moment later light appeared as he struck a match. We were in the underbelly of Crimson Hall, which housed his library. The library of the First and Second.

It was not what I'd expected. First off, it was an enormous underground cave with stone pillars, as beautiful as any natural wonder of the world. Second, this was no mere library. Along with books, it housed endless rows of art.

"I have no words. This place is amazing. I wonder if the castle was built here originally because of this cave."

"It was, we believe. This place is unique, with unique properties."

"Such as?" I asked, gawking at the vast art and artifact collection.

"The only way in or out is the way we came, even in the dreamscape."

I wondered if that were true. Maybe I'd test his theory.

"Even you can't get in. And though I'm sure that sounds like a nice fat challenge, it is not. Unwelcomed visitors have died upon trying to break-in. Every time."

"Oh. Good to know." Maybe that's why Adam was never willing to sneak into this fortress. Not worth the risk. "But I thought museums and libraries were for general learning and improvement. Isn't it kind of mean to have all these books and works of art, and hoard them?"

"It would be cruel to unleash most of what's in here on the world. We find tainted artifacts and bring them here."

"If they're dangerous, why not get rid of them?"

"Sometimes we do, but many poisoned objects don't work that way. To destroy the case in which they are contained is simply to set them free. It's what they want."

"You mean this comb wants something?" I laughed, pointing at a beautiful silver comb, brush, and hand mirror set lying on top of a mahogany vanity.

"Anna, don't touch anything here!" he commanded. "Yes, you picked it out. It's not the brush or mirror, but the comb. Just one pass through your hair and you'd be mad."

I dropped my hand, but couldn't deny I had a strong desire to use it. Wouldn't that feel so good right now? I could imagine the pleasure of the comb running along my scalp and pulling it through my hair

"Anna! Stop looking at it," he snapped

"Trippy," I said, shaking my head. "Uh, why are we here? Why did you bring me here?"

"Think of it as a gesture of good faith. My olive branch to you. I know, given the past, you're not sure whether you can trust me, even though I've pledged myself to you. I am your best bet."

He followed as I wandered through the stacks. Turning a corner I stopped, startled. One entire bookshelf was on fire. My first instinct was to call out, alert Mr. Seacrest, but then I looked again. The fire burned and burned, as if on repeat, but it wasn't spreading. The books were charred and ruined, but not disintegrating.

"That is why you shouldn't act in anger," Mr. Seacrest said, hand on my shoulder.

"You did this?"

"Too many years ago. But what is done is done, and the consequences continue. There lies the prophecy about you," he said, wistfully. "A Fifth born from Second and Third. In my rage and sorrow, a lifetime ago, I did this, and it cannot be undone. Whatever was gathered is lost. There is no help there, but I am committed, Anna, to you."

I thought for a moment, hoping it was true, that I could trust him. And then a question popped into my head. "Do you have a book called *Dream Killers*?"

Mr. Seacrest was surprised. His titles weren't common knowledge.

"I do. Why do you ask?"

"When Adam was attacked, last year, I found an old book that looks like it would be at home here. But the really weird thing was, when I asked Adam about it, he didn't know what I was talking about and it wasn't in his bag anymore."

Mr. Seacrest turned pensive and walked off to find the volume. He returned empty-handed.

"It's not here. He didn't have permission to remove it."

"It wasn't Adam. He was genuinely confused."

"Let's hope he's a good liar. Because if he's not, things are much worse than I'd imagined."

"I don't suppose you're going to explain that to me."

"Suffice it to say, let's be on the same team."

In a rare moment of utter honesty with him I laid out my worry. "I'm afraid I will say something that I don't understand the meaning or significance of, and you'll take it as a sign of your sworn mission, and you'll kill me. Like you tried to before. You have no idea how much I want to trust you. I really do. But I know your first allegiance is to your mission, and if you decide I need to die to achieve it, you'll kill me or order me killed."

"I won't pretend. You're right. But this extends beyond you. I am willing to give my own life if it means the destruction of the Fourth. I will do what it takes."

"And I won't. I mean, there are some prices too high. I think we have different ideas as to what's okay to do to achieve a good goal."

"You are right again."

"How can I trust you?"

"We do have the same goal, right?"

"Yes."

"And is this a cause you are willing to die for?"

"No. I won't die for an ideology. But, I would give my life to save others."

"Yes. We agree there, I think it's just a matter of semantics. Even I, jaded and old and worn thin by this work, see what it's for. The final goal. It's to save the lives of innocent people."

"How about this? I will tell you everything, if you are completely present, unveiled. You have to let me probe what you're thinking, how you're taking what I'm saying."

"No," he said flatly, ending the discussion. "Follow me." He blew out the lantern he'd lit.

I knew I'd offended him, just like I often offended Adam. Come to think of it, I also offended Maggie. It was them! They wanted me to capitulate. Do whatever they wanted on their terms, with no regard for my own mind and desires.

To hell with them ordering me around!

We ascended the winding path, emerging through a doorway. I expected to be back in the throne room, but we weren't. We were in the training cave where we regularly met, our chairs waiting for us.

"I thought there was only one way out?" I asked, confused.

He decided not to answer my question. "Take a seat, please," he said gruffly, pacing. "You are extremely frustrating and perplexing, Anna Rose Ellingwood. You expect to be treated as a peer when you are not. You want from me what no one has ever dared to ask. It's highly improper."

"And I've never been held at the edge of a knife before I met you. But since I met you, it's happened plenty of times. I am asking for transparency. That's all. If you want me to trust you, you need to show me. It's the only way I see forward."

"You ask the impossible. Be careful. I'm on your side, for now."

"Exactly! There you go, threatening me! When will you learn that if you want to work with me - if you want me to really tell you what I know, what I can do, what I see - I've got to trust you? You will not get me with threats. I'd just as soon take my chances without you."

"Then you'd die. You'd already be dead."

"So be it," I said, resolved.

Mr. Seacrest sat down, deep in thought. And then I felt it. The shield he held around him, keeping me and others like me at bay, was down.

"I do not like being pushed around."

"Same here," I said.

"But since I am on your side, and given our past, I think your request, while highly disrespectful, is reasonable. It's your turn."

It really seemed he was being genuine. I didn't feel I was being tricked. And while I knew he was making this concession because he wanted my secrets, he wanted them not simply for power's sake. His ultimate goal was to rid the world of those associated with the curse.

I laid it all out, starting with Jade, the ghost, and how I'd saved him. Mr. Seacrest produced pen and paper, writing it all down. He explained that taking notes would help him remember details when he awoke. I told him about my energy experiments and about the time I'd turned watery in the field after being chased by the homicidal Fourth. On and on, giving him everything I could think of, all the parts of the story we'd kept from him, even things that seemed small, like the appearance of Andrew.

"I am aware of Andrew," Mr. Seacrest said with a deep admiration. I could tell he hadn't heard of his change.

"Well I don't know anything about Andrew. But I do know that he is not what he once was. He's changed."

Of all the things I told him, this bit of information threw him.

"Impossible," he muttered.

"I don't have anything else to add there. But lastly, I think we actually made progress when it comes to the Gold Ghosts."

"Tell me."

"We have a lead. Apparently one of Jade's ancestors was related and best friends with the Gold twins. She died on the manor property shortly after they did. According to the stories Jade grew up with, his great-great-great-grandmother went looking for something of theirs or she had it. We plan to investigate. And, um, she was buried beneath the tree where she was found dead. I can't help but feel that is the tree I've been dreaming of in the reoccurring nightmare of Emma.

"And that's it, I think. At least that's all I can think of right now."

"You've given me much to consider. I'm going to wake and record."

"That's it? What do you think? Any insights?"

"What do you feel coming from me?"

"You seem really unsure. It's like you weren't expecting what I gave you and don't know what to make of it."

"Precisely."

"So I laid myself bare for nothing?"

"Sometimes, when solving a puzzle, you have to look at the pieces for a long while until the solution becomes apparent."

"Will you tell me when you figure it out?" I asked, his barrier still down.

He looked at me, deciding if he should tell the truth.

"The best I can honestly say is, it depends. I deal in information and secrets, as you know. I hold many secrets and covenants. You are not my only concern. I am bound to others. But you, this, is my primary responsibility. I will do what I can."

"Please do," I implored, feeling exhausted and mildly defeated. I hadn't accounted for all that he knew and undoubtedly had promised others.

"Let me give you a piece of information. In my long years, as far as I know, we have never tried to engage with ghosts. We've had little interaction with them, and when we did try to fight them, we've lost. They've been deemed toxic. We drill that into all our people. But you were not raised like us. You are free, able to see creatively, in a way we are not. It's true you miss much because you don't understand the structure of the Families, but you also have a fresh perspective. For example, all of us working with the Fourth on set. I have to believe that has not turned into a war due to your influence."

"It's not just me. I don't think people my age think in terms of enemies and allies being ethnic. It's about choice."

"Maybe, but that's a dangerous way to live. When you give someone the benefit of the doubt, you also give them a chance to stab you first. And the most vicious are not the young, but those who were there that day hundreds of years ago."

"Like yourself?"

"Yes. We are unnaturally strong and live a life of torment. Every time I close my eyes in sleep, I see the massacre. It's fresh. It always will be. Don't underestimate the effect that has on us."

Mr. Seacrest left me in the training room. Though I worried about giving him so much of myself, I also felt free. I was working on putting the pieces of the puzzle together, too. Which one of us would see it first?

Chapter Forty-Two

I awoke with a twofold mission: I had to figure out Jade's connection with the ghosts and what Emma wanted from me.

Summing up the mission to myself, I was struck with an epiphany: the Jade problem was the Emma problem.

They were two sides of the same coin.

I knew, *knew*, if I pulled on one side of the knot the other side would unravel as well.

Chapter Forty-Three

Sylvia had stepped up the production schedule, leaving no time for a team meeting. It just about killed me, having this new knowledge and not being able to act on it. Instead, I had to act in front of a camera.

I was filming tennis scenes, and the guys were out in the caves. I wasn't really surprised to learn our off-camera tennis coach, Maggie, had to leave town suddenly. I was surprised to see Andrew was taking her place, albeit temporarily.

"Wow. I must really be out of it. I didn't even know you were in town," I blurted out. He was helping Meg with her swing.

"I arrived last night. Seems a lot was going on around here, so I'm not surprised you didn't hear."

His cryptic response made me wonder if he knew what had happened.

"Can we talk later? I … saw one last night. In my room," Meg leaned in and whispered.

"A ghost?" Andrew spat, angry and way too loud.

"Not here," I said, looking at him hard, trying to bore holes into his skull with my eyes.

"He knows?" Meg asked, stunned and clearly still shaken from whatever had transpired last night.

"Not here, okay?" I said to her much more gently. "We'll take care of it."

"'Cause I didn't sign up for this, Anna. I can't take it. It's constant! I thought if I moved out of the manor I could get away from it, but it didn't work."

"I promise, as soon as we get a break we'll talk. But please don't talk to anyone else about this."

"Why? Everyone else seems to know."

"No, not really. Just disregard Andrew on this," I said to comfort her, which pissed him off. I didn't know I'd be doing so much personality management at seven in the morning!

"Little one, don't speak to me that way."

"Listen, Andrew. I'm not trying to be disrespectful, but it seems you only have one concern, and here she comes," I said as we all turned to see Katie walking through the grass, innocently twirling her racket. "So please, keep this stuff on the down low, okay Mr. Temper?"

As Katie got closer, she saw us all staring at her and she smiled wide. Her presence was like a drug for Andrew. He instantly relaxed and smiled right back at her.

"I'm sorry, ladies. I will do a better job of containing myself. I will not be a problem," he said, walking off in Katie's direction.

We both watched as Andrew greeted Katie with a slight bow of his head. Something had changed between the two of them. They were starting to own their intense feelings for each other.

"I wish someone would look at me like that," Meg sighed. Before I could even respond, she said, "Oh, no you don't. I don't want a love pep-talk from you. You're worse than they are! And besides, I already know. I'm a great catch and someday I will find the right guy. So there," she teased, sticking her tongue out at me.

"You don't need a guy anyway, right?" I encouraged.

"I certainly don't. But who's to say I don't have one?"

"What?" I asked, all curiosity.

"Dom. We're kinda back together."

"After the way he treated you? I'm shocked!"

"Yeah, well, nobody's perfect. Anyway, it's not serious. I'm just giving him another chance."

I wanted to be happy for Meg, but I knew this was a bad move. There was something wrong with Dom. I didn't care that no one else saw it, that I didn't have any evidence beyond how he'd reacted when Emma got hurt and my *extremely* accurate feelings.

It was a grueling eighteen hours on set. Sylvia had gone insane. I mean, Meg had days like this, but not the rest of us. I sat with Lucy as we waited for our afternoon barn shoot and she gave me her latest theory.

"It's like she finally did the math or something. Yeah, I mean, it costs to bring on more boom operators and such, having more equipment here, but if we can get more done at a faster pace, she'll save in the end. She's so tight. Ever meet anyone so tight?"

I knew she wasn't really asking, but I responded anyway. "My dad doesn't like to depart with money."

"Oh, well, anyway, I'm glad to speed this process along."

"Really? Why? I thought you liked working on *Ghost House*."

"You know I do. No, I'm not talking about that. I have other opportunities. If we can wrap the season earlier than expected, that really works with my plans."

"Are we wrapping early?"

"Why else would she bring more crew in? No, I'm sure of it. I bet we'll be done by end of January. Mid-February at the latest. Why are you smiling like a fool?"

I felt it all over my face. This conversation with Lucy, who I was really growing to dislike, was great! Lucy was the easiest person I interacted with on a regular basis. She was an open book – simple, no hidden agenda. My brain didn't have to do any work. Lucy was always on point; everything she did was selfish. All her actions, her choices, her maneuvers; there was no questioning her motives. She was all about personal advancement, all else be damned. She was my anti-role model. And I was thankful.

"Oh, it's nothing. I was just thinking about Adam," I lied.

I lied. Easily.

Lucy had gone back to her world, and I was left with a mini crisis of my own. Was this who I was now? A liar?

But what was I supposed to say? If I'd told her the truth, it would've been rude. And besides, I'm not at liberty to explain what I really meant anyway, I rationalized.

"Is this what it's come to?" I whispered. "Lying to others and myself?"

For the rest of the day I felt low, knocked down a peg. I didn't like Lucy and what she was all about, but at least she was consistent. For as long as I could remember, my mom and dad had talked about being a person of integrity. Someone with integrity chooses virtue, regardless of what others are doing or choosing. Integrity is a choice, a daily choice. The hardest. And sometimes the loneliest. But who was I if I couldn't trust myself?

Around ten p.m. I finally had a break so I called my dad. I knew if I told Adam or anyone else how I was feeling, they'd tell me not to be so hard on myself. But what good would that do?

I told him about my conversation with Lucy, then got to what was bothering me. "So I lied to her. And then I felt like a fraud. I mean, Lucy's a snake, but I want to be something more." There was silence on the other end. "Dad?"

"Why did you lie?"

"That's just it. I don't know why."

"Come on, dear, you know why. Honest people don't usually lie for no reason. Is there more to the story?"

"No," I said sheepishly.

"Then I think you already know the answer. And frankly, Anna, I'm shocked."

"But you have no idea how hard it is! There is so much I can't say to most people. One thing to this person and something entirely different to someone else. It's frustrating!"

"That is precisely why honesty is the best policy."

"But I can't be honest."

"That's not true and you know it. You can always tell the truth or remain silent. Don't delude yourself into thinking you must lie. There are other viable options."

"It's getting unmanageable! I can't do it!"

"Yes you can, honey. You've been doing it since you were little."

"I have?" I asked in confusion.

"Your eyes. You had to keep them a secret and you managed to do it without lying."

"Yeah, but this is now *so* much more involved."

"Life is hard. I am confident you can navigate these waters with grace. Do you think your mother and I would have sent you off with the Hollywood wolves if we didn't have full confidence in your abilities?"

"But I feel like I'm always screwing things up!"

"Welcome to the human condition. We all struggle, we all fall. But we can succeed. The amazing part of life is we get to choose to get it together and pull ourselves up again. But, Anna, you know this; this is your life. No one else's."

"Yes, Dad." Here it came. Dad never got tired of his "You're an individual" speech.

"You're an individual, Anna. You decide what kind of person you're going to be. That doesn't change just because you're involved in a high stakes supernatural world. You're still a person, and at the end of the day, you have to decide who that person is going to be."

"I want to be a person of integrity. But it's hard."

"Of course it's hard. Why would it be easy? Why would it not be painful and cost you? If that is what you really want, act like it."

"But sometimes I don't even know how. I don't know what to do."

"You are always welcome to ask me if you have any questions. Is there anyone there you can talk to? I mean an adult."

I didn't know why he popped into my head, especially considering his bad behavior towards Adam, but Andrew came to mind. He was clearly a broken man, but he still seemed full of wisdom. He also came with the bonus of knowing about the Families, but not caring about them.

"I think there is someone."

"Good."

Talking to my dad almost always made me feel better. And because I wasn't such a bad person I actually thought to ask him about how things were with him. Since I'd been back on set, our contact had slowed to random texts back and forth every few days.

I was sad to find out he'd been dating. No one person in particular, but he was looking around. His wife had not been dead a year, and he was dating.

"Happy for you, Dad. Kinda," I added, working on being honest.

"I know, honey. I'm conflicted too. No one will ever replace your mom. I'm trying to move on, but I don't know if I can."

"Me neither," I mumbled, trying not to blubber and mess up my make-up. "Thanks, Dad. Thanks for listening to me. I've got to go. Talk to you soon."

Chapter Forty-Four

I'd thought a lot about what my dad said. Mr. Seacrest had his way of getting things done, but I disagreed with his methods. However we solved the problems facing us, I wasn't going to win the war only to lose myself in the process.

It had been a few days since I'd had my revelation about Jade and Emma being connected before we were all able to find an extended time to gather. We found an opening in the middle of the day with the house completely empty.

We had the house because the crew, including Sylvia, had been called away to an event in Memphis for two full days. This was the reason for the extra crew. Sylvia and her team had been requested by Teen TV to shoot a civil rights documentary-ish special for Black History Month. She had agreed, but asked for extra help to make up for the time lost on set. Per usual, she got the better end of the deal. We'd had insane hours for weeks, all of us, just so this two-day hiatus wouldn't interfere with her production schedule.

The gang assembled: Adam, Echo, Suzanne, Corey, and me. I toyed with asking Jade to come, but we agreed it was better to keep him in the dark for as long as possible. I actually gathered up the courage to ask Andrew to join us.

He was surprised by the offer. He returned the surprise by saying he wasn't interested.

When I asked him to come to the meeting, what I was really asking was for him to be part of my inner circle. I took his refusal personally. I hadn't really considered he'd say no.

Adam was the only one I'd shared my epiphany with. He didn't see the connection between Jade and Emma, but deferred to me. Since Adam didn't see the connection, I'd delayed this meeting and spent most of my free time thinking about what I felt, and how to put it into words so others would see it too.

I puzzled, for the millionth time, through the various encounters with the ghosts; what they'd said and done. What was it about Meg? Why had they shown us the cave of Samuel Perry, the Third who was my father? This last point I didn't feel at liberty to bring up. Samuel as my biological father was still a guarded secret, and I didn't want to help anyone else make that connection.

"Okay," I began the meeting. "I've got something to tell you, but I need you to keep an open mind. In fact, I want you to be so open, you just pretend to believe what I've got to say. I know it's going to sound crazy and all but, well ...."

This was not going well. I was rambling. I closed my eyes and took a breath. When I opened them, I saw nothing but openness looking back at me.

"What's going on with Jade and what happened with Emma is related," I rushed, expecting one or all to shut me down, or at the very least shake their heads in unanimous skepticism. I got nothing of the sort. Only curiosity.

"So Jade, I know you heard about his great-grandmother and her friendship with the Gold twins and that she was buried on the property under a tree that is now missing. Okay, so there's that. Then there's Emma. She'd been invading my dreams. Those reoccurring nightmares, somehow she'd gotten in my head. She was trying to kill me."

"But she didn't," said Corey, thinking back to the horror on the plane.

"No. And I didn't say anything at the time, but she's dead."

"We haven't been able to confirm her whereabouts. I just got an updated report. She supposedly went home to Italy. Not surprisingly, the address was bogus," Echo reported.

"Trust me on this one. It was going to be me or her. I saw it only at the very end. Her plan was to take over my body. Possesses it. Unfortunately for her, she didn't know what I am or what I could do. She was utterly surprised I bested her. It never entered her mind she wouldn't win."

"She wanted your body? For what reason?" Suzanne asked.

"That I don't know, but it has to be tied to the Families. The main clue is the krim. How would she know about krims? Know to use that imagery? And there's the tree. I've been buried so many times under that tree. How can it be just coincidence, the tree in my dream *and* Jade's relative, who died a mysterious death, being buried under a tree in this forest, the location of which has been entirely lost!"

"Leaving Jade aside, as to the krim, I don't know if it was only imagery. Krims are mysterious weapons, used for many purposes depending on how they are spelled," Echo said.

"Spelled? Like by a witch?" I said, disgusted.

"What's up with you and witches?" Suzanne asked, a little bit offended.

Adam brought us back to the topic on hand before we got sidetracked. "The point is, Anna thinks when Emma was unsuccessful in taking over Anna's body, whatever Emma was using to do that backfired and killed her."

"I know she's dead. I was there. And the more I thought about her and the dream, trying to figure out what she wanted, the more frustrated I became. I mean, the dream took place in the Manor woods, but what else? And then Jade told me about his great-great-grandmother. That she was buried in the woods. The same woods in the dream and where the Gold Ghosts roam. His great-gran went to the house, maybe to get something, and then died. She was best friends with the twins when they were alive. Her burial in the woods, the location forgotten. Emma in the woods, me being buried."

I stopped. They were all looking at me, trying to see what I was putting together.

"Adam, I found one other key piece. When I awoke from my dreams, I always wondered why I allowed myself to be buried. Why didn't I fight back? Why didn't I claw my way to the surface? And that's the missing piece. I felt it, in my hand. I was holding on to something so important that I couldn't lose it. In the dream, thinking back, focusing, I can remember the feeling of utter terror if I let it go. I had it. I had found it and I couldn't give it up."

My crew were on the edge of their seats.

"What was it?" Corey asked.

I shook my head. "I have no idea. But whatever it is, Jade's great-great-grandma had it, and Emma died for it. And Emma knew about krims, so it's a pretty safe assumption that it's Family business."

"I think maybe it's time to have a serious conversation with Dom," Adam said.

"No. And I've really thought about this. He's bugged me from the beginning, but only me. Why is that? I think if we come at him directly, we won't get what we want."

"You misunderstand me. I mean it's time to take Dom out," Adam said gravely.

"Oh," I said, sitting down, feeling his anger. Talk about a misunderstanding! Adam was seriously considering killing Dom, and not in a hyperbole kind of way.

"No, you're right, Anna. He claims to be Emma's brother. And from the start you haven't trusted him. That almost cost your life. They must be in this together. He will pay for his part in the attack."

This was getting out of hand. I had brought everyone here to form a plan, not go on a witch hunt. But the others fell in line behind Adam. Not just Suzanne and Echo, but Corey too. Corey wanted to cause Dom pain.

"Not you too," I pleaded with him.

"You didn't see what I saw, A. You were in and out of consciousness for hours, blood and … I almost saw you die. You don't know how close you were, or what I vowed to do if I ever got my hands on the bastards who did that to you. I guess it's payback time."

"No!" I yelled at him. "Stop it! This is not how civilized people deal with problems."

"You just don't get it. Some people can't be reasoned with," Suzanne sneered.

"Hey! Don't talk down to me! I was the one attacked. Me, not you. I'm the one who's been hunted in my dreams for months. In the day I deal with my mom's death and at night I'm taken against my will to a nightmare puzzle. So back off. I'm telling you right now what we're going to do. We are, all

329

of us, going to work on the new puzzle before us. None of you will touch Dom. You guys will continue to be buddies. And we will plan."

"I don't mean to be obtuse, but I don't understand what you want us to do," Echo said.

"We are going to use the power of observation to figure out what's right in front of us. Now that we suspect Dom is up to no good, he can be watched. We won't rush to anything for the same reason you didn't take off Finn's head on sight - we don't know what Dom is part of. And until we do, we'd be wise to be careful. We don't want to bring this house of cards down. So, please, let's pull ourselves together and pay attention. Let's see if we can find out more about the ghosts and Jade's great-gran. Let's see what the Family can tell us about Emma, following that trail. Okay?"

Corey nodded at me, but Suzanne and Echo looked to their leader for direction.

"Fine, Anna. But he deserves what he's got coming to him," Adam consented.

"Maybe so, maybe not. I don't believe in guilt by association."

"All things being equal, your approach sounds sane. But the moment he threatens you, he's gone. Understand?" Adam wanted to make his stance clear.

"Can't we at least hope for a peaceful resolution?" I asked, looking at the grave eyes on me.

"There is peace only in death," Suzanne said, concluding our meeting.

Chapter Forty-Five

I'd thought that when Sylvia returned from her stint in Memphis the pacing of the shoot would return to normal. No such luck.

When I complained to Meg, she said, "Welcome to my world. This is how it always is for me. You're just noticing it now because, well, this season isn't just about me. The writers have really filled out the other characters and you're not such a zombie – uh, no offense."

"None taken. I guess you're right. When I'm not filming, I'm learning lines, rehearsing, being fitted or something. I had a lot more free time last year."

"Enjoy it while you can. In our line of work you never know when you'll be in demand or a has-been."

"True enough."

Meg was in a chatty mood as Drake made her change into a different outfit. "Then there's the problem Dom's having."

At the mention of Dom, I felt the hairs on my head stand up. Smoothing them down, I nonchalantly inquired, "What's up with him?"

"He's pissed he doesn't have a bigger role. It's like everyone has so much more screen time than him. Even Jade. He's now a principal player, while Dom has fewer lines this year than last season, if that's even possible."

"Hmm. Wonder why?" I had noticed this, but hadn't given it much thought until now. Why was Dom's role getting smaller? Was he being phased out?

"Lucy said –" but she stopped, realizing we weren't alone.

"Ladies, gossip away. My lips are sealed. I promise," Drake guaranteed.

He was someone I trusted, so I encouraged her. "What did Lucy say?"

"I don't want this getting out," she said, still looking at the back of Drake's head.

"Hate to break it to you, but if Lucy knows, it's out!" I joked. Whatever it was made Meg sad, so I added, "But you know, Lucy isn't always right. She doesn't know everything. In fact, I would bet against her if I were you."

I wasn't sure if I believed that, but Meg looked really upset.

"Thanks, Anna. Well, Lucy told me she was talking with one of the writers who spilled that Dom's getting killed off. And soon. Not even in the season cliffhanger or anything."

I was genuinely surprised. "You've got to be kidding me! Does he know?"

"No clue. I really like him too. He's got all these plans. I know he thinks he's going to be around here for a while. He's even been looking for a house to buy."

"Really? Next door to you?" I kidded.

"No," she laughed. "He likes the country."

"Dom?" That was clearly false. He was a fancy, big city guy. He didn't like bugs or wildlife. There was no way he really liked country living. He must have been looking for something.

"Yeah. People don't know him like I do."

I nodded, playing along. "Have you gone looking at houses with him?"

"No. I've been right here. On set. He's been spending a lot of his time getting to know Martin and the area. He takes long rides around and goes out with his realtor sometimes, when he comes across a house he likes."

"Interesting."

"I know you don't like him," Meg said, looking at me.

"Not everyone gets along with everyone else, you know," I said to her.

"He does. Everyone loves him but you. What gives?"

"I don't like the way he's treated you. It doesn't matter that he's not my favorite person, but he really treated you like crap and you just forgave him. Why?"

"People make mistakes. Adam hasn't always been a prince."

"True. Just… I don't want to see you get your heart broken. Keep your eyes open."

"Of course. Just hope you take your own advice."

Chapter Forty-Six

It's amazing what you can see when you focus. With our attention on Dom, he outed himself as engaged in several suspicious activities by the end of the week.

I paid closer attention to his interactions with Meg. Whatever he wanted from her was not what she wanted from him. He was using her. That was not a new piece of information for me, but now it seemed important since we suspected him of... what exactly? Being a killer, or part of whatever Emma was involved in. Before she lost her battle with me on the plane, Emma said that "they" said this wasn't supposed to happen. She wasn't in it alone.

Finn seemed to notice my fits of abstraction more than others. Was he watching me?

So now I added Finn to my watch list. Was it possible Emma and Dom were in league with Finn? It was certainly possible, but that explanation didn't feel right. They didn't fit. Finn was one thing, Emma and Dom were something else. They seemed like normal humans, but they were up to something; related to the Families, but not Family themselves.

I began watching Finn intently. The weeks passed, and though the evidence mounted heavily against Dom, I got nothing new on Finn. Just a confirmation: He was in love, totally smitten love, with Suzanne. He wasn't here for his career. He was here for her.

For her part, Suzanne was careful around me. I totally got it. She was a private person and certainly didn't want me in her most private business. But unfortunately, and ironically, I had to film an intimate scene with them. The scene was simple. I'd invited Suzanne, Meg, Katie, and Lucy over for a sleepover. My big brother was there, being aloof, but watching Suzanne.

"Cut," Sylvia yelled. "For Pete's sake, Suzanne. I want you to look at him with the realization that you're attracted to him. Stop looking at him like he's your brother. Got it?"

Suzanne nodded and, looking right at me, whispered, "Screw it."

She let her guard down, let go of her pretend indifference. And wow. Suzanne was completely in love with Finn. The look she gave him was incredibly intimate, and his response was palpable.

"Cut! Suzanne, that was way overblown. Hold back. You only want to give the impression that you're interested, not in love with him. Okay? Can you do that? Find that sweet spot halfway between indifference and infatuation. Okay people. Let's do it again."

Suzanne got it right the third time, but now Finn was rattled. He'd come here with only the slightest hope that she had a shred of feeling for him. He was in shock because he'd felt it. And I could feel how much they still meant to each other.

Still shooting at the farm house, I watched from my chair as Finn and Suzanne filmed a scene that takes place later in the evening of the sleepover. There's a small fire in the kitchen and Finn comes to Suzanne's rescue. They exchange flirty banter. The first take was perfect, if a little intense. Their chemistry couldn't be denied, except of course by Lucy.

"She's awful. How can he stand it?" Lucy said, eyes on her phone.

"Oh, he looks like he's enjoying himself just fine," I said.

"Really?" she asked, pulled from her online world. "There's no way he'd go for her, like, for real. Who is she, anyway? She's a mediocre actor and he's amazing. And rich and famous."

"She's a friend of mine, Lucy," I responded coldly.

"Oh, really? I thought you were best friends with Corey. Hmm. Guess your friendship isn't worth that much. Excuse me," she said, getting up, her rebuke stinging.

I'd gotten so caught up in Suzanne and Finn's magic, I'd momentarily forgotten the price Corey was about to pay.

I went back to watching the scene. Sylvia wanted another take, unhappy with the lighting. As the set crew cleaned up the mess and reset the scene, Sylvia gave the actors a new set of directions.

"This time, when you grab the fire extinguisher, make it look out of control, Suzanne. Finn, she'll bump into you, you behind her. Wrap your arms over hers and help her put the fire out. Then finish as before."

Both looked at Sylvia with gaping mouths.

"Is there a problem?"

"No. Fine," Suzanne said, trying to stuff back inside what she'd let out. She was terrified of herself. She threw Finn a biting look which confused the hell out of him.

"Action," Sylvia yelled.

The fire started and the scene unfurled like a dance.

When his arms wrapped around her, she reacted stiffly but melted into him as they worked to contain the fire.

The kitchen covered in soot and foam, they collapse, laughing at the mess. This is my cue to enter. I find them on the floor together, staring into each other's eyes, the kitchen a disaster.

"Cut!" Sylvia yelled.

I turned my head, feeling Dom was now on the set. When I turned back, Finn and Suzanne were still looking at each other.

"I think we need to get ready for the next scene," I said. Suzanne looked up at me and the spell was broken.

Finn got up and offered her his hand, to which she replied, "I think I got it."

Miss Sassy Pants was back, her mask of disdain perfectly back in place. She walked off. Poor Finn's head was spinning.

"What'd I do?"

"She's got a boyfriend," I said, trying to explain.

"Yeah, I know," he dismissed, which made me go on the defensive.

"And that doesn't bother you?" I chided. "You know he's my best friend."

"Are they serious?" he asked with so much earnestness, it was hard for me to stay pissed.

"Listen, I like you, Finn. And usually I like helping people out. But not with this. Corey really is my best friend. Got it? You're on your own with this."

"What's new?" he muttered.

I decided not to let his statement go. "What do you mean?"

"It's nothing," he sighed.

"I don't think it is," I said.

"Well, if you must know, I'm kind of the black sheep of my family."

"Oh, you mean because you're rich and famous?" I teased.

"I'm on the outs with my family. They don't care about the things I care about. Funny, isn't it? What one person considers success another person sees as failure?"

We were walking out to the trailers for wardrobe. He needed hair and make-up too. We passed by Dom and Meg, who were in the middle of an intimate conversation. I involuntarily shivered.

"What was that for?" Finn laughed.

"Don't care for Dom."

"Really? I thought you liked everyone. Why not?"

I could see Finn had bought whatever Dom was selling.

"Hard to explain. But he's hurt Meg before. I just don't trust him," I answered.

"Maybe he's changed. Maybe he's sorry," Finn said, thinking about himself and his botched relationship with Suzanne, no doubt.

"Maybe. But methinks he's a player."

Finn didn't have a response. I left with a weird feeling. Despite the centuries of anger emanating through his ancestry, I liked him. He was not warm and fuzzy. I knew he was a killer, trained by ruthless cutthroats, and it would be easier to hate him. But I liked him.

There was still the real possibility Adam would decide Finn had to go. Or Mr. Seacrest might see to it, and there was nothing I could do about their decisions. There was also the matter of the Fourth who wanted to hurt and kill me, no doubt brought to town because of Finn Varga. And on top of it all, I simply couldn't root for him. I loved a good love story, but not at Corey's expense. And even if Suzanne was interested in Finn, was a relationship between them even possible? Suzanne was a traitor. Wouldn't his people come after her?

I couldn't see a scenario that ended well. No happily ever after for those two.

Chapter Forty-Seven

"Turns out Dom's an ambitious, conniving jackass," Corey said, busting into my room.

"What are you doing up? It's not even 7 a.m." I said, blurry-eyed. I'd been up until nearly dawn. Adam and I had visited 4 a.m. for clarity and made a bit of progress.

"I'll tell you what. He convinced Sylvia I was leaving the show. She believed him!"

"What? Why would he do that?"

"Oh, I don't know. Maybe because he heard he was being killed off."

"He heard this? From Lucy? Where did you get your info?"

"Same source," he said, fuming, missing the connection.

"Calm down, Corey. Sit," I ordered, and he complied. "Okay, so, let's figure this out. If it's true he's being written off, that's clearly good for us, but bad for him. He obviously wants to stay on and is grasping at straws."

"Totally not cool. I thought we were buds. Guess it's every man for himself."

"I told you he's up to something."

"Yeah, well, I believe you now. So what do I do?"

"I highly doubt Sylvia would take Dom's word that you're leaving. She doesn't work that way."

"Except she hates to waste time. And if she got the info confirmed by Lucy... I mean, Lucy always seems to know what's going on, right? Who knows? I bet the writers are busy writing me out and Dom in!"

"I seriously doubt it. It's 5 a.m. in L.A. Just go talk to Sylvia."

"Now?"

"Yes, now. Go! But come back and tell me what happens," I shouted as he hurried out of my room.

I wondered if this was the break in Dom's armor that would be his undoing. For my part, I had plenty of evidence.

I wrote in my diary as I waited, my eyes swollen from lack of sleep.

Not fifteen minutes later, Corey reappeared at my door, this time knocking.

"Come in."

"It was all a misunderstanding. I squared it up with Sylvia."

"A misunderstanding?" I was puzzled.

"Yeah. No harm, no foul."

"Wait. You're not pissed at Dom?"

"No, of course not. He was actually trying to do me a favor. He'd heard I was going and he knew it would be a bad career move to leave the show midseason, not to mention the serious breach of contract. He was trying to put things right for me."

"That is such a load of crap!" I said, getting mad.

"What are you talking about? I got it right from the horse's mouth."

"Sylvia?" I asked, seriously confused. What the heck was going on?

"No, A. Dom. He was watching the shoot. You know Meg was doing that big scene this morning, and he was there to support her."

In the span of a few minutes, Dom had gone from villain to hero in Corey's eyes. What the hell was going on?

I took a close look at Corey and saw that something was off. He had a goofy expression on his face. "Hey, well that's cool, I'm glad you got it worked out," I said, playing along. "Come here. I think you've got something on you."

I wanted an excuse to examine him closely. How was Dom able to change Corey's mind?

He came closer. "Yeah. I'm covered in dust from the tunnels."

"Let me get it." As I brushed him off, I felt it. There was something other than dirt sticking to him. "Let me see your hands," I ordered, no longer acting.

Corey stuck out his hands and I laid mine on top of his and closed my eyes.

"What are you doing?" he asked.

"What he said," Echo chimed in, standing in my doorway. I'd forgotten to cancel our daily running plans.

"Shut up, both of you. I'm concentrating."

It didn't feel like he was being messed with telepathically. It was different. Like he'd been drugged.

I opened my eyes and looked at his hands. There was a thin layer of something on them. But was it just dirt?

I had an idea. I propped up my phone and set it to record my experiment.

"Echo, Dom tried to get Corey fired. He told Sylvia that Corey was leaving the show, and he tried to get Corey written off. Corey just went to tell Sylvia it wasn't true, that he had no such plans. And get this, Corey just came back and told me that Dom wasn't going behind his back, but was the hero in this scenario, trying to help him out."

"That's messed up," Echo said, seriously concerned. "You were right, Anna. That certainly counts as fishy behavior."

Corey was about to set the record straight, but I said, "Shut up, Corey. Echo, come over and take Corey's hand."

"You want me to hold his hand?" Echo scoffed.

"Okay, I'm so tired. You two just need to do what I'm telling you. Now do it."

As soon as Echo touched Corey, Echo's countenance shifted. It was very slight. I don't know if I would've noticed if I hadn't been looking for it.

"Echo, what do you think about all of this with Dom?"

Echo blinked and sat in my chair. "Always good when someone has your back."

I couldn't believe it. What the heck was going on?

"Okay. You two stay right here. Got it? Stay?"

"Yes, ma'am," Corey said, picking up Entertainment Weekly to flip through.

I woke up Suzanne and Adam and pulled them into my room.

"Suzanne, I hate to do this to you, but will you be the rat in my experiment? It won't hurt, I don't think. And it's important."

"Fine, what is it?" she asked, plopping down on the bed next to Corey.

"Oh, no, no. You sit here," I said, pointing to the chair Echo was occupying. "Echo, move."

"Pushy this morning," Suzanne complained.

Even though I'd just pulled Suzanne and Adam from sleep, they didn't act it. They were ready to go. Years of training, I suppose.

The camera still rolling, I told them about what had happened with Corey and Dom this morning.

"What do you think?" I asked. "And no comments from you two," I said, pointing at Echo and Corey.

"Something's not right. That doesn't seem like something Corey would say, even if there were a genuine misunderstanding. Which seems highly improbable. No, it sure sounds like Dom was trying to get Corey fired," Adam concluded.

"What a creep! I'm gonna have my own special talk with him," Suzanne said, ready for a fight.

"So, you both think Dom is scheming, or in the wrong somehow, right?" I asked to clarify. They both nodded.

"Okay, Corey, put your hands out. Suzanne, I want you to take his hands."

Suzanne approached Corey slowly, and it wasn't lost on me that there was a hesitance to her movements. I could feel that she was just about ready to break it off with him.

She squeezed his hands and sat back down. "And?" she asked, looking at me.

"What do you think about Dom and what he did to Corey?"

"Did to Corey? Not too many people would go out of their way to help someone else like that."

"What the hell? You think Dom was helping Corey?" Adam asked, baffled.

"Of course. I mean, come on. Dom's a good guy," she responded, Corey and Echo nodded in agreement. "Can I go now? I don't have to be on set until noon."

"Yeah, thanks. Corey, I'll talk to you later. And Echo, I'm too tired to run today."

Adam stood there slack-jawed as they left.

"Come here," I said, pulling him onto my bed. I handed him my phone and pressed play. I lay down, eyes closed, listening to the crazy exchange as Adam watched.

"Unbelievable," I said, the show over.

"Insane. I wonder how many times he's tricked us."

"Whatever it is, it doesn't work on me. I think it's a contact thing. Corey had something on his hands. When the others touched him, they instantly changed their minds. The scariest part is that I don't think the effects wear off. I think it permanently changes a person's mind or perspective."

"That's pretty powerful stuff. He must be working with someone. There's no way a guy like that could be in possession of something so strong on his own. I didn't want to believe it before, but you must be right. Dom and Emma are – or were – working together to bring you down."

"No, I don't think it's me they're after. I think they are looking for something. I think they want what the ghosts are after. The other day Meg was gushing about how supportive Dom is, and she said that she'd told him about the ghosts. He took it well and told her he'd help her sort it out. But guess what? She told him about the ghosts, or hinted about them, the first time they were together. Dom has known about her connection with the ghosts almost as long as he's been here."

"I can't believe I've been so blind!" Adam said, feeling bested.

"It's not your fault. I'm just glad I've been immune so far. I'm thinking that whatever he's using works primarily on Family."

"Why do you think that?"

"Lucy doesn't seem particularly in love with the guy and neither does Jade."

"I thought Jade liked him."

"Jade's too polite," I said, smiling fondly.

"You sure think a lot of him," Adam said with a hint of jealousy.

"I do. He's a great guy. Nothing for you to worry about. You know that."

Adam sighed.

"What is it?"

"It's not that I don't trust you. I've just seen it before."

"Seen what before?"

"When the war becomes too much. Suzanne happens."

"I'm not running away."

"You say that now, but I know you. If you think leaving would save me, you'd leave in a heartbeat. Just like Suzanne did. That's why I took her in. She's incredibly loyal."

"Let's not worry about the future. Today has more than enough worries. Can you feel it?"

"I honestly have grown a bit numb."

"I alternate from all the feelings to none. We can't go on much longer without some sort of resolution. I hope it can wait until the end of the shoot when I'm rested. It's hard to think on such little sleep."

"It will come when it does. But I could use a few more hours of shut-eye before facing the world. Shall we?"

I cuddled up next to him and drifted off with the Dom puzzle spinning in my mind.

Chapter Forty-Eight

Half a day later I was sitting in hair and make-up when a depressed Corey took the chair next to me.

"It's officially over," he said, looking at his phone but talking to me.

"I'm so sorry. How are you?"

"Honestly, I don't know. It'd been coming for a while, even before Mr. Perfect showed up. She took it pretty well."

I hadn't seen that coming. "*You* broke up with Suzanne? Why?"

"You did know she was still in love with Finn Varga. I thought as much. I'm pretty pissed you didn't tell me."

"It wasn't really up to me. I mean, I know she likes you too. But, why did you break up with her?"

"Besides the fact she's still into Finn? We don't have a lot in common."

I thought that was such a strange reason. From my perspective they had loads in common. They both acted, had Fourth blood, big personalities, and were funny.

"Oh, well, if you're happy."

"Not happy, but better off. We weren't going anywhere. And I was already picking up on the 'I'm in love with my famous prince of an ex-boyfriend' vibe. I'm not dumb. There was no way I could compete with that, and when I thought about it, I didn't want to. Just not that interested, I guess."

"Oh," I said, feeling uncomfortable. It'd been easier to be around Corey and have our friendship work when he started dating Suzanne. But now that they were no longer together, what would that do to our relationship?

"A, stop it. I know you're in love with what's-his-face. Hey, I did get a piece of good info. Lucy said she heard Dom might not be gone after all."

Since Corey was under Dom's spell, I didn't make a negative comment. I was proud that my eyes didn't even roll. "Strange. Anyway, back to you. Are you okay?"

"I will be. Maybe it's time to play the field," he said thoughtfully.

I gagged on the sip of water I'd taken.

"Oh, that's so not happening," I laughed, once I'd stopped coughing.

"What? You think I can't get a girl?"

"You can get all the girls, that's not it. You're just not that guy, hate to break it to you."

"What do you think?" he asked Meg, who'd just walked in. "I could play the scene."

"What scene?" she asked.

"You know. *The* scene. I could be a player."

"Naw, don't see it. You're too nice."

"And that's the meanest thing anyone has ever said to me," he retorted.

"I doubt that," she teased back. "Where's Koyte? Isn't he doing my hair today?" she asked Carrie.

"I'll go check if you'd like," she said.

Once Carrie was gone, Meg asked Deb if she'd be a "dear" and get her a cup of tea and orange slices. Meg closed the door, leaving me and Corey alone with her.

"I hope that wasn't too obvious, but I had to tell you guys. I've been shaking since last night. She said she was going to kill me if I didn't give it to her. I don't know what to do!"

Corey didn't know what Meg was talking about, but it didn't matter. He got out of his chair and put his big arms around her. He let her cry and feel safe at the same time.

Once she calmed down, I asked her what'd happened.

"You know I'm talking about the ghost. You always seem to know, Anna. The ghost said what she always does, like I understand it!" she exclaimed, exasperated. "She said, 'Go to the grave, to the tomb. The fifth from the third. Find and know or she will die and all is lost. Stay and die. Stay and die. Stay and more will die.' And I don't think I can stand anymore. I can't! It's even in my dreams!"

"I'm really sorry, Meg. We've been keeping you out of it because you made it clear you don't want to have anything to do with the ghosts."

"Yeah, well it doesn't seem to matter anymore. What have you kept from me?"

"Not much," Corey replied, still holding her. She rested her head on his chest in a rare show of vulnerability.

"We are trying to figure out what the ghosts want, and we're getting closer. Would you mind telling me what you're leaving out?" I asked.

"How do you always know?" Meg asked, searching my eyes. "Scratch that. I don't want to know. But, that's what I wanted to tell you. Last night was different. The ghost added something new to her message."

"What did she say?" I asked.

"Indulge me. What do you think she added?" Meg asked, testing me.

I closed my eyes and breathed in my surroundings. She was feeling both scared and curious. "My best guess? She wants you to follow her. You didn't, but you think she'll be back."

"Damn, you're good! How does she do it?" Meg asked Corey, finally letting go of him.

"Well, uh…."

"No, no. Stop. Don't want to know. But yeah, you're right. I didn't, of course. Follow a ghost? I know I've gone crazy, but I'm not daft."

"You want this to be over, just like us. But to get rid of them, we need to find out what they want."

"Maybe they just want to suck my blood," she said, shivering.

"They're not vampires."

"But you don't know they won't harm me, do you?"

"In fact, they are dangerous," Corey said. "You shouldn't go alone, that's for sure, if you do go."

"What about this. Would you consider the next time she shows up texting me so we can follow you?" I suggested. "I'd bring everyone I can."

"Can you guarantee my safety?"

"No. But we will all be better off if we can figure this out. There's a lot of other stuff going on too, you know," I said, considering telling her about Emma.

But she shoved her fingers in her ears. "La la la la la la la la la. Really, I want to stay out of it. Got it? I'll think about your idea," she said, unlocking the door. Two hair stylists and one not-so-happy make-up artist were on the other side, waiting for the diva to let them in.

Meg took a chair unapologetically, but squeezed my hand and mouthed, "Thank you."

Chapter Forty-Nine

I was on a walk in the woods with Adam. It was beautiful. It was romantic. It was perfect, until I felt them.

"Maybe we should go the other way," I said into his ear, as we felt the Fourth, Suzanne and Finn, a mere football field in front of us, on the outskirts of the Gold Manor cemetery.

"We don't need to hide. In fact, I'd like to see if they are hiding," Adam said.

"Mean," I teased and kissed him.

"On second thought, maybe we can leave that for another day."

"Onward," I said, letting curiosity get the better of me.

Neither Suzanne nor Finn had our gifts, and thus didn't sense our approach. They were fully immersed in an intense conversation.

"Hey, guys. What are you doing out here?" I asked pointedly.

Suzanne jumped, but Finn was all ease and smiles. He looked like he'd just received excellent news.

"Suzanne was showing me the old cemetery. Have you walked through?"

"Yes," Adam said. He was holding back. I was surprised he wasn't feeling out, sizing up Finn for ulterior motives. As much as I wanted to forge ahead and read what was on Finn's mind, if possible, I held back too.

"You following me?" Suzanne asked, getting angry.

Her question was directed at Adam, but I pretended it was for me. "No. Just enjoying this cold, crystal clear night."

Just then my phone buzzed. It was a text from Meg.

"FYI. Saw what we talked about. Will follow. Don't come. Dom's with me. Will be ok."

I showed the text to Adam.

"Like hell she will be," I spat.

"What is it?" Finn asked.

He'd barely finished speaking when I felt Meg and Dom heading our way.

"Everybody hide," Adam whispered.

"What's going on?" Finn asked.

"Just shut up and do it," Suzanne said, grabbing his hand.

I think Finn would've done just about anything to keep Suzanne close, so he went along.

We ducked behind the mausoleum, but that didn't block our view of Meg and Dom following the gold ghost.

I looked at Finn, who was ashen, but composed. His playfulness was dead, his smile replaced with stone. I would not have to worry about keeping him quiet.

Then there were Meg and Dom. Meg was scared but drawing strength from Dom. He, on the other hand, looked genuinely shocked. I doubted he'd ever encountered the supernatural before. Or at least not like this. Powers and potions and spells are nothing compared to being face to face with a specter.

The ghost passed by, not paying attention to us.

Meg and Dom walked through the cemetery and into the woods. We followed as close as we could without calling attention to our presence.

Not too far into the woods, the ghost stopped. The gold ghost was changing from her usual color to silvery blue. As she changed, the smell of roses filled the air.

"Go to the grave, to the tomb. The fifth from the third. Find and know or she will die and all is lost. Stay and die. Stay and die. Stay and more will die," the ghost said into the night.

"I know, but what do you want now?" Meg pleaded.

The ghost flew to within inches of Meg's face, studying her. Slowly she flowed back, pushed by that unseen current. "Dig!" the ghost commanded, pointing to a tree.

I almost lost it. The ghost was pointing to the tree I'd been buried beneath countless times. It was the tree from my nightmares. And it hit me, seeing the tree from the outside with chunks of weathered stone at its base, that this was the tomb from the ghosts' riddle.

I looked back to the ghost who was still studying Meg.

"Do you believe me now?" Meg asked Dom.

Dom took a step toward the ghost. "This time we came prepared for you." He threw a powder at the ghost, causing her to disappear on contact.

"I always believed you, bitch," he said, slapping Meg so hard she fell. "My family and I thank you for your service."

Meg was on the ground, not moving. He'd knocked her out cold.

"And thanks to you, Emma's dead! You killed my sister! That wasn't supposed to happen. How did you do it? They said you must be incredibly powerful to have taken Emma out. But look at you, all crumpled up on the ground, helpless. You and your kind, you will never find peace. We will see to it. The curse will never be lifted! Our ancestors will be avenged. The butcherers will suffer forever. But you half-breed scum? We will hunt you down and kill you all. You know, I thought you'd be harder to trick. Disappointing, really. Oh well. "

Dom reached into his backpack and put on a pair of gloves.

"What the...?" I mouthed to Adam. He put his finger to my lips and shook his head. He was good at waiting for just the right moment.

"Now where are you?" crazy Dom said to himself. "Oh, there you are," he said, producing a krim. "Off to hell, then. Nighty-night!"

Chapter Fifty

Suzanne charged from her hidden spot. Unfortunately he saw her and planted his legs, ready. She managed to knock the krim to the ground, but Dom wasn't hurt. He grabbed her around the waist and landed a hard punch to her gut, causing maximum pain.

Finn was just seconds behind Suzanne. He was about to grab the weapon but Adam called out, "No, it's a krim. Don't touch it!" as he charged on the scene.

In a blur of motion, Finn had his shirt off and round the hilt of the weapon. Dom was on top of Suzanne, beating her. In the next second Finn had plunged the krim through Dom's back with enough force to spear and shred his heart.

Finn kicked Dom off Suzanne. "Are you okay?"

"I had a plan, you know. He just thought he was winning," she wheezed as she tried to prop herself up. "Ow, not yet. Think I'll just lie here."

I ran to Meg. She was unconscious. "She's breathing, but we need to get her to a doctor."

I looked to Adam, who was checking Dom's pulse.

"Did you have to kill him? I mean, you didn't even hesitate," I said to Finn.

"He would've killed Meg. He would've killed Suzanne too. I did what I had to," he replied. I could feel the adrenaline running through his body. I could feel the Fourth hatred in him.

Adam gave me the not-now look, earning Finn's attention. "How do you know about krims?" Finn asked, standing up and tensing. He started backing away from us.

"What's going on here? Are you, are you… one of them?" Finn spat at Adam, his hostility growing.

Suzanne managed to drag herself upright, putting herself between the man she loved and the one she'd pledged her loyalty and life to. "Please, please, not now. Finn, I'll explain. It's okay."

"You know it's not. It's kill or be killed, same as it ever was," he said, ready to take Adam on.

Suzanne reached out and put her hand on his heart. "It's not what you think."

Her touch calmed him down a little, but he was still gearing up to kill. "I see now, it's exactly what I think. Stand aside."

Adam pulled out a pocket knife.

Before I could tell them to stop, I was gagging. Someone, some Fourth, had me in a choke-hold.

"Drop it or she dies!" Colby called out. "I'm gonna snap your little neck," he whispered into my ear.

"You think I travel alone?" Finn sneered, feeling in control of the situation. "Kick your knife over, now!" he commanded.

Adam complied.

"I like to play nice, when I can. Now everyone calm the hell down," Finn said.

"Let Anna go," Adam commanded.

"Colby," Finn nodded to him, implying it was time to free me. But I already knew that wasn't going to happen. Colby had decided he was going to kill me. He was looking forward to it.

"Yes, sir," he replied with mock deference.

I felt his grip tighten so he could free one hand to get his knife. I closed my eyes and tried with all I had to tell Adam what was happening. *Please, please, please hear me*, I said in my mind to him.

"No!" Adam called out, feeling something, seeing Colby was about to hurt me.

My savior came from behind. As soon as I felt him my heart sank. I didn't want him here. If he weren't here, he wouldn't get hurt.

Corey, never one to overthink, jumped out of the brush and took Colby by the neck, snapping it with such force that his head came off.

Echo leapt from behind a tree, cold-cocking Finn with a tree branch. He crumpled to the ground.

"That's gonna leave a mark," Echo said, enthusiastically. "Oh," he faltered, seeing Colby's headless body.

Suzanne crawled over to Finn. "Why did you do that?" she seethed, concerned only with Finn, not thinking about the irreparable damage done to Corey.

"You're welcome," Echo said sarcastically.

"How are you even here?" I asked Corey, my brain trying to catch up.

"Adam texted us. And Colby was going for his knife, A. He was going to kill you."

"I know," I conceded, not wanting to make this anymore awful for him. This wasn't the first time someone had tried to kill me, but it was the first – and hopefully last – time Corey had killed. He had killed a person.

A deep silence fell.

"Dom thought Meg was me. He thought Meg was one of the Family," I said, pulling my eyes off the headless corpse.

"But what was Dom? Who was he working for?" Echo asked.

"He wasn't Family, but he knew about us, knew about the curse," Suzanne said, stroking Finn's hair.

"He mentioned his ancestors. Wasn't the origin of the curse the massacre of an entire village? If they were all killed, how could he be a descendant?" I asked.

"All but one were killed," Adam said, the pieces of the puzzle coming together. "Dom is either a descendant of or working for the one who placed the curse. The Seer."

This didn't sound good. A new ancient enemy. More people intent on our destruction.

"We really need to get Meg to a doctor, and I think Suzanne needs to get looked at too," I said, surveying our scene. "What are we going to do with Finn and the bodies?" I turned my mind to the practical to keep from losing it.

"Echo and I will take care of Dom once we get Finn into Suzanne's room. Suzanne, sorry, mate, but you don't have time to sit around at the hospital. You are on Finn duty. It's up to you," Adam said to her.

It was up to Suzanne if Finn was going to be allowed to live.

"You understand the stakes and what you've got to do? Yes?" Adam asked, making his intent crystal clear.

"You're really going to leave this up to her?" Echo asked, aggravated.

Adam threw him a look that said *don't ever question me*. Echo ducked his head in submission.

"Corey will need to bury Colby. It's the way," Adam said, looking at me and feeling my pain for Corey.

"And I've got Meg. But the tree. It's here. Dom wanted this. This is what he was looking for. This is what's been in my dreams. I mean, look at it! It's where Jade's grandmother was buried. If we leave now, I'm afraid we'll never find it again," I said, pointing at the weathered, broken pieces of tombstone. I brushed the debris from the pile of stones. Hidden in the bramble was my scarf. The scarf I'd wrapped around a tree last year. This tree. I held it out for Adam to see, unable to speak.

"You decide what you think is best," Adam said, kissing my forehead. He was leaving it to me to decide whether we'd take care of Meg or finally solve the mystery.

The others were getting a move on as I considered my choices. She'd survive, I decided. It was just a bump on the head, right? We'd get help soon enough.

Then I felt the lie. This place, wherever it was we were, was not in our time. When the ghosts were involved, time sometimes seemed to stand still. It was not predictable. Meg could've been out for just a few minutes or hours. Was whatever was buried beneath the tree worth risking Meg's life?

I watched as Adam left with Dom's body over his shoulder, and Echo carrying Finn, Suzanne leaning on him for support. It seemed so cruel to make Corey carry Colby, but that was their way.

"Fine," I muttered to the universe, scooping up Meg and leaving the tree and its secrets behind.

Acknowledgements

This is my sixth book. It has taken nearly a full year after it was written to get it into shape for you to read. Why so long? Life, I suppose. In addition to writing I have a full-time job, a family, and a whole host of obligations (just like you!).

But it's finished, and I do love it. I hope you do too. I love the world of the Four Families. Maybe because it's set in my sweet little corner of the world, Martin, Tennessee, and when I drive around town I think of Anna, Adam, and the rest, what they are up to, and how they are going to solve their problems and keep what's worth saving.

It is the case this book would've never seen the light of day without the help of my peeps, primarily Lisa Smartt, Chris Brown, and Jennifer Newton.

Lisa, my writing partner, without you I'd probably still be in bed with the sheets over my head. I might be caught up on my Netflix queue, but no writing would've taken place. Word to the truth! Thank you.

Chris, my husband and BFF, without you I'd be wandering in some distant wilderness. Thank you.

Jennifer, without you my dyslexia would be on full display for the world to see and this book would be fairly unreadable. Or at least not an enjoyable read. Thank you.

A shout out to Stephanie Richardson, my first reader. I love your enthusiasm and appreciate your kindness. I always look forward to handing my books off to you!

Thank you, Alison Page, for being one of my last readers, helping to rid the work of typos!

Lastly, I am grateful to be part of a university (University of Tennessee at Martin) community that has a space for and recognizes the writing of fun pop-culture books.

 Born and raised in Bakersfield, California, Merry Brown now lives in the northwest corner of Tennessee with her husband, three boys, and cat. She teaches philosophy at the University of Tennessee, Martin, where she counts it a great privilege and joy to introduce students to perennial questions about the nature of the universe, meaning, morality, and the human condition. Merry Brown's love of philosophy and young adult paranormal fiction inspired her to write her first novel, **THE KNOWERS**, book #1 in **THE EXILED TRILOGY**, published in 2012. She has since published five additional books, completing the **EXILE TRILOGY** and three books in **THE FOUR FAMILIES** series.

To learn more about **SILVER TREE GHOST HOUSE**, book #3 in **THE FOUR FAMILIES** series, and forthcoming books from Merry Brown, visit her on Facebook at facebook.com/MerryBrownBooks or Twitter @merryebrown.

Made in the USA
Columbia, SC
03 August 2017